THE WONDER OF LOVE

Book of Love, Book Eleven

Meara Platt

ARE YOU SIGNED UP FOR DRAGONBLADE'S BLOG?

You'll get the latest news and information on exclusive giveaways, exclusive excerpts, coming releases, sales, free books, cover reveals and more.

Check out our complete list of authors, too!

No spam, no junk. That's a promise!

Sign Up Here

www.dragonbladepublishing.com

Dearest Reader;

Thank you for your support of a small press. At Dragonblade Publishing, we strive to bring you the highest quality Historical Romance from the some of the best authors in the business. Without your support, there is no 'us', so we sincerely hope you adore these stories and find some new favorite authors along the way.

Happy Reading!

CEO, Dragonblade Publishing

Additional Dragonblade books by Author Meara Platt

The Book of Love Series
The Look of Love
The Touch of Love
The Taste of Love
The Song of Love
The Scent of Love
The Kiss of Love
The Chance of Love
The Gift of Love
The Heart of Love
The Hope of Love (novella)
The Promise of Love
The Wonder of Love
The Journey of Love

Dark Gardens Series
Garden of Shadows
Garden of Light
Garden of Dragons
Garden of Destiny
Garden of Angels

The Farthingale Series
If You Wished For Me (A Novella)

The Lyon's Den Connected World
Kiss of the Lyon
The Lyon's Surprise

Also from Meara Platt
Aislin

CHAPTER ONE

Taunton, England
June, 1821

S HAYNE BRAYDEN GROWLED as heat, flames, and the throat-clogging scent of burning leather swirled all around him. But he also caught the orange blossom scent of Willow Farthingale, which he would have considered quite pleasant if her fist did not happen to smash into his face at just that moment. She followed it up with a swift kick to his shin. "That does it." He scooped her up by the waist before she landed another punch. "Hit me again, and I vow I shall drop you into the horse trough."

They were standing outside the Ashcott Inn where Willow, her aunt, and youngest sister had stopped on their way to London. They were meant to leave today, but the fire consuming the Ashcott Inn's carriage house that he and the inn's staff were furiously fighting to douse would now change all that.

"You don't understand! I need to get that book!" She tried to squirm out of his grasp once again to run into the burning carriage house.

"Are you two cards short of a full deck? You'll burn alive." He firmed his grip on her waist and heaved her over his shoulder, determined to carry her away from the fire that was only now starting to burn itself out, unfortunately not before several of the guest carriages stored in this outlying structure had been torched beyond recognition.

Someone had purposely set this fire, and he expected it was another of Lord Belfy's jackals, intent on causing trouble now that Lord Belfy and most of his rabble were imprisoned and awaiting their sentences to be carried out.

Willow pounded on his back. "Let me go, you brute! I have to get that book!"

"Is it worth more than your life?" He paused at the horse trough filled with water that was located just off the entrance to the inn. Oh, he was itching to toss the little hellion in. Willow Farthingale was quickly becoming the bane of his existence.

Not that he detested her.

Sadly, he did not.

Indeed, his dreams had suddenly been taken up with visions of this slight and slender girl with hair the reds and golds of a sunrise, and eyes the vivid blue of a May sky. He'd met her only a week ago and had not been able to think of any other woman since.

He did not care for her invasion of his dreams, did not care for it at all.

She gasped. "Don't you dare toss me in!"

He hadn't planned to, merely intended it as a threat. But in frantically trying to get out of his arms, she landed an inadvertent kick to his privates. He howled and released her on protective impulse—his protection—and she dropped into the trough with a splash.

Bloody hell.

She came up sputtering a moment later, her hair now partly fallen out of its pins so that one sinuously long strand was pasted to her breast.

Not just pasted to it, but curled around it, lovingly cupped over it.

All he could do was stare.

How in blazes did this girl manage to have this effect on him?

He did not mean to stare at all.

But how could any man resist her incredible perfection?

"I hate you, Shayne Brayden!"

"I'm not too fond of you at the moment, either." Bollocks, his nuts were throbbing and not in any pleasurable way. But he was going to say no more, not in front of an inn full of spectators who had been watching helplessly as their carriages went up in flames and were now gawking at him and Willow.

Well, probably mostly at Willow, who was luscious and wet.

Her chest heaved in anger.

"Calm down," he growled, knowing he should be the one taking his own advice. "Let me help you out. I didn't mean to drop you." He took a painful step toward her and held out his hand. "I apologize, Miss Farthingale."

He was the respected Taunton magistrate.

A former agent of the Crown, one of the king's best men when he had been in service.

He was not an addlepated, pimple-faced, fourteen-year-old boy to be bested by a hot-tempered innocent.

Willow regarded him with heat in her exquisitely expressive eyes.

"No," she said quietly, surprising him when she suddenly seemed to calm down and now looked upon him with embarrassment. "I am the one who owes you the apology."

He shook his head, certain he had heard wrong. "What?"

"I said I am sorry, Magistrate Brayden. I did not mean to hit you so hard." The girl actually appeared contrite.

He choked back his grin.

Oh, she'd meant to hit him. She was obviously not sorry for that, only for hitting him in the *wrong* spot. He removed his jacket and wrapped it around her shoulders as she awkwardly climbed out.

Her gown was sopping wet.

So were her boots and stockings.

He glanced at the men still working frantically to subdue the fire. Their efforts appeared to have paid off, unfortunately too late to save the structure and its contents. "Let me take you to the inn. There's no saving those carriages now."

All in all, the damage was manageable. No deaths or injuries. No other outbuildings set aflame. The stables were safe. So was the inn. They had even managed to pull out a few of the carriages, but the Farthingale's conveyance was too far back and not among those rescued.

She squished as she walked beside him. "I have something to tell you."

He sighed as they continued toward the inn's kitchen door, going in the back way to avoid ruining the elegant carpet in the formal front entry. "If you mean to berate me for dunking you in the trough, I've already apologized, and I am not going to do it again."

She cast him a wry smile. "Not going to dunk me again? Or not going to apologize to me again?"

"Apologize. I've told you I'm sorry. That's all you'll get. I never meant to dunk you in it in the first place."

"I know." She nibbled her lip. "I also know who set the fire."

He stopped abruptly and turned to face her. "So help me, Willow. If this is a jest—"

"It isn't." She frowned at him, puckering her lips in a pouting way that made him want to kiss her and taste the pink perfection of her shapely mouth.

But he was the Taunton magistrate and not about to make a fool of himself over a girl who was on her way to London to enter the marriage mart and probably land herself a duke. The sooner she was away, the better. "Who did you see?"

"I don't know his name, but I've noticed him around the inn this past day or two. I'm not sure he is a guest. That's the odd thing about it. I don't think he is. So, what was he doing lurking around here? I also saw him eyeing your office early this morning. I happened to walk outside for a bit of air, and there he was. He ducked behind a tree as soon as he spotted me."

Shayne frowned. "Then he saw you."

"Yes, but I don't think he realized I had seen him first. I pretended that I hadn't. Afterward, I was in my room when I happened to peer out the window and saw him running from the carriage barn moments before the fire started. I can describe him for you. Perhaps you can put a name to him with my description."

He nodded. "I'm going to escort you upstairs. Change out of your wet gown, but wait for me in your room. Keep your door locked, and do not open it to anyone but me or your family."

He led her into the kitchen, pleased to find it a hive of activity as the Ashcott cooks prepared meals for an inn full of elegant guests. "Just make sure Cammy and your Aunt Charlotte are alone before you open the door to them. Afterward, the three of you are to remain put until I return."

She considered him an oaf. Perhaps he tended to be overly protective. But she was young and slender, a little thing, and no match for a man's strength. He was not going to hurt her, of course. But Lord Belfy's friends, angry over Lord Belfy's downfall at the hands of Juniper Farthingale, Willow's eldest sister, would have no hesitation in coming after Willow to avenge that worthless lord.

He took her up the servants' stairs, grabbing her hand when she almost stumbled because her gown nearly tripped her up as it clamped to her legs.

To his surprise, she did not jerk out of his grasp.

When they got to her room, he went in first and looked around, giving every possible hiding place a thorough inspection. "It's safe. Bolt that door and let no one in but me or your family. I won't be gone long."

"Where are you going?" She started to remove his jacket and meant to return it to him, but he stopped her.

"I'll pick it up later. Right now, I have to get back to my office. The fire was meant as a distraction. I've left Lorcan and several of my guards on duty to watch the prisoners. Why do you think this man started it if not to create a diversion while he helped Lord Belfy and his foolish friends escape?"

Her eyes widened. "Of course! I ought to have realized."

"My brothers and I expected Lord Belfy's jackals to try something like this. I'm sure he hoped we would all run out to douse the flames. We knew immediately something was wrong. A carriage barn doesn't just catch fire on a beautiful summer's day."

The magistrate's office was next door to the inn.

He gave Willow a final warning, waited to hear the latch fall into place, then strode to his office. It took Shayne no more than a moment to reach it. His brother Lorcan stood exactly where he had left him, positioned to keep an eye on every window and door, his rifle in hand.

He had posted another two guards to remain with him and the prisoners. They were armed as well.

Shayne released a breath. "All quiet?"

Lorcan nodded. "Was the fire an accident?"

"No, it was set on purpose." He glanced at the weapon in his brother's arms. "I'm sure one of Lord Belfy's friends set it, hoping we would run out and leave the prisoners unguarded. He'll probably try something again tonight."

Lorcan had a lethal glint in his eyes. "Unless we catch him first."

"I'll leave that to you. I have a witness I'm about to question. I'll give you a description of our arsonist shortly. Where's Donal?"

"Right here," their other brother said, striding in behind him. His face was covered in soot, for he had been fighting the fire as well. "I'll wash up and ride off to the Earl of Monkton's estate. I wouldn't put it past those lords to threaten him next. After all, Lord Belfy is his brother, and he helped turn him in."

Shayne snorted. "No matter that it was the right thing to do."

Donal nodded. "That rabble care for nothing but their own pleasures. They were no tamer in London, just played their depraved games where no one cared who they harmed when their amusements got too rough."

Shayne took another moment to make certain their prisoners were secure. He was eager to have them all shipped to Exeter where there was a proper prison to house them, not this flimsy magistrate's gaol designed for harmless sots who needed a night to sleep off their overindulgence. That move to Exeter was not likely to happen until next week. "I'll be back shortly with a description for you, Lorcan."

His brother arched an eyebrow. "Let me go with you."

"No. I need you here. I'll give you details later."

He took a moment to wash the soot and grime off himself, then grabbed a pencil and sketchbook and returned to the inn. He went up the back stairs, preferring to be seen by as few people as possible. "Willow, it's me. Let me in," he said, knocking lightly on her door and hearing her scrambling toward it.

She raised the latch and opened it a crack to peer out. "Mr. Brayden. Come in."

He watched her set aside the hearth shovel she had taken in hand as a precaution and then step back to allow him entrance.

He glanced around, not liking that she was alone and definitely not liking that she had taken off her soaked clothing and was wearing only a thin robe to cover that breathtaking body of hers. Her gown and unmentionables were set out on two chairs beside the unlit hearth, but rays of sunlight streamed in at just that spot, which was likely why she'd positioned them there. "Where are your sister and aunt?"

"Still downstairs, I'm sure. They're watching the men put out the remains of the fire. They won't stray far from the inn." She went to the open window to glance out of it. "See, there they are. Do you see them standing in the courtyard among the inn's other guests?"

He joined her at the window, careful to keep his distance. Willow was little and sweet…the scent of her skin, that is. In all other respects, she was a firebrand and not at all the sort of woman he would ever want to marry.

Bloody hell.

Where were these thoughts coming from?

She had taken the pins out of her wet hair and brushed it out so that it fell in damp, red-gold curls to her waist. He noticed she had a handkerchief in her hand. On closer inspection, he realized she had been crying into it. "Willow," he said, his tone gentle, "shall I have Mrs. Ashcott bring up some tea for you? I know the fire must have been frightening for you. Can you give me a description of the man you saw? I'd put it off for later, but the sooner I have it, the sooner I can send my men off to search for him."

"I wasn't crying about the fire." Her eyes began to water again. "It's the book."

"What book?"

Her body seemed to crumble, her shoulders sagging and her eyes filling with sorrow. He hated to see her so defeated, her beautiful vitality gone. *The Book of Love.*

He emitted a choked cough. "The one with the red leather binding your sister June was toting around when she met General MacLauren?"

She nodded. "It's magical. Now she's married to General MacLauren, and he's as madly in love with her as she is with him. All our cousins and their friends have made love matches after reading it, and now it has gone up in flames. It's my fault. It was my turn. How can I go to London now? My family will despise me. Cammy will despise me," she said, referring to her younger sister, who was outside watching the fire with their Aunt Charlotte. "I've ruined her chances of ever finding love, too."

He tried not to appear impatient. *A magical book? Finding true love?*

Nor did he intend to take her in his arms to comfort her.

No, definitely not that.

"You haven't ruined anything. No one in your family is going to turn against you because of that book. Losing it was not your fault. I can write a letter attesting to it if you wish." The notion was absurd, but if it would make her feel better, he would do it. This girl was so strong-willed, he sometimes forgot how young she was—only nineteen, almost twenty, and as pure as a gently fallen snow.

He was hardly ancient himself, not yet thirty but by no means pure or innocent.

It wasn't merely the years that made a difference. It was the life experiences. Willow and her sisters had led sheltered, genteel lives in the quiet Devonshire town of Barnstaple. Traveling to London was their first major excursion. They had not even made it halfway there and were already homesick.

He had fought in wars, worked as an agent for the Crown, traveled throughout Europe on behalf of the Crown, and was now Taunton's magistrate.

Right, he was the magistrate.

This shook him back to his purpose in coming to her bedchamber in the first place. "Have a seat, Willow."

She settled on her bed.

He hadn't meant there. But he supposed it made sense since there was only one unused chair in the room now that she had commandeered the others for her wet clothes.

He drew it up beside her bed, trying to ignore how lovely she looked with her legs curled under her robe and her hair tumbling over her shoulders. "Start with a general description of the man. His height, his weight, his approximate age."

She nodded. "He is tall, about your height, but slender. Not muscled like you."

He stifled a grin.

She'd taken notice of him.

"He appeared to be about your age, too. Well, I'm not sure. How old are you?"

"Twenty-nine."

Her eyes rounded in surprise. "Oh, you seem…older…not older really. That is…more imposing." She shook her head and continued. "He had a long face. Blond hair that fell just above his shoulders. Styled curls about his forehead. I'm sure it is all the fashion in London, but I don't find it attractive at all."

He started to draw as she spoke. "Go on."

"Clean shaven. Thin eyebrows. Thin lips."

He glanced up. "You noticed his lips?"

She frowned at him. "Yes. So what? I wasn't planning on kissing him. Don't you notice things on a person?"

Like her robe drifting open and exposing the swell of her bosom? He lowered his gaze and stared at the sketchbook before some untoward organ in his body ruptured. "Get back to the details. High forehead? Low forehead? Close-set eyes? Wide-set eyes? Shape of his ears? Shape of his chin? Any prominent marks on his face? Thick neck? Thin neck?"

She gave him the rest of her description, which was surprisingly detailed. Well, these Farthingale sisters were quite clever. He'd noticed it with Willow's elder sister Juniper, who they commonly referred to as June. She had married Augustus MacLauren a few days ago and was now on her way to Scotland with her new husband. "Here, look at this drawing. What do you think?"

She stared at his handiwork, and her mouth dropped open in amazement. "It is excellent. I had no idea you were so talented. That is him exactly. Do you recognize who he is?"

Shayne nodded. "Lord Manton. One of Lord Belfy's friends. You know of Lord Belfy and his pack of scoundrels because of your sister's unfortunate encounter with them."

"Yes, but I only know of the five you've captured. Thank goodness they never managed to hurt June."

"Indeed. Your sister is one of the bravest women I have ever met. Clever, too. I shudder to think what they might have done to her had she not outwitted them."

"Thank you, Mr. Brayden. We think so, too."

"Well, I suppose all of you Farthingale women are quite extraordinary."

She laughed and clutched her heart in jest. "Wait? Am I hearing right? Was that a compliment? I feel giddy. I think I shall faint."

He smiled. "No, it wasn't a compliment, merely a statement

of fact. As I was saying, there are eight depraved lords in all. Worthless younger sons, born in privilege and given every advantage by their titled fathers, and yet they feel nothing but envy and contempt for all around them. Thanks to your sister and General MacLauren, we now have five of them in custody, three of them already tried, convicted, and awaiting their sentences to be carried out. The other two will rot in my prison until they are tried and convicted, which they will be."

"That leaves Lord Manton and two others on the loose. Do we know if the others are here?"

He shook his head. "I haven't seen them. Believe me, I've been looking."

"I hope they're not. You would think one or two of them would have the sense to walk away from a bad circle of friends."

"I'm sure we'll find out soon enough." He closed his sketchbook and rose to leave. "Lock up behind me. Same caution applies. Let no one in but your aunt and sister. I'll be back as soon as I've given this sketch to Lorcan. I'll do up a few more for my other trackers, too."

He walked to the door.

She scrambled off the bed and followed him, placing a soft hand on his shoulder when he reached for the latch. "Mr. Brayden, I know we got off to a bad start. Well, a most unpromising start. I think you do not like me very much. I suppose I am too outspoken. But I want you to know I appreciate all you've done for me and my sisters."

"It's my job."

She nodded, now staring up at him with those big, blue eyes capable of drowning a man if he weren't careful. "I'm sorry if I behaved like a banshee earlier. That book…I wish I could make you understand how important it is to me. I promise you, I am not as demented as you believe me to be."

He grinned.

"Cammy and I are on our way to London to be thrown into the marriage mart. We don't know the first thing about men, about finding the right one and falling in love. This is why we desperately needed the lessons in that book."

He cupped her cheek and gave it a light caress. She was standing in her bare feet, a thin robe wrapped around her slender body, and that wild tumble of molten hair spilling over her shoulders. "Willow, you are wrong, and I will prove it to you."

She nipped at her lower lip. "How will you do that?"

"If you can abide to be in my company, I will tell you all you need to know about men. Believe me, we are simple creatures. Our discussions shouldn't take long."

She eyed him dubiously. "You would help me?"

"Yes, despite your attempts to maim me," he teased, slipping his hand off her cheek before she noticed how much she affected him.

She groaned lightly. "I've already apologized for that. But I don't think you appreciate the importance of that book."

"And I think you are placing far too much importance on it." He knew he ought to get back to his office as soon as possible, but leaving Willow was surprisingly hard to do. "There are just a few things to remember when dealing with men."

"Such as?"

"Do not ever be alone with a man."

She nodded, obviously overlooking that they were alone and in her bedroom of all places. Alarms should be going off in her head, the blare of a warning trumpet. The bang of a drum. But she appeared not at all concerned.

He did not know whether to be grateful she trusted him or angry that she considered him safe, which he decidedly was not. "Do not ever be alone with a man while you are undressed."

She nodded again.

Lord, have mercy!

Did she think he was a eunuch?

"Do not ever let a man kiss you."

She frowned. "That cannot be right. How am I to know if our senses are compatible? Why can I not allow him one kiss?"

"Because…it isn't safe. It isn't wise. You cannot go around kissing men."

She tossed her hair back and tipped her head up in a huff to mark her indignation. "I haven't kissed any men yet. But I should be permitted to kiss any man I consider marrying, don't you think? Not that I am rushing to do it. I don't even know what a kiss feels like. And you needn't worry because I am not going to kiss you."

He placed his hand on the door, knowing he had to leave right now, or this was not going to end well. "Nor would I ever consider kissing you." Blatant lie, of course. Capturing her lips was all he'd been thinking about for days. "You needn't worry that I ever will."

He expected her to kick him out right then and there. Instead, she turned so quiet, he could feel the silence prickle between them. "Willow? I'm sorry. It came out wrong. Any man would be delighted to kiss you."

"Just not you." She emitted a ragged breath. "I knew you did not like me. What is it about me that puts you off? You needn't be kind to spare my feelings. It is important for me to understand. *The Book of Love* says we must always be truthful. So you can be honest with me. Do you not like the way I look? My hair is a little too red, I think. I know I am far too opinionated for most men's tastes. I can't seem to keep my mouth shut even when I know I ought to clamp it tight. What of the five senses, sight, touch, taste, hearing, and scent? Is there anything you do find pleasing about me?"

He laughed and shook his head. "I had better go."

"But you haven't answered a single question."

"Latch the door after me. Put some clothes on. And don't go around kissing men. I'll see you later."

He should have walked straight out and not looked back. But he did look back, and she hadn't moved. She stood there with her head down, and her hands were trembling. Did this girl not realize how beautiful she was?

He felt like a wretch.

Well, how was it his fault? Wasn't she opinionated, outspoken, too independent for her own good? There were dangerous men lurking around, and she was too little to defend herself if those fiends ever got their hands on her.

How was he to protect her if she insisted on doing whatever she wished? Not that he wanted her to be biddable or timid.

He gave a silent oath and turned to her. "You irritate me to no end."

"You are no garden of delight either. Does this mean you are going to answer my questions? Why are you looking at me like that?"

He cupped the back of her head and drew her close. "How am I looking at you?"

She swallowed hard. "Like you want to—"

He kissed her as he'd longed to do from the moment he had set eyes on her and kept kissing her even though his brain was warning him to stop. But he was listening to his body that was screaming for fulfillment.

No.

No.

This was not what he'd planned.

This is not what he wanted.

Her soft, giving lips yielded to the press of his mouth. Her fingers clutched the front of his shirt, grabbing onto the fabric to draw him toward her. They were so close…too close. He inhaled the scent of orange blossoms on her warm skin.

Why was he kissing this little nuisance?

Worse, what was he going to say to her once he pulled away? After an achingly long moment, he eased his lips off hers and took a step back. "Willow…"

"You needn't apologize. I understand the lesson you were trying to teach me." She pursed her lips and continued. "The book warned about this very thing."

"What very thing?"

"Men will kiss women they do not like. They separate the physical urge from the bond of love. To a man, one has nothing to do with the other. It is merely their low brain responding to a female they perceive as desirable, and they perceive thousands of women to be desirable. Nothing to do with the higher act of love. Is this what you were trying to point out to me?"

He could have nodded and blithely gone on his way.

But this was her first kiss ever. He was not going to ruin the memory for her. "No, Willow. That kiss was from my heart. It was me kissing you because I like you and think you are beautiful."

She mistook his words as a jest at first.

Had he been that much of an ogre to her?

"You're serious? You like me?"

He clutched the sketchbook in his hand, relieved he had kept hold of it. If he'd had both hands free, that robe would have been off her, and he would have been busily kissing more than her lips.

She suddenly shoved him out the door, shut and latched it firmly, then began to chatter at him through the door. "Do you realize what this means? It is impossible, you know. It is not to be considered. Are you still there, Mr. Brayden? No, do not answer that. I want you gone. Do not darken my door again. You have no idea what you've just done. But do not apologize to me for that kiss. It was wonderful. However, I am still overset and angry."

He leaned against the door, trying to make sense of what she was going on about. She'd liked the kiss. No apology required, although he had been out of bounds and did owe her one even though she had forgiven him. "Willow, why are you angry?"

"Isn't it obvious?"

He groaned, for this is what came of growing up with only brothers. Bedding a woman was a far different thing from building a life and being a good husband to the one you loved. Outside of bed, women were a mystery to him. "Not in the least. Would you care to enlighten me?"

"No, Mr. Brayden. Go away now. But rest assured, nothing has changed between us. One splendid kiss does not change anything. I am still certain I do not like you, and I hope you still do not like me. I expect that is all right with you. Is it, Mr. Brayden?"

He should have responded with a simple yes.

She would be on her way to London to snare a titled idiot for herself, and his life would return to normal.

Only, he did not want normal.

He—*Lord help him*—wanted this fiery Farthingale.

"No, Willow. It is not all right."

CHAPTER TWO

SHAYNE BRAYDEN HAD kissed her!

That big, handsome hunk of an ogre had taken her in his arms—well, one arm, since the other held his drawing pad—but the point was, he'd put his mouth to hers, and that certainly counted as a kiss.

Willow sank onto her bed and groaned.

How could such a thing happen?

He did not like her.

She was certain he had not wanted anything to do with her when he had first walked into her guest-chamber to question her. What had changed? Why was he now being difficult and insisting it was not all right that they revert to how things had started off between them?

Their first meeting went badly, to be sure.

Nothing had changed for her part.

She fell back against the pillows and groaned again. Well, everything had changed. Their carriage had gone up in flames, and she had lost *The Book of Love*. All their clothes, which had already been packed in the carriage from the night before for the sake of efficiency, had burnt to ashes.

She, Cammy, and Aunt Charlotte had nothing left but the clothes on their backs, a nightgown and robe, and a few unmentionables that fit in their small travel pouches. Fortunately, those were still here in their guest chambers.

Now, she did not even have clothes on her back because her gown was soaking wet and set out to dry. How were they to leave for London today without a carriage or clothes? If not for the pin money Aunt Charlotte kept on her person, they would be destitute.

She glanced at the foot of her bed and realized Magistrate Brayden had forgotten to take his jacket. She supposed he would be coming back anyway to have her sign her witness statement.

A sudden ghastly thought struck her. "Oh, no!"

Would they be required to remain in Taunton until the villain was put to trial? This trip was turning into a disaster.

A rattle of the door brought her back to the present.

She rolled off the bed and grabbed the hearth shovel. "Who is it?"

"It's me, Cammy. Let us in."

Us?

She meant Aunt Charlotte, no doubt.

To her surprise, Shayne Brayden followed her in. He remained standing by the door, completely blocking it with his size and brawn. He folded his arms across his chest and maintained a stony expression, as though he hadn't been kissing the daylights out of her only moments ago.

There was not even a glint in his dark silver eyes to give him away.

Goodness, that combination of dark hair and silvery eyes was devastating to her senses. Why did he have to be so handsome?

Was it possible not to like him and yet want to kiss him again?

"Willow, Mr. Brayden has kindly offered to purchase new gowns for each of us." Cammy stared at the wet clothes spread across the two chairs. "Your needs are especially urgent. He's asked Mrs. Albright to come here and take our measurements. You remember her, the nice lady from the fabric shop who made the faerie wings for us for the Midsummer's Eve celebration last week? Isn't it thoughtful of him?"

Willow glared at him. "It is not thoughtful at all. An unmarried gentleman purchasing clothes for us? We will be ruined before we ever reach London."

Cammy frowned at her and then flitted to the window to peer out. "Well, it's too late. There's Mrs. Albright, and she's chatting with Aunt Charlotte. You are making too much of it. Everyone knows we lost everything in the fire. Papa will repay Mr. Brayden once we get word to him."

Cammy was right, of course.

But the thought of this man purchasing gowns for her felt so intimate. "He will repay you, rest assured, Mr. Brayden."

His expression remained serious. "I have no doubt of it. But it is not necessary. I am not lavishing an entire wardrobe on you, only a gown or two to get you to London. You'll need a carriage as well. And do not insult me by suggesting you will ride the mail coach."

She was going to suggest just that but snapped her mouth shut because he did not seem at all pleased with her just now.

How could he kiss her with such ardor and still appear so indifferent?

What did he mean when he'd earlier told her it was not all right for them to return to their respectful dislike of each other?

"I'll come back to finalize your witness statement once Mrs. Albright has finished with you ladies." His eyes now revealed his amusement. "Keep away from horse troughs, Willow."

He put his hand on the door, apparently ready to leave. "Latch this after me, even if your aunt and Mrs. Albright will be up in a few minutes. Do not take Lord Manton's malice for granted. These are not nice men."

"And you are?" Oh, why could she not keep her mouth shut?

He cast her a fiery look that did not strike her as angry so much as...hot. *Sweet heaven.* Perhaps this is why her own blood was now pumping wildly through her body. Her legs felt as though they were about to buckle. "Yes, Willow. I can be very nice."

Her eyes widened.

What did he mean by that?

He shut the door behind him as he left.

Cammy crossed the room to latch the door and then burst out laughing. "You are not going to win if you try to match wits with him. He's too clever. Why are you so prickly with him anyway?" She grinned at Willow. "Admit it, you like him."

"He threw me into a horse trough!"

"You shouldn't have been fighting him, even if it was to save that book. We've read it with June. Discussed it. Dissected it. No one will blame you for its loss. Did you seriously mean to run into the carriage house to try to retrieve it? You would have died, and that is a far greater loss than any book." She ran to Willow's side and hugged her. "Don't you dare do anything so foolish again. Whatever possessed you?"

"Honestly, I don't know." She hugged her sister back. "It was as though the book was calling to me. Seriously, I think I could have rescued it without getting injured."

Cammy's eyes widened in horror. "Do you hear yourself? Running in through those flames? Through that thick smoke? Mr. Brayden was right to dunk you in the water. I would have done the same."

Willow could not be angry with her sister, for everything she had said was right. "Once my gown dries, I want to sort through the embers and see if we can find anything of the book. Perhaps a few of our clothes survived. I feel utterly naked right now."

"That's because you are. If you think that thin robe hid anything from the magistrate, you are sadly mistaken."

Willow gasped. "Are you jesting? Please say you are in jest. How much do you think he saw?"

Cammy was laughing again. "Probably not enough."

Honestly, sometimes her sister was so irritating. "Cammy, stop laughing at me. This isn't funny."

"I can't help it. Don't you remember what the book said about men and a lady's body parts? Especially her bosom. His gaze will continually stray *there* until his eyes fill in what they cannot see. He must have been in spasms over you."

"Hardly."

But he had kissed her.

Their aunt knocked at the door. "Girls, do let us in."

"Right away," Cammy said and bounded to the door to open it. "Good morning, Mrs. Albright. Have you ever seen such excitement? Thank you for coming straight over. Poor Willow is in desperate need of a gown or two."

"So are we all," their aunt said, sounding remarkably calm despite their having lost everything in the flames. "But Willow first. She cannot go about as she is, lacking even a decent pair of walking boots for her bare feet since those she had on are now soaking wet."

"Indeed. What size are your feet, Miss Farthingale? I'll ask one of Mrs. Ashcott's boys to run over to the shoemaker. I'm sure he'll have something suitable for you. Perhaps not as fine as you are used to wearing, but more than adequate for your journey to London."

"Assuming we ever get there," Willow muttered.

Mrs. Albright set out her notebook and measuring tape. "Oh, my. Yes, the magistrate may want you to remain here another week or two. You'll need to identify the man you saw running from the carriage house."

Willow took in a sharp breath. "How do you know I'm the one who saw him?"

"Well, my nephew is one of the guards at the magistrate's prison. Not much of a prison, really. More of a holding pen attached to his office. He said the magistrate had a witness. Then one of the girls who sews for me said she saw you and the magistrate looking out the window of your room. Since he isn't the sort to dally with…well, the only reason he was here had to be because you were the witness."

"Willow, is this true?" Her aunt stared at her in alarm.

She nodded. "Mrs. Albright, who else do you think realizes I am the one?"

The kindly woman shook her head sadly. "Oh, I expect by midday everyone in town will know. This isn't London, Miss Farthingale. We all know each other in Taunton. Word spreads fast."

"How soon before the culprit learns of it?" Cammy wondered, her face now ashen. "Did you recognize him? Who set the carriages on fire?"

"I gave Mr. Brayden a description of the man. He drew a fine portrait of him. He says it is a friend of Lord Belfy's. One of his dastardly friends, Lord Manton."

Mrs. Albright grunted in disgust. "That rabble. Of course, we all suspected one of them was involved. I hope they catch him soon and toss him in with the rest of that bad lot. Thank goodness they were stupid enough to go after your sister and General MacLauren. Not that I'm glad they did. But those wretches finally tangled with someone powerful enough to bring them down. No wonder your sister fell in love with that handsome Scot. Indeed, I think half the ladies in town fell into a swoon over him when he rode in along with his Royal Scots Greys."

She continued chattering while taking Willow's measurements. "But he had eyes for no one but your sister. Those Scots are like that, I've heard. Loyal, faithful. His heart will always belong to her. He must have fallen in love with her at first sight. Isn't it wonderfully romantic? I hope you girls find good men for yourselves as well."

"Thank you, Mrs. Albright," Cammy said.

"I doubt it," Willow said at the same moment.

All three women stared at her.

She frowned at all of them, although the impact of her displeasure was lost on them since she was presently at the mercy of Mrs. Albright, standing with her arms outstretched while the woman measured her shoulders, hips, waist, and bosom. "Well, June was fortunate. How often do you think love strikes like that?"

"Honestly, Willow." Aunt Charlotte shook her head in disapproval.

"How am I wrong? What about all we've been taught?" she continued, feeling like a scantily dressed scarecrow standing in a field of corn. "Do not leap into love. Get to know the nature of the beast before you allow him to court you."

"Beast?" Her aunt arched an eyebrow. "When did you grow so cynical?"

"It is merely caution. If we all fell in love at first sight, then there would be no need for the marriage mart or long engagements. We could all leap into unbreakable commitments like bounding hares and then spend the rest of our lives regretting our hasty actions."

The three women broke into laughter.

"What did I say that you all find so humorous?"

Aunt Charlotte patted her cheek. "You are afraid of falling in love."

She could not even manage an indignant toss of her head since Mrs. Albright was now taking measurements of her neck. "I am not. But I will not be swept off my feet by a handsome boor who does not even like me."

Oops.

She cast Cammy a warning glance to keep her mouth shut, but her irritating sister ignored her. "Not even one with silver-gray eyes?"

"If you mean Lorcan Brayden, no. I am not referring to him."

Mrs. Albright snapped her tape and then began to roll it up. "Then you must be referring to the magistrate."

Willow arched an eyebrow. "Are his eyes gray? I hadn't noticed."

Which brought another burst of laughter from the ladies.

"Fine, so he has nice eyes. But he is still an overbearing know-it-all who expects a woman to keep her mouth shut until spoken to. He doesn't like me, and I don't like him."

Cammy swatted her backside. "He is nothing like that, and you know it."

Truly, did her parents have to conceive their youngest sister? Could they not have stopped at her and June?

"Why are we even speaking of the magistrate? Mrs. Albright, surely he has a sweetheart in town. A man with his good looks and importance must have women flocking to him."

The woman looked up from the notes she was jotting in her book. "He does."

Willow's insides did a little flip. Did this mean he had a sweetheart? Or only that women flocked after him?

She refused to ask for the clarification.

She would go to her grave not knowing.

Aunt Charlotte asked the question she refused to ask. "Then he is courting a young lady?"

Mrs. Albright glanced up again. "What? Oh…no. None that I am aware of. It isn't for lack of trying on the part of the local ladies. He hasn't taken an interest in anyone here. I'd heard there was someone in London, but I expect that has come to an end since he hasn't gone there in months now. Poor man, I suppose she must have broken his heart."

"Do you know who she was?" Cammy asked, and Willow decided perhaps younger sisters were not so annoying after all. She did want to know more about Shayne Brayden.

"No, he never speaks to anyone about her." Mrs. Albright gathered her belongings. "The daughter of a marquess is the rumor. Lady Felicia…or Fenice…perhaps Felice…well, something-or-other like that. Beautiful, of course. Elegant. Graceful. But who knows?"

"And who cares?" Willow immediately berated herself for tossing the remark. Why could she not keep her mouth shut?

Cammy had that broad, cat grin on her face again. "Jealous?"

Mrs. Albright patted her hand. "Do not be ashamed of it, my dear. We are all jealous of the woman who will capture the magistrate's heart." She then took Cammy's measurements and those of their aunt. "I'll put my best seamstresses to the task. Miss Willow's gown first. I should have it ready by late this afternoon and will bring it around myself."

"Thank you," said Aunt Charlotte, reaching into the coin purse attached to her belt.

"Oh, dear me. No. Magistrate Brayden has taken care of all the expenses. I'm not to take anything from you."

Her aunt gave an appreciative nod.

"It is very kind of him," Cammy said.

"It is," Mrs. Albright agreed. "But he's a good man and often generous to those in need."

"Ah, he's a spendthrift then," Willow muttered, more to herself because she wanted to find a reason not to like him.

"Well, he does spend quite a bit. But I would not call him a spendthrift."

Willow tipped her chin up in the air. "What would you call him then?"

Mrs. Albright grinned. "Since he's probably the largest land-owner in the area, and his business enterprises seem to make him money hand over fist, I would call him…rich."

CHAPTER THREE

S HAYNE HAD WAITED until early evening to return to Willow's guest chamber for the purpose of finalizing her formal witness statement but was surprised when he was met by her blazing stare. What had he done wrong now?

When she told him the reason, he ran a hand through his hair and laughed. "You are angry with me because I am not a pauper?"

She was dressed this time, a becoming gown the color of apricots that Mrs. Albright had managed to whip up in a matter of hours. The girl looked spectacular, but he was not about to give her the compliment while she was busy scolding him because he was wealthy.

She tipped her impertinent chin into the air. "I thought the office of town magistrate was an unpaid position."

"It is." He silently swore to himself that he was going to kiss that little dimple on her chin, along with many other spots on her exquisite body, before she left Taunton. "I do it out of a sense of duty to the good people of this town."

He thought he heard a squeak of dismay slip out between her clamped lips.

Her chin was still tipped up, and she was too busy being indignant to notice his gaze dipping to her chest each time she emitted a light heave. Earlier, Willow had muttered something about a man's low brain. He supposed this was it in action, this need to soak all of her in, and his frustration in not getting enough of a good, long look.

Bloody hell.

Is this what he had become? A leering dolt? He had not been raised this way and had never behaved in such unseemly fashion around any other woman before. Willow had a way of getting under his skin.

She was doing it again, her eyes still blazing and her soft lips pinched tight as she hurled her next barb. "I had no idea I was in the presence of a saint."

He folded his arms across his chest and stared down at her, uttering a low growl. "I am no saint. Do not ever mistake me for one."

Her eyes widened, and she licked her tongue along the seam of her lips, a quick, light flick that had his body in sudden combustion. He took a step back, needing this distance between them before he made an obvious fool of himself in front of Willow's chaperones.

He and Willow may have been alone in her guest chamber, but the connecting door between her room and her Aunt Charlotte's room was open, as he had insisted upon to protect her reputation. Both Charlotte and Cammy were in there and obviously listening in if their giggles, snorts, and chortles were any indication.

Cammy called to her sister from the other room. "Willow, stop being so mean to Mr. Brayden."

His lips quirked in a grin. "Thank you, Cammy."

"You are most welcome, Mr. Brayden. I like you, even if my sister tries to pretend she does not. Ouch! Aunt Charlotte, why did you pinch me?"

Willow's face turned a strawberry red, and she began to squirm uncomfortably. Finally, she emitted a sigh. "I have been mean to you. I don't understand why I am so prickly around you. You've been nothing but kind to us."

"We are all on edge because of Lord Belfy and his so-called friends. The danger is real, as you have experienced. But my men and I will do our best to catch the last of them." He motioned for her to sit on the chair beside her bed. "I've prepared your witness statement as you've told it to me. Take your time reading through it. If it is in order, then I will ask you to sign it."

He moved to the fireplace to put some distance between them, but her unmentionables were still set out beside it, delicate and small. He strode across to the window to peer out into the courtyard. Wisps of smoke still trailed upward from the burnt structure that once housed the guest carriages.

He would sift through the remains tomorrow, assuming the heat had subsided enough to allow them to walk through the rubble. He scanned the courtyard and beyond, his eyes immediately looking for anything out of the usual.

All appeared quiet.

But it was still daylight despite it being evening, for darkness fell late at this time of the year. He did not think Lord Manton would dare return here to cause more mischief while the sun was still out. Having set the fire, one would think this lord would now be running as far away from here as possible no matter the hour. But this pack of eight lords did not behave like normal people.

These were cruel, heartless men.

They operated like an ancient cabal.

He would not be surprised if they'd taken oaths to destroy all who got in their way. All for one and one for all, like a Dumas novel, except their minds were twisted, and they had no noble cause to bind them, only evil.

He did not care what they attempted to do to him. He was trained to defend himself. But these Farthingale sisters had unwittingly come to the attention of these jackals, and he was truly afraid of what the last three who had not yet been caught might try.

There was also the Earl of Monkton to protect, for the leader of this immoral pack was the earl's own brother, Lord Belfy. The earl, in helping them capture Lord Belfy, had now earned the vengeance of this wicked cabal.

Fortunately, both Donal and Lorcan were here to help him combat whatever mischief might be planned. They had come for what was meant to be a family visit, but both were trained, active agents of the Crown. He was glad for their presence because his regular guards were not up to the task of outwitting that pack of jackals.

He had assigned Donal to guard the Earl of Monkton and his family. He would now assign Lorcan to escort the Farthingale ladies to London. Willow's witness affidavit was enough to hold Lord Manton once they caught him. If her presence was required in Taunton at a later date, he would ask his cousin, Joshua Brayden, a captain in one of the king's elite army regiments, to return her under the protection of his soldiers.

He had also sent out men on his night watch to try to hunt down the last two lords who had not yet made their presence known. But Shayne knew they could not be far and had to be planning more trouble.

Adding to his headache were the newspaper reporters who were following Lord Belfy's demise. During that lord's trial, Shayne had detained two suspicious men in the courtroom. But he'd had to let them go once he was able to verify their credentials. Those men had since returned to London to provide their stories to their paper, a sensational account of Lord Belfy's attempted courtroom escape. Except that miscreant hadn't been trying to escape so much as attack Willow's sister, June, whose testimony had sealed his fate.

Once the ladies were on their way, he would join his men in hunting down the last of Lord Belfy's friends still at large, Lord Simmel, Lord Kearns, and Lord Manton.

However, for now, he meant to stay close to the inn because these innocents, Willow and Cammy, were likely to draw these men back, and he was bloody well not going to let either of them be hurt.

He rubbed the nape of his neck as he continued to stare out the window and formulate his plans. He had everything organized and operating efficiently except for one thing. He had not planned on his heart responding to Willow the way it had done.

He liked her even when she was fiery and hurling insults at him, but he was in greatest danger of falling in love with her when she was soft and showed her vulnerability. Not that he ever wanted her to be meek and scared. But a softer Willow was the sort of woman who could be a partner to him throughout their lives, the sort with whom he could share his concerns, ask for her thoughts.

The sort he would never tire of holding in his arms.

He turned when she cleared her throat and walked to his side. "It is very good, Mr. Brayden. You've accurately set forth everything I have told you. I'm ready to sign it. But I have no inkpot or quill pen at hand. Unfortunately, those all burned along with our clothes and carriage. I can sign it downstairs by Mr. Ashcott's desk. He keeps his pot and pen there."

She looked down at herself when he hesitated. "Am I not presentable? I can do up my hair now that it is dry. At least I still have my brush and hair pins. Give me a moment to put on these new walking boots."

Her aunt and sister, having overheard them, came back in. "Indeed," her aunt said, "we shall soon be going downstairs for our supper. Will you join us, Mr. Brayden?"

"No, thank you." He motioned to the parchment in his hand. "I'll take this back to my office once Willow signs it, then I must attend to securing my prisoners for the night. But I will stop in once again before you retire."

Willow's sister helped her pin her hair while he continued to speak to their aunt. "I keep a carriage at my estate. I will send word to have it brought to the inn. My driver should arrive sometime tomorrow afternoon. He will take you to London the following morning. Lorcan had better ride with you for the added protection. Your driver, that Pierson fellow, seems to be drunk more often than he's sober. I do not like him, nor do I trust him to protect you."

"Oh, he isn't so bad. I'm sure having to wait around here is wearing on his nerves. He isn't a very clever fellow and not much at holding a job. But he is harmless and needed the money, so we decided to do him the favor."

Shayne frowned. "All the more reason for Lorcan to escort you. Mr. Pierson can ride with my driver, but he isn't to touch the reins. If he'd rather return to Barnstaple, I'll put him on the next mail coach headed west. In truth, I would rather he not be around you in his drunken state."

"That is most kind of you, Mr. Brayden. Truly, I do not know what we would have done without your generosity."

"I'm sure the people of Taunton would have chipped in to help you out. It is usually a peaceful town. Lord Belfy and his friends spend most of their time in London, thankfully. But you had the misfortune of arriving just as a Monkton family wedding was taking place. Since those lords travel with Lord Belfy wherever he goes, they were all here. Well, six of them that we know of. I haven't seen the other two yet, but it does not mean they aren't around."

"My nieces and I shall remain vigilant. We shall sleep with fire irons beside our beds if we must."

He liked Willow's aunt. She was clever and had as much spirit as her nieces. Indeed, despite losing everything, the three of them had remained remarkably poised...if one overlooked Willow's moment of madness over that book. "Willow, are you ready?"

"Yes, just lacing up my boot." She was bent over, her delightful backside on display.

He stifled a groan and turned away.

Willow's aunt had her gaze on him.

Did he say he admired her cleverness? He took it back. He wished she was dense as a doorstop. But no, his luck was not that good. Despite being a spinster, she understood exactly what was going through his mind.

He marched to the door, opened it, and checked down the

hall for anything out of place. "It's safe. Cammy, stay with your aunt. I'll return your sister here in a few minutes."

Willow took his arm as they walked along the hall and down the steps. "I should have asked earlier about those last two friends of Lord Belfy's. What are their names? What do they look like?"

She was right.

He should have told the ladies.

He corrected the oversight now. "Lord Kearns is about my height but quite thin. Do not mistake his frail appearance for weakness. He may dress the height of fashion, but at heart, he is a barbarian. Wiry red hair. Green eyes. Thin face and pointed chin. Pale skin, the sort of pallor one achieves from dosing themselves with laudanum. These lords were schoolmates, so they are all about the same age."

"And the last lord? What does he look like?"

"That's Lord Simmel. He's about a head shorter than me. Stocky. Dark eyes. Dark hair that he wears long, falling below his shoulders. He has a scar on his chin in the shape of a crescent moon. I put it there during our last encounter."

Willow gasped and looked up at him. "Then he will be here for certain, won't he? The way you describe these men, they will not be satisfied until they've wreaked ruin and destruction on anyone who has ever crossed their path."

"I am not afraid of him. I've been besting him for years. I can only hope he will come after me first and not anyone else. Bloody hell, I'll toss his bony arse behind bars so fast, he—" He sighed. "Forgive my language, Miss Farthingale."

She smiled up at him. "In this, you are wholeheartedly forgiven. My father is a perfect gentleman and the kindest man alive, but he swears like a pirate. June, Cammy, and I adore him and used to hang upon his every word as we were growing up. Needless to say, as infants, we started repeating everything he said. We were little and just learning how to speak. Imagine my mother's horror when the most blasphemous oaths came out of the mouths of her three little angels."

He laughed.

They were now at Mr. Ashcott's desk.

Shayne asked for the use of his quill pen.

"Of course," Mr. Ashcott said, eager to accommodate. "Come around, Miss Farthingale. You'll be more comfortable seated in my chair."

She scooted around his desk, dipped the quill in the inkpot, and signed her name in perfect penmanship.

Shayne waited another moment for the ink to dry, then rolled up the parchment and escorted her back to her chamber. She had taken hold of his arm again as they walked upstairs, so he now placed his hand over hers before they reached her door. "Willow, promise me you'll be careful. Return here immediately after supper and don't go wandering the halls. If you need anything, ring for one of the staff to fetch it. Do not open the door to any voice you do not recognize. I will be back later tonight and again in the morning to look in on you."

"I will. Please don't worry about us. We'll be careful." She paused a moment and smiled up at him. "Thank you for everything you are doing for us. It is a wonder you will even speak to me after my surly behavior toward you. I think losing *The Book of Love* has affected me more than I ever expected. Mostly because it was my responsibility to protect it, and I failed."

She shook out of her momentary wistfulness and continued. "Perhaps we are alike in this, both of us taking our responsibilities quite seriously. Well, until later then, Mr. Brayden. Do you think you might take me through the carriage house remains tomorrow morning?"

"Yes, if I deem it safe enough. Enjoy your supper, Willow."

He watched her enter her room and heard the latch fall on the door before he turned to walk away. She was going to haunt his dreams again tonight, assuming he got any sleep.

When he returned to his office, he sent an eager Lorcan off to join his regular guards in tracking Lord Manton. Donal had already gone off to protect the Earl of Monkton and his family. It was left to him and the remainder of his night watch to guard their five prisoners. He could have left it to his men alone, but his instincts warned something would happen tonight.

As they tightened the noose on the three remaining lords, they had to be growing desperate. If they were to help their friends escape, it had to be done before they were moved to the sturdier Exeter prison.

Since it was still daylight and his men appeared to be suitably diligent in guarding these unholy five for the moment, Shayne went into his private back office and stretched out on the cot he kept in there. His turn at night watch would be in the wee hours when all the world would be asleep. This was the most dangerous time, for the taprooms closed down for the night, and the town was draped in darkness. No one trustworthy would be up and about at that hour.

As was often their routine when watching the more hardened prisoners, Shayne stood guard until daybreak when one of his men took a turn in relief. He and his brothers were trained in such matters and prided themselves on their keen eyes and good instincts.

Those instincts warned he would be kept busy tonight.

He sank onto his cot and had managed a good hour of sleep before one of his guardsmen woke him.

"Shayne, Mrs. Ashcott is here with supper for the prisoners. You asked to be told when she arrived."

"Yes. Thank you, Ezekiel."

He shook off the haze of sleep and strode out of his office to greet her. "Mrs. Ashcott, is it the usual fare?"

She nodded, her plump cheeks still ruddy from the heat of the inn's kitchen. "Just as you instructed. Food they can eat with their hands. No utensils. You aren't taking any chances with these lords, are you?"

"No, not a one. I'll be glad to have them safely stowed away in Exeter."

"So will we all," she said with a solemn shake of her head.

"How is Miss Charlotte? And her nieces?"

"They've had their supper and are now back in their rooms."

He nodded. "I'll walk over in an hour for a final check on them. I'm hoping Lorcan will return with Lord Manton in hand by then. If luck is on our side, he'll have Simmel and Kearns in custody as well."

"One can only hope." She lumbered out to return to her guests, for the inn was full, and the carriages were lined up in the courtyard since there was nowhere else to house them yet. Fortunately, the skies had remained clear of rain.

Shayne hoped the weather would cooperate for the next few days, not only for the sake of the carriages. Lorcan needed to follow untouched tracks. Rain would wipe them all away and make his task more difficult.

As night fell, Shayne decided he had put up with as much grumbling from these pampered lords as he could tolerate for an evening. They had eaten their meals, thrown the bones at his guards, and were now shouting to be released.

They would grow hoarse shortly and quiet down.

In the meanwhile, he and his men swept up the mess, then he took the dirty dishes back to the inn.

He left them in the kitchen for the scullery maids, who greeted him with welcoming smiles and eye flutters.

After a few polite words, he strode through the inn to make certain there was no trouble. Mr. Ashcott nodded to him as he marched upstairs to look in on the Farthingales. "Willow, it's me."

The door quickly opened.

Willow was in her robe, this time with a nightrail under it, but looking no less enticing despite the additional layer of clothing. Her hair was brushed back in a loose braid that draped over her shoulder in a wave of golden red. Cammy was similarly attired, her blonde curls also braided. Charlotte strolled in from her connecting room, also in her robe and wearing a hideous white sleeping cap over her dark hair that was peppered with gray. "Mr. Brayden, rest assured we are all fine. I shall keep our connecting door open, and we will all have weapons close at hand."

Willow grinned and reached over the side of her bed to hold up her weapon of choice, the hearth shovel.

Cammy did the same, scurrying to her bed and holding up a fire iron.

It pained him to think they had to resort to this protection in an elegant inn, especially in *his* town. "I have a few men posted around the grounds, but this does not mean you can let down your guard."

"We won't," Willow assured him.

"Then I will bid you a final good evening. I'll see you in the morning." He strode out, not daring to turn back for a glance at this exquisite girl. She was already etched in his memory. Big eyes, soft lips, pink cheeks. Little ears.

Beautiful body.

His chest felt as though he'd just been hit with a cannonball.

This is what a mere glance at Willow did to him.

He strode out of the inn and was about to walk back to his office to secure the prisoners for the evening when he heard a shot ring out followed by the smash and tinkle of glass falling like raindrops onto the courtyard.

Willow.

He shouted for the two guards he'd posted at the inn. "See to the Farthingale ladies. Summon a doctor if any of them are hurt."

He withdrew his pistol from the lip of his boot and took off in the direction of the hill just behind the now burned-down carriage house. The shot had to have come from there. But as he ran toward it, he heard the thunder of hooves and knew he would not catch up to the culprit while he was on foot.

He cursed and hurried back to the inn, taking a closer look at the broken window.

Yes, it was Willow's window.

He tore upstairs and hurried through the open door. "Charlotte, are the girls all right?"

But he feared the answer, for Charlotte was holding a weeping Cammy in her arms. His men were kneeling beside the damaged window and now looked up at him in dismay. They were kneeling over a body, they had to be.

His heart shot into his throat.

Lord in heaven.

"Willow?"

CHAPTER FOUR

SHAYNE'S HEART WAS in his throat as he rushed to Willow's side. His men moved out of his way to give him access to her, where she sat crumpled on the floor amid shattered glass. "I'm all right, Mr. Brayden," she said, her voice and body trembling to reveal that she was quite the opposite of all right.

A light breeze blew in from the shattered window, carrying with it the warm night air and a lingering scent of the acrid, fire-ravaged carriage house.

"Some pieces of glass dug into your arm," he muttered, his voice husky from anger. He ran his hands down her body to make certain she'd suffered no other injuries.

Whoever had fired that rifle blast had missed her.

Thank goodness for little mercies.

Judging from the residue now staining the counterpane, it appeared to have been scattershot, more likely to wound than kill, although that flying glass might have killed Willow if it had severed an artery.

Her arm had caught the worst of it.

Thank heaven it missed her face.

"Jasper, fetch the doctor for Miss Farthingale. She will need a few stitches once the glass is taken out of her arm. Martin, I'll need bandages and some brandy. I'm sure Mrs. Ashcott will have both available."

Willow sat quietly as his men ran off to attend to their tasks.

He knew she was trying to remain stoic, but she had to be frightened out of her wits and could not stop trembling. Worse, she was in obvious pain. "Willow, you will definitely need stitches," he said, sweeping aside the shards of glass to kneel beside her.

"But will she be all right?" Cammy asked, openly weeping.

He nodded. "Yes. However, she has some nasty cuts. Willow, I'm going to start pulling out some of these shards from your arm. I'll be as gentle as I can. The doctor will take over once he arrives. But I dare not wait. Let me know if I hurt you."

He knew it was going to hurt, but it couldn't be helped. The glass had to be removed as soon as possible.

She nodded and cast him a brave smile even as tears rolled down her ashen cheeks. "Yes, go ahead, Mr. Brayden. I won't complain."

"I'm so sorry. I would do anything not to…"

He must have appeared quite pained himself, for she put her uninjured hand on his arm. "I know. It is all right. None of this is your fault."

This girl affected him deeply.

Her gentle strength tugged at his heart.

She closed her eyes and clenched her teeth as he proceeded to draw out the larger pieces, for those were the ones that had pierced through her robe and now dug into her flesh. "Miss Charlotte, get me any clean cloths you can find. I have to stanch the bleeding."

Cammy sobbed again.

But Charlotte immediately hurried to the task and returned with several.

"Thank you." He worked quickly to also remove the remaining smaller pieces. Thankfully, there were not too many of those. As soon as that was done, he unfastened Willow's robe and gently slipped it off her arm. He tried his best to ignore the delicate curves of her body, especially the lush mound of her breast that was too clearly outlined beneath the sheer fabric of her nightrail.

"Cammy, bring me the ewer and basin. But mind the glass."

She nodded and quickly did as bidden. "I'll ask Mrs. Ashcott to send up a maid to sweep away this mess." She set down the ewer and basin beside him and hurried downstairs before he could stop her. He supposed she would be safe enough with his guards down there and the Ashcotts and all their staff on alert by now.

Half the inn would be up here in a few moments.

Willow winced as he applied a damp cloth to her arm and then held it there to maintain pressure on the spots that were bleeding most. Two cuts appeared deep enough to warrant the doctor's tending. The others were minor and had only a spot of blood where tiny shards had struck her flesh but not really pierced the skin. Those marks would disappear within a day, but not so for the deeper wounds.

Droplets of red fell onto her white nightgown.

She laughed softly. "I shall have no clothes to wear if this keeps up."

This was not the time for lewd thoughts to hop into his brain, but of course, they did. Willow without clothes? His dreams were haunted with that vision. "Mrs. Albright must have a nightrail or two of suitable size in her shop. She'll provide something for you. Whatever you need. I will work it out with your father afterward."

He'd only said the last to appease her.

He had no intention of ever asking her father for repayment on any purchases.

His men returned with the bandages and brandy. Mrs. Ashcott ran up along with them, broom in hand, and quickly swept away the broken glass.

Willow called out to her. "I'm so sorry, Mrs. Ashcott. We've caused you so much trouble."

The woman frowned. "None of this is your fault. You poor dear, stopping here on your way to London and now losing all your belongings and getting injured because of those knaves.

They've been plaguing us for years. Small things mostly, but every year they grow bolder and meaner. First, they try to harm your dear sister, June. Good thing General MacLauren was there to protect her. And now they've turned their malice on you."

She gave a *harrumph* and glanced worshipfully at Shayne. "But our magistrate is not going to let them get away with it. Those fiends will get what they deserve, and we'll all be cheering loudly for it. Don't you worry about us. We have a longstanding arrangement with the Earl of Monkton. He pays for any damage done by his brother and those friends of his. Ugly pack of wolves they are."

Mrs. Ashcott glanced at Shayne again before continuing. "Mr. Brayden will be looking after you now. You'll be very nicely cared for while you are here. You can have no better protector, I assure you."

She swept up the last of the shards, still chattering. "Mr. Ashcott will be up here shortly to move you and your family to another set of connecting rooms. I'll be back as soon as I get rid of these nasty pieces of glass."

Shayne watched her scurry out.

Willow cleared her throat to regain his attention.

He turned to her and grinned when he noticed her expression. Despite her pain, she had an eyebrow impudently arched and was smirking at him. "Is that right? Will you nicely care for me?"

He nodded. "I've already assured you I can be very nice."

"Obviously a statement fraught with double meaning. What exactly does that entail?"

He gave her cheek a light caress. "Let's get the bleeding stopped, and you stitched up, then we'll see."

By the time the doctor arrived, Shayne had settled Willow in a chair beside a small side table since the doctor would need to set his medical instruments within easy reach while he stitched her wounds. He remained kneeling by her side, his arm around her as she leaned against him, obviously scared and grateful for his support.

He held her while the doctor examined her arm. "You did a good job, Shayne. Let me put a couple of stitches in each cut. I'll be as gentle as I can, Miss Farthingale." He took out a bottle that held a clear liquid and uncorked it, immediately releasing a pungent smell. "This will help numb the area of these cuts."

Willow glanced at Shayne worriedly.

He understood her fear. "I won't leave you. I'll be right here the entire time, holding your hand. Dr. Stratton is the very best. He'll be done before you know it."

The doctor nodded. "I've had a little too much practice for my liking, lately. Those cowards are going to get what they deserve. First trying to shoot General MacLauren, and now trying to hurt you. I hope they hang the lot of them."

The doctor kept chattering as he worked, continually asking Willow questions that she was able to respond to with short answers. No doubt, he meant to distract her from the pain of his necessary ministrations. "I hear you are from Barnstaple, Miss Farthingale?"

"Yes," she replied, wincing as he tucked a stitch in her arm.

Shayne had his fingers wrapped in hers and felt her squeeze them hard with each pinch of the needle. Seeing her hurt was a hundred times worse than any injury he had ever endured. He wished it was him and not her suffering through this.

"Devonshire's a lovely area. My wife and I considered moving there, but her family has been settled here in Taunton for generations, so we ultimately decided to remain." He sewed two more stitches. "And now you are off for London. Have you ever been to London before?"

"Once when I was a child." She gasped as he pricked her with the needle again. "But my sisters and I were too young to be taken around to see the sights, so I hardly think it counts. Most of our travels were to join the family for Christmas up north in Coniston. It is a Farthingale tradition."

"Ah, yes. I know of Coniston. It is in the Lake District. How lovely. My wife and I went up there on holiday once. Beautiful scenery. Those lakes and hills are magnificent. And there are excellent walks. My wife prefers the shops, but I prefer the bracing air and climbing those hills."

He went on and on about his travels in the Lake District until putting in the last stitch. "All done, Miss Farthingale. The worst is over now. I shall give you some laudanum for the pain that you will likely experience tonight and tomorrow. Hopefully, it will only be a mild discomfort that will pass quickly. I will take the stitches out in a week's time."

"Oh, I don't think that is possible. We ought to be in London by then," Willow said, accepting the little bottle of the drug and taking a spoonful of its contents, which she obviously found distasteful by the grimace she made after swallowing it. "We have a doctor in the family, George Farthingale. He's the best in London."

"Indeed, I know of him. Never had the pleasure of meeting him." He stowed his supplies in his medical bag and rose. "Miss Farthingale, please have me summoned at any time should you feel the need, especially if you develop a fever. I am at your service at all hours."

Willow smiled at him. "Thank you, Dr. Stratton. That is very kind of you."

Shayne turned to her once the doctor walked out. "Let me take you to your new chambers. Do you want to take a quick look around to make certain your sister and aunt left nothing behind?"

"Would you mind doing this for me? We have almost nothing anyway, and Mr. Ashcott's workmen will let us know if they find anything we've overlooked. I'm sure they'll be here soon to fix the window." She took a deep breath and groaned. "Mr. Brayden, I don't think I have the strength to stand on my own at the moment. I think my legs will give way if I attempt to get out of this chair."

"Then stay seated, Willow. Take all the time you need. You

were incredibly brave. I would have been howling like a baby."

She laughed. "I doubt it sincerely. I don't think I've ever met anyone more stoic than you."

He nodded. "I'm not an expressive man by nature."

She laughed again. "That is quite an understatement. You hide your every thought so well. You rarely talk unless you have something specific to say. I've dubbed you the grunting man because that is all you seemed to do when I first met you."

"I am touched by your flattering description of me." He gave her chin a gentle tweak. "Let me take a last look around, then I'll carry you into your new quarters." It took him less than a minute to accomplish the task. "Seems everything has been accounted for. Put your good arm around my neck. Can you do that?"

She nodded.

He picked her up and held her to him for a moment, partly to steady himself against the perfection of her body and partly to give her time to get comfortable in his arms. "All right?"

She nodded again. "Do all the women in town get this excellent service from you?"

"It hasn't come up before. But if they were hurt and bleeding? It would be my duty to help."

She looked disappointed.

"Willow, you are not a mere duty to me." He carried her out into the hall.

"Are you suggesting that you might actually like me?"

He arched an eyebrow and laughed. "Was I not clear on this point? I've never kissed a witness other than you. Nor do I randomly go about kissing women. You have a way of growing on a person. Slowly, quietly."

"Me? quiet?"

He smiled broadly. "Perhaps not so quiet. But you do have a way of creeping up on a man."

"Be still my heart. You sound like you're describing fungus around a tree. Do you think you might be a little more flowery in your description?"

He chuckled as he marched down the hall, pausing as they neared the door to her new guest chamber. "No. I'm not the poetry-spouting sort."

"I did not mistake you for one of those romantic gentlemen. I doubt I'd ever come across you in a literary club. You are a man of action." Her fingers teased the hair at the nape of his neck. "You could kiss me again. That would not require talking."

"I could, but I am not going to do it now."

She blushed. "Does this mean you might consider doing it at a later time?"

"Yes, when you are healed and not drugged with laudanum." His expression turned serious. "I would be honored to kiss you then."

She nestled against his shoulder. "Thank you, Mr. Brayden. Is that a promise?"

"You are most welcome, Miss Farthingale. Yes, it is a promise."

"Good. I need to rest my head against your shoulder. The world seems to be spinning around me. I'm so dizzy. It hurts to keep my eyes open." She yawned. "It is the laudanum, I think."

"It will put you to sleep and ease your pain." He could have kissed her now because there was no one else in the hall, and they would have had a modicum of privacy, but it did not feel right. He'd stolen their first kiss and did not intend to steal another that she might regret once on the mend.

He wasn't sure why he felt it was important, only that he did not want to take advantage of her while she was in this delicate condition. Pain had a way of tearing down one's defenses, and Willow had to be feeling a considerable amount of it right now.

He doubted the laudanum had fully worked its way through her body yet, or she would be unconscious in his arms. However, the numbing solution the doctor had poured on her arm might have enhanced the unpleasant, dizzying effect and quickened the impact of the stronger drug. She was now rambling, talking at him rather than to him, and asking him for more promises that she would never have asked for if she had been thinking clearly.

She giggled and told him he was extraordinarily handsome.

"Thank you, Willow."

He hoped she would forget this conversation had ever taken place come morning because she was not yet finished expounding on his merits. While he much enjoyed the truth of her feelings spilling out, he knew she would be mortified once the medicine wore off and she realized what her unleashed brain had revealed.

She began to nuzzle his neck. "I think you kiss very nicely, Mr. Brayden."

He tamped down a smile, not wanting to encourage this conversation, especially once they were in front of her aunt and sister.

She closed her eyes and sighed against his throat. "It was my first time," she said in a whisper. "Kissing you, I mean."

"I know."

"I will try to do better next time."

He wanted to capture her lips and kiss her into eternity. This girl was so soft and sweet. "Nothing wrong with that first time. Just be yourself, Willow. You'll be perfect."

He knocked on the door that was left slightly ajar and waited for Charlotte or Cammy to let him in. Cammy did so immediately, her eyes red and swollen and tears still running down her cheeks. She was another sweet one, very caring of her sister, and quite distressed to see her suffering. "Come in, Mr. Brayden. Is Willow sleeping?"

"Not quite yet, but the doctor gave her some laudanum to ease the pain, and it might be starting to work. It has made her drowsy."

"Drowsy and talkative," Cammy muttered, leaning in to hear what Willow was going on about. "I can't understand what she is saying."

"It is just nonsense chatter." He hoped she would stop talking soon.

He glanced around the well-appointed room, pleased to note

it was as fine as the one she'd been staying in up to now. The connecting door to the adjacent room was open, and Charlotte came scurrying through it.

"Where shall I set her down?" he asked. "She cannot remain in these nightclothes."

Her robe and nightrail were stained with blood, the ominous patches of red so stark against the white of her nightrail and the darker cream shade of her robe. Both garments needed to be removed. Of course, the task could not fall to him.

"She can sleep in her chemise," Cammy said, quickly searching through the small pile of clothing on one of the beds and pulling out the delicate undergarment. "I have it right here. It's dry now. This ought to do for the evening."

The fabric was sheer and delicate.

He refused to think of how spectacular Willow would look in it.

He needed only to glance at the dark stitches on her swollen arm to push all wanton thoughts from his brain. "I'll wait outside your door until she's made comfortable. Call me if you need my help." He cleared his throat. "In case she falls. Be careful. She might pass out because of the medicine she's taken. Be gentle. Her arm has to be quite sore."

Cammy cast him a consoling smile. "We will be, Mr. Brayden. I'll call you in once we have her settled. I think she would like to say goodnight to you. Thank you for worrying about her."

He groaned and raked a hand through his hair. "I feel responsible for this."

Charlotte frowned at him. "You are doing everything you can, but how can anyone control the bad behavior of those villains? They've left us all overset and apologizing left and right. We feel awful about the damage to the inn. The Ashcotts feel awful about the loss of our carriage and belongings, and now Willow's injury. You feel as though you've let us all down. And I feel to blame for delaying us in Taunton when we should have been safely in London by now. But I did so want June to have her chance at love with General MacLauren."

"And she did," Cammy interjected with an emphatic nod. "My sister left here happier than I've ever seen her. It was worth our staying a few extra days. She found true love and married General MacLauren. It might not have happened otherwise. I'm glad we remained. I only hope Willow and I find love matches."

A sly smile suddenly crossed Cammy's lips. "You've been awfully nice to Willow, Mr. Brayden."

He cleared his throat. "Right, well. I'll be standing just outside your door."

He left before Cammy got any matchmaking ideas in her head. Not that he wasn't interested in Willow. His body was a riotous mess over her. But he did not need her family meddling. He would go about it in his own good time.

Or not go about it at all if he thought his interest in her would put her at further risk. Seeing her in pain tonight was unbearable for him.

He could not live with himself if his actions made her a prime target for these villains. They all needed to be caught, put on trial, and sentenced to banishment from England. Of course, Lord Belfy would face the stiffest penalty for the attempted murder of General MacLauren. It had been ruled an act of treason, and he was sentenced to hang for the offense since Augustus MacLauren was one of the king's closest confidantes, leader of England's military forces in Europe, and top advisor to Lord Castlereagh at the Vienna conferences.

Lord Belfy might have taken the assault as a lark, another one of his wicked games, but no one else in England was laughing about it.

No one outside his tight circle of friends was sorry he would pay for it with his life.

The Ashcotts and their staff were still hurrying about, tending to their other guests, and also attending to the broken window and blood stains in the other room. He watched them run back and forth, but it wasn't long before the door to Willow's new quarters opened, and Charlotte motioned for him to come in.

She stepped aside as he strode in. "She's barely awake but still chattering. Mostly nonsense. I'm sure she will drift off at any moment. Pay no mind to what she says."

"I won't stay long." He nodded as he moved a chair beside Willow's bed and took gentle hold of her hand. "Willow, are you comfortable now?"

She looked beautiful, her skin pink and delicate, what he could see of her now that she was neatly tucked beneath her blankets.

Her eyes flickered open, and she cast him a genuine smile. "Yes, although my body feels as though it is floating. Will you still take me to see our carriage tomorrow?"

He stifled a sigh of frustration. Sifting through those ashes would only upset her, and yet she would not let go of the hope of finding that book of hers until she saw that it was truly gone. He did not want to do it, but how could he deny her request after all she had been through? "If it is safe, yes. We'll do it in the afternoon if you are feeling up to it."

"I will be."

"We'll see. I want you to get a good night's rest. Sleep late. Mrs. Ashcott will bring breakfast up to your room in the late morning."

"I don't think I can hold down food."

"She'll bring up something light. You don't have to eat if your stomach is too queasy to manage it. Don't think about it tonight. Just rest."

"I'll think about you. Do you mind?"

"No, I don't mind." He kissed her on the forehead, no longer caring what anyone thought. The gesture was innocent enough.

Willow cast him a sleepy but still impertinent smile. "That doesn't count, Mr. Brayden."

"What?"

"That doesn't count as a proper kiss. It must be a kiss on the lips, or it doesn't count. You have very nice lips. Has anyone told you that?" Her eyes were now fluttering closed, and she was beginning to slur her words.

He hoped she would drift off before she gave away that he had already kissed her. Not that he regretted it or particularly cared if others knew. But he did not want her to get in trouble over it. He did not know her aunt and sister well enough to be sure how they would take it. Nor would he succumb to threats to marry her over a simple kiss.

"Very nice lips, indeed," she murmured. "I'm sure lots of women have told you that."

Laudanum affected everyone differently, mostly putting those who took too much of it into a catatonic stupor. The doctor had given Willow just enough to make her talkative.

Mercy.

"No, Willow. They haven't."

"Then they are very silly women. I think it would be very nice to fall asleep to your kiss. To be in your arms and kissed."

Cammy and Charlotte were listening in on their conversation and had to be wondering about it. Let them think whatever they will. First of all, he was not going to deny Willow any request in her condition. Nor would Cammy and Charlotte make too much of it even if he agreed to kiss her now. They would likely believe he was humoring her.

Earlier, he had promised to kiss her.

He meant to keep that promise, preferably not while she was drugged and rambling.

He leaned over and kissed her on the cheek.

Truly, she was soft and sweet.

He would worry about the repercussions of this light kiss afterward. "Go to sleep, Willow."

"Your eyes are nice, too."

"So are yours. No more talking, Willow." He rose from her side. "Latch your doors, ladies. I'll be at my office standing watch over the prisoners tonight. Summon me if she takes a turn for the worse."

"We will," Cammy assured, walking him to the door. "She's right. You do have nice eyes."

He groaned. "Don't you start on me."

She laughed and thanked him for all he'd done.

He walked downstairs, made certain his men were standing guard, and then walked next door to his office. "Any problems with the prisoners?" he asked Ezekiel.

"No, Shayne. All quiet. But that puts me all the more on edge. Do you think their friends will try to break them out tonight?"

"Yes. They must, for they are running out of time to accomplish it." He had no sooner uttered the words than he heard the rumble of horses approaching. "Bloody hell, could this be them now?"

Ezekiel strode to peer out the window while he rushed into the back room to grab their rifles. "Shayne, look at this. I don't believe it."

Shayne handed him one of the rifles and joined him in looking out the window. "I'll be...Lorcan's got them. All three of them."

He and Ezekiel rushed out to greet his brother and the night watch guards who had been searching with him. While the guards took care of locking up these last three villains, Shayne took his brother aside and clapped him on the shoulder. "Well done, baby brother."

Lorcan cast him a smug grin. "Was there any doubt I'd find them? Those men left tracks a blind man could follow. We would have been back sooner, but my horse threw a shoe, so we were delayed in Monkton while I had it replaced."

"So, Manton got as far as Monkton? Where did you find the others?"

"They were with him. Three rats all hiding in the same hole, a rundown tavern in one of the less elegant parts of town. How are things here? Quiet?"

"No, there was an incident." He frowned, wondering how

Lorcan could have found them all in Monkton. Perhaps his sense of timing was off. "One of these villains tried to shoot Willow. The scattershot missed her, but the window shattered, and shards flew into her arm. The doctor saw to her. She needed stitches, but she'll be all right."

Lorcan frowned. "When did this happen?"

"About two hours ago."

Lorcan stared at him. "Hell, that can't be right. No wonder you're frowning at me. Seriously, that can't be right. I've had all three lords in custody since late this afternoon. Manton, Kearns, and Simmel. If someone took a shot at her only two hours ago, then they could not have been the ones to do it."

A knot formed in Shayne's stomach. "You're jesting. Tell me you are jesting."

"I wish I were."

Shayne stared at his brother. "If they aren't the culprits, then who is?"

CHAPTER FIVE

ILLOW AWOKE TO a throbbing arm the following morning. She yelped when she accidentally leaned on it while attempting to sit up. Then a blinding light struck her as her sister opened the drapes to allow the sun to spill in, revealing another beautiful summer day.

She blinked to adjust her eyes to the sudden brilliance. "What did you do that for?"

Cammy came to her side. "How are you feeling? The room was dark as a mausoleum. I thought the sunshine would cheer you."

"I think this must be what a hangover feels like. I don't know what hurts worse, my throbbing arm or my pounding head. What time is it?"

"Just shy of noon." She sat on the bed beside her and put a hand to her brow for a closer inspection. "Good, no fever. We didn't want to wake you. Mrs. Ashcott brought up a breakfast tray about an hour ago. The tea might be tepid by now, but I'll ask her to brew another pot for you. Are you thirsty?"

She nodded.

The laudanum had dried out her mouth and left her throat raspy.

"She also brought you Devonshire buns. Those are still warm and should be fine to eat. Would you like me to put a little strawberry jam on them? There's also clotted cream, but I know you are not too fond of it. There's also marmalade cake. Would you like a slice?"

She smiled at her sister when she poured her a little of the tea. Willow eagerly took a few sips, then handed the cup back to Cammy. "My stomach is still in a roil. I don't think I can hold down anything too rich. A slice of marmalade cake will do for now. And never mind about a fresh pot of tea. I prefer to have it tepid this morning, since I'm likely to spill most of it on myself anyway. Look." She held out her hands to show they were shaking. "I'm not at all steady yet."

"Oh, dear." Cammy cast her a worried look. "Do you need more laudanum? Would you like me to feed you? I saw you wince when you moved your arm."

"No more laudanum for now. It made me feel so odd. I could hear myself chattering, but I don't remember much of what I said." She carefully shifted to a more comfortable position and set the plate of cakes Cammy now handed her on her lap. The marmalade cake was still warm, and she caught the fragrant scent of peeled oranges as she took a bite of it. Little bits of dried fruit were also in the cake, apricots, raisins, and plums.

Cammy chuckled lightly. "You were a chatterbox last night. Especially with the magistrate."

"He was here? I didn't dream him?"

Her sister nodded. "Poor man, he was so worried about you. You put on quite a show for him."

Willow groaned. "What did I do?"

"It's more what you said to him. *Ooh, Mr. Brayden, you have the nicest lips.*" She made smacking sounds that were obviously supposed to be kisses. "*Ooh, you have the finest eyes.*" She batted her eyelashes as though caught in a dust storm and furiously trying to keep the dust out of her eyes. "*Ooh, may I touch your body?*"

Willow choked on her cake. "Tell me I did not say any such thing!"

"Well, a slight exaggeration, but I'm afraid you said most of it. You definitely wanted him to kiss you."

"I did?" She groaned again and sank back against her pillows. "He already considers me a ninny."

"He does not."

"Do you think he'll say anything to me about it? How can I ever face him again?" She emitted a pitiful wail. "He'll know I am the biggest idiot ever to walk the earth. This is awful. We must leave right away."

"We cannot. You have no clothes."

"Nonsense, I have two gowns. The one I was wearing yesterday morning ought to be dry by now. And there's the apricot gown Mrs. Albright made for me yesterday afternoon. Those will be enough to get me to London."

"How? By walking? Mr. Brayden's carriage won't arrive until this afternoon. And since when are you the sort to run away from a challenge?"

"Since it means facing Shayne Brayden. This is awful."

"I don't think he minded your compliments at all. It is obvious he likes you."

"Perhaps he was starting to like me, but how can he not change his mind after this?"

Cammy's expression turned serious. "He was beside himself with worry when you got hurt. He did not want to leave your side. He would have sat with you through the night if he could have, which reminds me! You'll never guess what happened after you fell asleep!"

"Wasn't my getting shot enough?" Willow stopped feeling sorry for herself and sat up again. "What else happened? Out with it, Cammy. What have I missed?"

"Lorcan Brayden caught the last three of Lord Belfy's group of miscreants and returned with them last night. Lords Manton, Kearns, and Simmel are now behind bars along with their partners in crime. The magistrate means to keep them locked away. Now that he has them all, he plans on moving them to Exeter as soon as possible. He and Lorcan can make the ride in a day. But they will do it in shifts, taking a few prisoners at a time. They are planning it now."

Willow breathed a sigh of relief. "Do they know which of them fired that shot through our window?"

Cammy took her hand. "There's a slight complication about that."

"Cammy, I am going to throttle you if you don't tell me right now. What sort of complication? My head may be a little foggy, but I can still put coherent thoughts together."

"The thing of it is, none of them did. Lorcan had them all in custody in Monkton when that shot was fired. Obviously, it could not have been one of them."

A knot formed in Willow's stomach. "Was it someone they paid?"

"The magistrate doesn't think so. These men act together and never let anyone into their inner circle. Besides, Lord Belfy's allowance has been cut off. And Mr. Brayden doesn't think any of the others have the blunt to pay someone to commit this crime."

Willow gaped at her sister. "If not them, then who would want to hurt us? Or was it perhaps someone seeking vengeance against the Ashcotts and just happened to hit our window?"

"He is looking into it. I get the sense he has his suspicions, but he won't saying anything until he is certain."

She set aside her plate, feeling too ill to take another bite.

"Mr. Brayden wanted me to let him know when you woke up. Would you mind if I went to fetch him now?"

"You can't." She put a hand to her hair. "I must look a mess. No, don't let him in here. Where's Aunt Charlotte?"

"She went to Mrs. Albright's shop to see about her new gowns. And mine. It is awfully nice of Mr. Brayden to take care of our expenses. I'm going to fetch him. Don't get all worked up. You look beautiful."

She hurried out before Willow could stop her.

Not that she had the strength to hold her ebullient sister back while lying here weak as a mouse.

She wasn't even able to move the tray of cakes off her bed or get out of bed to brush her hair and make herself presentable. The tragic heroines in the romantic books she and her sisters loved to read always managed to look magnificent as they lay dying.

Well, she supposed it was not very romantic to die, even if you managed to look spectacular in the arms of the man you loved. It seemed awfully wasteful to die just when you'd found your happiness.

Not that she was in love with Shayne Brayden or considered him her hero in any way.

She just thought he looked magnificent.

Well, he had been wonderful to her last night—caring and compassionate.

It wasn't at all the same thing.

As for her, she merely hoped to look halfway decent and not die.

She tried once again to get up, but her legs were too wobbly, and her body felt weighed down by boulders.

She fell back with a sigh and closed her eyes to keep the room from spinning.

Now her arm felt like daggers were being stabbed into it.

There was nothing she could do but lie in bed like a useless lump.

She would have to face him as she was. If he was a gentleman, he would not make jests about her behavior last night.

One thing for certain, she was never going to take that horrid laudanum again unless Cammy muzzled her. She remembered talking to him about kisses, but had she really said all those embarrassing things? *Ooh, Mr. Brayden…*

Would she ever learn to keep her mouth shut?

She breathed a sigh of relief when the handsome magistrate strode in a moment later with Cammy. By his worried expression, she knew he had no intention of teasing her.

He looked big and wonderful, and his gaze held nothing but

warmth and concern.

"How do you feel?" he asked, drawing up a chair beside her bed.

He was looking at her as though peering into her soul.

Indeed, his look felt like a hot caress.

How was it possible to actually *feel* his look?

The touch of his hand felt fiery against her cheek. Fiery and yet exquisitely gentle as his calloused fingers slid lightly along the line of her jaw.

Her body began to tingle.

Could he see the effect he was having on her?

Did he know?

He must.

Women would have fallen at his feet when he was in London. Had he gone there for the season? This man, dressed in formal evening wear, would have looked spectacular. He was big and muscled. His shoulders were broad, and his body, hard and lean.

His eyes were dark silver and dangerous.

"Um, how do I feel?" Is this what he had asked before her mind had wandered to the handsome contours of his body?

He took her hand in his. "You look pale, Willow. Did you pass a bad night?"

"I'm a little sore," she said, sounding like a bullfrog, "but otherwise all right. I don't remember anything of last night after I took that drug." Well, this wasn't quite true. She remembered being carried in his arms. She remembered him kissing her on the forehead and then on the cheek.

And she remembered going on about wanting him to kiss her on the lips and making him promise to do it. She would never mention it again. It was too humiliating. "Do you think you might take me to sift through the remains of the fire later?"

He ran his thumb lightly over the top of her hand. "I don't think you should get out of bed today. Laudanum takes time to work out of your system."

His voice was as smooth as melted chocolate.

Warm and silky.

"Oh," she said with her bullfrog rasp.

"Your eyes look glazed, and you look a bit…"

"Beautiful?" she suggested.

He grinned. "I was going to say hazy. But you also look beautiful. You always do. Even when soaking wet."

She laughed.

"The ground is still hot. Not all the wood has burned itself out yet. The Ashcott staff is keeping an eye on those embers and still tossing water on the remaining hot spots. I wouldn't risk exploring for another day, at least. We'll see how you feel tomorrow."

"All right. But I understand you've ordered your carriage to be brought around, and we're to leave for London tomorrow. I don't want to go until I see for myself about that book. I cannot leave here until I put it to rest."

"All right. I know how important it is to you. Willow, tell me truly. How are you feeling? My heart is still lodged in my throat. I would have done anything to spare you the injury."

"I know. Please don't fret. I will recover soon, and I promise to resume plaguing you as soon as I am back on my feet." She cast him a warm smile.

He laughed softly. "I look forward to it."

"Cammy said Lord Belfy's friends were not the ones who shot out the window. Do you have any idea who is responsible?"

Speaking of Cammy, where was her sister? She had walked in with the magistrate but had somehow slipped away now that he was settled by her side.

She supposed it did not matter.

Nothing was going to happen now anyway.

The door to their aunt's guest room was open, and she realized Cammy must have disappeared in there to lend her and the magistrate some privacy.

"I have my suspicions," he said, regaining her attention, "but nothing solid yet. I will let you know as soon as I have more information. I don't think this incident is connected to Lord Belfy at all. Amazingly, this is one crime for which he cannot be blamed."

He kept hold of her hand as he spoke.

Was this of any significance? Ordinarily, she might think so. She doubted magistrates were in the habit of holding hands with the victims they questioned. But she dared not make too much of it. Mrs. Albright had mentioned something about a young woman he'd met in London.

Had he loved her?

Had she spurned him?

Did he realize he was still holding her hand? "Please tell me who you suspect."

"All right." He shifted uncomfortably and sighed. "I'm looking for your driver, Mr. Pierson."

"Mr. Pierson?" Her eyes rounded in surprise. "You think he did it? But why?"

He shrugged. "I don't know his motive. He's been drinking quite a bit lately, obviously not happy to be stuck here in Taunton. Or he may be completely innocent and simply got tired of waiting around here and rode back to Barnstaple."

"Are you suggesting he is gone? You think he abandoned us and took off for home?"

"It is possible. The man did not strike me as particularly loyal or clever."

She nodded. "He isn't clever, but neither is he mean-spirited. He likes his ale a bit too much, that is for certain. But my parents trusted him, so did my aunt, or they never would have given him the responsibility of bringing us to London. I cannot believe he would ever harm any of us. He's known us since we were children."

"I'm not rushing to judgment, Willow. But I have to investigate all possibilities. One of your carriage horses is missing as well."

"This is why you believe he rode off and left us behind? I suppose the important question is, when did he leave? Mr. Geoffries, the inn's ostler, might know. Or one of his grooms might have seen something."

"I've asked them. Unfortunately, with the inn so busy, they paid him no mind. I'll ask the tavern keepers in town. One of them or their serving maids might have noticed him drinking there when the incident occurred."

"But where does that leave us if you rule him out? Do you have any other suspects?"

"None yet. I am also looking into anyone who might hold a grudge against the Ashcotts or one of the guests in the neighboring rooms. It is possible the culprit simply miscounted the windows and fired the shot into the wrong room."

She closed her eyes a moment, suddenly overwhelmed by all that had happened. "I suppose this new investigation will keep you busy today."

When she opened her eyes again, he cast her a wry smile. "Is that your hint to kick me out of here?"

"No, I like your company." She glanced down at their entwined fingers, surprised he did not seem inclined to release her. Her hand was small and almost lost within his grasp, and yet they seemed to fit together so perfectly. "This is the sensation of touch. *The Book of Love* explained it."

"Do you mind?"

"Not at all. I like it. I remember you holding me in your arms as the doctor stitched my cuts. It helped me tremendously. Truly, I thank you for that."

"Yet you are frowning."

"I'm just confused."

"What confuses you?"

"All these sensations running through me." For one, the soothing timbre of his voice. She found it so deep and gentle. But he was affecting all of her senses, just as the book said would happen. He was undeniably handsome, too. The look of him was quite pleasing. His touch was wonderful. She had meant what she'd just told him about their holding hands. Also, being held in his arms had eased her pain considerably.

She had loved his strong, healing touch.

Splendidly comforting.

His scent was appealing, as well, clean and male. He sat close enough for her to breathe in the alluring aroma of sandalwood soap on his skin.

That covered four of the senses, hearing, look, touch, scent.

She was missing the taste of him, something to be accomplished with a kiss on the lips. This must have been why she was going on about it last night.

"Willow, tell me what you are feeling."

"No, it will embarrass me. Have I not made enough of a fool of myself?"

"Don't ever feel embarrassed with me. I promise not to laugh. How do you know I am not feeling the same thing?"

"I doubt you are. I was thinking your touch felt heavenly." She blushed, wishing she had not admitted it, but apparently, her mouth had a mind of its own and was going to spill everything she was thinking at his slightest prompting.

"So does yours, Willow. I mean it."

Her eyes widened. "You do? What exactly are you feeling about me?"

"Did that book not give you any indication?"

"Yes and no."

He grinned. "That is not at all helpful. Care to explain?"

She pursed her lips, wondering how she was going to boil down these chapters to their essence in a few sentences. "Do you really wish to know?"

"Yes, or I wouldn't be asking. This book is obviously important to you, and I am curious to know why. Not to ridicule it or you. I am not so full of myself as to believe I cannot learn something new."

He appeared sincere, so she nodded and began to explain.

"Did you know men have two brains? The low and the high. This is what the book says. A man's low brain is the thoughtless brain, it works on pure instinct, and that instinct is the urge to procreate."

He coughed.

"Oh, I'm being too forward."

He grinned. "No, go on. I'm curious to hear more. You have a way of surprising me. I'm never sure what's going to come out of your mouth next."

"I hope there was a compliment buried in there somewhere. Shall I stop? You don't look like the sort of man who likes surprises."

"No, truly. Go on. I find it oddly interesting. I've never had a conversation like this before, certainly never with a woman. So, we males have two brains."

"Yes, your low brain is the one that assesses every woman you meet to determine whether she is a suitable mate for you. Is she too young, too old, too ill, too frail? When you first meet a woman, your eyes take all of her in to make that initial determination. This is why men are so fascinated by the female body. They are instinctively drawn to those women who can give them children. Healthy breasts, large hips."

He coughed again. "Sorry. Go on."

She eyed him warily but continued. "Once a man has dismissed all unsuitable candidates, he must then turn on his high brain."

He sat forward, casually leaning his arm upon his thigh. "And what does the high brain do?"

"It helps the man determine the right woman for him to love. She is the one he will protect and the one with whom he will raise a family. He will protect them all in order to ensure the survival of his bloodline." She met his gaze, trying to determine whether he was truly interested or whether he thought it was just idiocy and would jest about it with his brothers later.

But he seemed sincere…although, how could she know for

certain?

"What confuses you about this process, Willow? You seem to understand it quite well. Obviously better than me. I never thought about relations between men and women that way."

She slipped her hand out of his. "What confuses me is that there are so many subtle layers to these theories. Nothing is straightforward. For example…you infuriate me, and yet I still like you. We have no obvious connections, and yet I feel so comfortable around you. You are the most overwhelming man I've ever met, and yet I feel I can speak freely to you, as I am doing now."

He arched an eyebrow. "That is good, is it not?"

"Only if you feel the same way about me. Otherwise, it is very bad. Hypothetically speaking, if I gave my heart to you, then you would have the power to break it. This is what *The Book of Love* is all about, understanding who is right for you, knowing whom to trust. It is about avoiding those prospective mates who may appear right for you but will only make you unhappy over the length of a marriage, assuming that person is even willing to marry you."

He rose and went to peer out of the window. "Are all women like this? Do you all think only about marriage?"

She did not understand why he had suddenly become so prickly. It wasn't as though she had proposed to him.

Goodness, perish the thought!

She liked him, but he was too much for her to handle.

Too handsome. Too experienced. Too smart. Too opinionated. And otherwise, too perfect.

"Spoken like a typical man," she said, irritated by his blindness about the inequalities that existed.

He turned back to her. "What do you mean?"

"What opportunities in life does a woman have? Most will never be educated beyond the most rudimentary skills. Even if we are educated, we are not allowed to hold important positions or inherit titles. How are we to make our way if we are always relegated to the lowest positions in life? We cannot be doctors. We cannot be judges or bankers or run our own companies except in rare instances. Most of us are not allowed to manage our own assets. Men are appointed to do this for us."

He hadn't said a word to stop her, so she continued. "What sort of life is available to a spinster? My aunt is one of the more fortunate ones. She knows she will always have a home with our parents and be treated with honor, not relegated to the role of servant. She also knows that if they pass on, we will provide for her. She will never be left destitute, assuming we are not in the same position, which we will be if we remain spinsters."

She tipped her chin into the air and huffed. "So do not condescend to me about marriage. It is often the only choice available to a woman, and if she chooses wrong, her life will be a misery. This is why *The Book of Love* is so important to me. I do not want to choose wrong for myself. I envy my sister, June. She met Augustus MacLauren and immediately knew he was the one for her. I wish I could be as sure for myself."

He cast her a look of surprise. "Then you don't think you have met the right man yet?"

"Maybe I have. Maybe I haven't. I just don't know. Were you ever in love, Mr. Brayden?"

He returned his gaze to the window which faced the rear of the inn and had a lovely view of the garden. "Call me Shayne, will you?"

She supposed it was all right after all they had been through. He had dropped the formality almost from the start by calling her Willow instead of Miss Willow or Miss Farthingale. She had assumed he'd done it because he still considered her a child. But he'd kissed her and often looked at her as though he knew she was a woman. "Very well, Shayne. Were you ever in love?"

He grunted.

"Is that a yes or a no?"

He ignored the question.

"Fine, keep it to yourself then. But answer me this…what is

love supposed to feel like?"

He laughed and returned to her side. "It's supposed to feel good. Easy. Not forced. And yet it also drops you upside down and turns you every which way so that you don't know whether you are coming or going."

"That is not helpful."

"I don't know how else to explain it. But be careful about those men who only spout compliments. The one who truly loves you will recognize your faults and love you in spite of them. Look for a man who will love you for who you are and not for who they want you to be."

She drew her knees up to her chest and tucked her arms around them. "It is obvious you have been in love before. Why won't you admit it? Love is not something one ought to be ashamed of."

"We've gotten off the topic. I had better get back to my investigation. I'll look in on you later."

"That's it? Conversation over? You are the one who asked to know more about this book."

"I know. But I had better go now."

"Please come back later. I like your company."

He laughed and leaned over to kiss the top of her head. "You have an odd pull on me, too. When I'm with you, I feel as though I am watching two speeding carriages about to collide. It is frightening and fascinating. You want to turn away, but you cannot. I don't think you can keep me away even if you tried."

Cammy scurried into the room the moment he strode out. "I cannot believe he just said that to you," she said with a squeal.

Willow shook her head. "What exactly do you think he said to me?"

"Are you daft? He has just admitted he is in love with you."

Willow fell back against her pillows and laughed heartily. "That is the most ridiculous thing I've ever heard. Have you been nipping into my laudanum? I think he would choke before he ever uttered the L-word."

"Fine, be that way. But I know what I heard."

"Cammy, stop. He does not love me. Could you not tell? He's been in love before, and I think she must have spurned him. I could feel his anger and frustration."

"So what?" She sat beside Willow on her bed. "He must have moved on by now."

"But what if he hasn't?" Willow's stomach began to churn.

She did not know why she suddenly felt so unsettled. She hardly knew this man, and they would likely be on their way to London tomorrow. But she did not want to leave before searching through the ashes for that book.

She needed it more than ever now.

She liked Shayne Brayden.

But she did not want to fall in love with him.

First of all, it was quite possible she would never see him again. Well, she might have to return to Taunton to testify against Lord Manton when he came to trial for setting the fire. Yes, there was that possibility.

Still, how could she let herself fall in love with someone whose heart might already be taken? "Cammy, he described me as odd and frightening. I think he is still in love with that elegant woman Mrs. Albright mentioned. The daughter of a marquess, I think she said."

Cammy looked stricken. "No, Willow. He has to love you."

"Why? Look at me? I look like something the cat dragged in from the meadow. What could he possibly find enticing about me? How can I compete with a *ton* beauty?"

"You can," she said, throwing her arms around Willow with care to avoid her stitches. "I think you are beautiful. Mr. Brayden has to think so, too."

"Thank you, my ever-loyal sister. But I truly think his heart is pledged to another."

"No!"

"Oh, Cammy. I appreciate your loyalty, but nothing is going to happen between Mr. Brayden and me. He isn't over this other woman yet, this darling of the *ton*." She leaned back and closed her eyes. "I wonder who she is?"

CHAPTER SIX

S HAYNE AVOIDED RETURNING to his office after leaving Willow. He preferred to take a walk, knowing he needed to clear his head. All this talk of love had rattled him. He was no pious monk and knew his way around a woman's body. Probably too well. And yet, he had gotten everything wrong when courting Lady Felice.

He hadn't loved her.

He understood that now.

He had chased her because she was the season's diamond, and every other buck was after her. He'd done it as a lark, said and did whatever he thought would please her, and turned himself into someone he did not recognize or particularly like in order to win her hand.

When she had chosen him over her other suitors, he had not felt victorious.

He had felt trapped.

A trap of his own making, to be sure.

He was too honorable to bow out, and so he had gone through the motions of courting her. They had started a physical relation early on and then met fairly regularly afterward, rarely talking. Just getting to it.

He knew they weren't a good fit…not even when making love that first time. It hadn't been special or memorable. He had not been deflowering a virgin. There had been no moment of wonder or hint of joy in her eyes. Just raw heat, and she'd been spouting instructions to him the entire time. Well, she knew what she wanted and had not been shy about asking for these more erotic and risqué diversions.

But there had never been anything more than physical gratification between them. Surprisingly dispassionate.

They'd certainly never had a trusting relationship.

She was not going to be faithful in the marriage. Apparently, this was common in *ton* unions. Discretion, not faithfulness, was what mattered.

But he wanted something real, something solid and true. The sort of marriage his parents had enjoyed when they were alive.

Ultimately, the conquest had felt empty. He had simply stopped making trips to London, and the affair had died of its own accord, to his great relief. Neither of them had been particularly broken up over it, and Lady Felice was now betrothed to an earl, or so he'd heard.

"Shayne! Hold on. Where are you going?"

His brother's shout brought him back to the present. He stopped walking and waited for Lorcan to catch up to him. "Care for company?"

Shayne snorted. "No."

Lorcan merely clapped him on the back. "Too bad. I'll join you anyway. You look troubled. What's on your mind?"

"Hasn't there been enough?" He marched on, taking one of the paths that led out of town and into the hills.

"Yes, I suppose." Lorcan fell into step beside him. "How is Willow?"

"Amazing," he said with a soft laugh, not breaking his stride. The dry grass crunched beneath his boots as he continued the gentle climb as the path sloped upward. "Bravest little thing I've ever met. I have to find the arse who did this to her. She might have been killed."

"You like her."

He sighed and ran a hand through his hair. "Lorcan, that is an understatement. I think I am falling in love with her."

His brother burst out laughing. "I knew it. I told Donal, too. But you cannot behave with her as you did with Lady Felice."

The air was warming, and the gentle breeze offered little respite from the sun beating down on them. "I wouldn't think of it. Willow is nothing like Felice. For one thing, she is irritating beyond belief."

"And Felice wasn't?"

He shrugged. "It wasn't the same. She never got under my skin the way Willow does."

"So, what are you going to do about her? Willow, I mean. Do you really want me to escort her to London tomorrow?"

They reached the pinnacle of the hill and paused beneath one of the nearby shade trees. "Yes, I want you to take her away. I still have to deliver Lord Belfy and his friends to Exeter. Donal will help me with that. Then there's the matter of Willow's injury. She doesn't think their driver, Pierson, is involved. So, I'm back to nowhere in this investigation."

"Perhaps it was just a mistake, and she was never the intended victim."

"I'm not about to take that chance." He looked down at the town below, noting the bustle of activity. Yet, Taunton was a quiet place for the most part. Neighbors were friendly, and the worst crimes were petty thefts and drunken brawls. "I searched the area where the bounder would have been standing when he fired the shot. There were too many footprints to single one out. The ostler and his grooms walk the horses back and forth along that stretch every day."

"I can take a look. I was always better than you at tracking." Lorcan cast him another of his smug grins.

Shayne punched him lightly in the arm. "That is up for debate, but go ahead and do it today. Maybe there is something I missed. I'm trying to keep an open mind, but who else could have done it if not Pierson? One of the Farthingale carriage horses is missing, and so is he. It is too much of a coincidence."

"I can track him down for you. He isn't the brightest fellow, is he? I'll bet a month's wages he rode back to Barnstaple."

"I expect so. I'll ride there after I deliver Belfy and his rabble to Exeter."

"Then what?"

They started back down the hill. "I don't know. Maybe I'll ride to London."

Lorcan frowned at him. "Maybe? You had better go after Willow and court her in earnest. Don't be an idiot. If you don't claim her, someone else will. Then where will you be? Old, alone, and miserable."

"It isn't that simple."

"Of course it is. Love is always simple, that's what Mum used to say. Trying to deny it is the hard part."

"I am not denying anything. I've hardly known the girl a week. Just let me deal with the investigation first."

"Fine. I've told you what I think. If you want to be an arse about it, who am I to stop you? I'll see you later." Lorcan strode off in the direction of the investigation site.

Shayne headed back toward town, deciding to stop by the local taverns. These would be opening up around now, and he could start asking the barmaids and tavern keepers questions about Pierson. He would also ask about anything unusual they happened to notice last night. A fight between two patrons. A theft. Any strangers in town.

He stopped at the tavern across from Mrs. Guinn's tea shop where the Farthingale sisters had stopped for cakes and refreshments on one of their shopping excursions when first arriving in town. He had seen their driver go into the White Horse Tavern for an ale while they had been having their tea and treats.

The man had come out too drunk to escort them back to the inn, so Shayne had taken over the chore.

He stepped into the tavern and was immediately assaulted by the scent of stale ale. The floor was sticky, and the tables appeared to need a good scrubbing. "Good afternoon, Mr.

Seaver."

"Mr. Brayden," the portly owner said, offering him a pint. "What brings you around so early in the day?"

He declined the ale. "Someone shot out one of the windows at the inn last night. Unfortunately, one of the young Farthingale sisters got hurt by the spray of glass."

Mr. Seaver was a decent fellow and had daughters of his own. "I'm sorry to hear that. How badly is she hurt? Will the poor lass be all right?"

"I think so. Dr. Stratton had to tend to her and stitch her up."

The tavern keeper looked sincerely contrite. "That's terrible. What do you need from me? Information, I suppose."

Shayne nodded. "Did you notice anything out of the ordinary last night?"

He paused and thought about it a moment. "Now that you mention it, their driver, that Pierson fellow, was in here mouthing off a little. He was going on about Barnstaple and how he never agreed to be sleeping in a stable while the ladies had the fanciest rooms at the inn."

He cast Shayne a look of alarm. "You don't think he's the one who shot out the window, do you? I feel terrible now. I should have had you summoned, but I had no idea he meant to do anything beyond grumble about it."

"How long was he in here?"

A couple of his maids strolled in with mops and buckets in hand. "Lasses, come have a listen. Mr. Brayden wants to know about that Pierson fellow. Did you notice when he walked in?"

One of them nodded. "Around eight o'clock of the evening, I would say."

"Thank you, Mary," Shayne said, familiar with Mr. Seaver's staff because of the brawls that often broke out, especially on Friday nights. "How long did he stay?"

She gave a moment's thought. "I believe he was here until about midnight."

"Bollocks," he muttered under his breath, running a hand

through his hair in consternation. Had he just lost his best suspect? No, he wasn't about to dismiss Pierson yet. "Did you notice him leave at any point in between?"

"No, I didn't. But we were very busy last night." She turned to her friend. "Did you, Betty?"

Betty tossed him a practiced smile and ambled closer. "I was out back talking to one of the patrons shortly after nine o'clock when I noticed him stumble out. I thought he was going to the trees to relieve himself. But I didn't pay him no mind as I was…um, deep in conversation with the other gent, if ye get my meaning."

"I see." Some of these girls exchanged their services for coin, a rather lucrative side business, and he expected Mr. Seaver took a small cut of their earnings. He would have shut the tavern down if he thought the man was forcing the girls. But he knew that wasn't happening. Mary merely served ale and other spirits to the patrons. If any man got too friendly with her, Mr. Seaver tossed him out. Betty was another matter. She was saving up her earnings to buy a farm outside of town and was quite clear-eyed in how she went about it.

He considered Willow's words about the options available to women. How had he been so thoughtless? He had no right to denigrate the marriage-minded mamas and the daughters they meant to shove at every eligible bachelor they could manage. Who could blame them when their choices were so limited, and the consequence of failure was sometimes dire?

"Did any other patrons catch your eye?" he asked all of them. "Anyone acting suspiciously?"

"No," they all responded in turn.

But Mary added, "Come to think of it, I did not see that Mr. Pierson for quite a while after nine o'clock, but he was definitely back here close to midnight, and he appeared to be crying. Some drunks get that way, you know. Crying into their ale. But he was particularly torn up about something."

He muttered his thanks and strode out to question the other

tavern owners in town. He'd gotten the confirmation he was hoping for but did not want to leap to a convenient conclusion. Just because the man had gone out to supposedly take a piss around the time of the shooting and did not return until much later did not mean he was involved. His decision to leave Taunton and take that horse could have been another coincidence.

Also, Willow's assailant had run off on horseback immediately after firing that shot. Did it make sense for Pierson to ride off then come back to town, plunk himself down at the same tavern, only to ride off again?

Shayne cursed under his breath.

It made no sense, but it was not impossible.

The man did not think clearly even when sober.

He shook his head and sighed as he walked along the familiar streets, stopping at several taverns to pose similar questions, but he got little helpful information.

Locals drinking.

No strangers that anyone noticed.

No one suspicious passing through town.

No fights.

No disgruntled drunks other than the usual ones who complained about their wives, their jobs, their children, and sometimes their cattle.

He returned to his office. "How are things, Ezekiel?"

"Quiet, Shayne." He nodded toward the cells where Lord Belfy and his friends were held. "I think the enormity of what they've done is now sinking in."

"Don't believe it for a moment. If they're behaving, it means they have a plan afoot. Those lords do not know the meaning of remorse. They will never feel contrition or seek to atone. Do not be taken in by them."

"Those scum? They won't fool me. I'd as soon shoot them as look at them," Ezekiel said with surprising depth of anger, then shook his head and sighed. "Warning received and duly noted."

Shayne regarded the man thoughtfully. "You all right, Ezekiel?"

"Yes. Fine. Just a little wound up, but aren't we all?"

"Yes. Just ignore them. Don't let them crawl under your skin. They are locked behind bars and can do nothing but hurl empty threats."

Lorcan walked in a few moments later.

Shayne cast him a questioning look. "Find anything?"

He held up a half-spent smoke. "This. Shall I show it to the Farthingales? They might recognize it as one of Mr. Pierson's."

"I'll go."

Lorcan arched an eyebrow. "You? Why? I thought you weren't interested in pursuing—"

"Shut up and stop being a pain in my arse. I am not going to discuss my life with you or anyone else." He held out his hand. "Give it over."

"No, but you can come with me." He strode out without bothering to wait for Shayne.

"Ezekiel," he said, feeling the man needed a reminder, "don't fall for any of their tricks. I'll be right back."

He followed his brother to the inn.

Cammy and Charlotte were in the dining room having afternoon tea.

Lorcan headed straight to them.

Shayne took the opportunity to go upstairs instead. He wanted a few moments alone with Willow.

He knocked at her door. "Willow, it's me."

He heard the scuffle of her feet, then heard her raise the latch.

She opened the door to him, staring up at him with trust and wonderment in her big, blue eyes. Yes, this is what he liked about Willow, the wonder in her eyes. "Mr. Brayden?"

She was still clad in her chemise and a robe that she must have borrowed from her sister since he did not believe Mrs. Albright had delivered more garments to her yet. Her hair was no longer in a braid but left loose to flow down her back in magnificent waves. Her feet were bare, since she'd obviously scampered out of bed to open the door to him without bothering to don slippers.

His heart tugged.

Despite having lost all, despite being injured and still in pain, she had never once complained.

She cast him a breathtaking smile. "Any breakthrough in your investigation?"

CHAPTER SEVEN

WILLOW STEPPED ASIDE to allow Shayne Brayden to enter her guest chamber, not sure why he had come to see her, but glad he was here. She expected he had more questions for her and hoped he would allow her some of her own. She wanted to learn more about his feelings for his former sweetheart, assuming she was in his past and not the one he hoped to marry. "You are not smiling. Does this mean more bad news?"

"Maybe." His lips were pinched, and he appeared tense as he now stood in the center of the room with his arms crossed over his chest so that he appeared quite massive next to her. She did not know whether to leave the door ajar or close it, so she left it open just a crack.

"Would you care to explain?" she asked, trying to maintain her composure as a tingling warmth spread through her body. Merely looking at this man got her heart pounding and the butterflies in her stomach fluttering.

He grunted, something else she was starting to find endearing about him. This habit he had of barely parsing out information used to frustrate her, but she was starting to find this back-and-forth tug between them somehow intimate.

"Lorcan found what might be a clue."

"What sort of clue?" Despite the seriousness of his expression, she could not help but smile. Only a small smile, of course. She understood the investigation was no laughing matter.

"Does Mr. Pierson smoke?"

She nodded. "These nasty looking, brown paper rolled up things that smell awful. Why? Is this what your brother found?"

"Yes."

She sank onto her bed in dismay. "Then you think he is our culprit? He cannot have meant to do it. Certainly never to hurt me. I don't know whether to be relieved or angry as blazes for his stupidity. Do you have him in custody?"

"Not yet. But I'm not worried about finding him. Where else would he go but back to Barnstaple? I'll ride there after I deliver Lord Belfy and his friends to Exeter."

"Must you go after Mr. Pierson?"

"Yes, Willow. He cannot go unpunished."

She sighed. "I suppose not. But please deal lightly with him. You must think us so stupid for engaging his services when we knew he was pretty much a wastrel. My parents are kind and compassionate people. They raised us to be the same way." She glanced up at him and winced. "Although I have not been very kind to you, have I?"

A smile tugged at the corner of his lips. "Most women tend to treat me better. I don't recall any sweet, young thing ever smashing a fist in my face until you."

Heat shot into her cheeks. "My point is, Mr. Pierson is not an evil man. I'm certain he feels remorse for what he has done. If we are able to forgive him, then so should you."

He remained standing, his arms still folded across his chest. "I'll think about it. How is your arm? Any better than this morning?"

She nodded. "A little. It's still quite sore. The stitches feel as though they are pulling on my skin."

"May I see?" He uncrossed his arms and stepped closer, sitting beside her on the bed, which was not at all proper, nor was his being alone with her in the room. Yet, being with him did not feel wrong to her at all.

She did not hesitate to allow him a peek since he was the one who had treated her wounds until the doctor arrived. He'd done everything but put the stitches in. "Just help me tug the sleeve off my shoulder."

His hands were warm and gentle.

She loved the soft way he touched her.

But she looked away when he drew the sleeve down, afraid to see the injury for herself. It had to be revolting to the eye. "What do you think, Shayne?"

She also liked the sound of his name. A good, strong name for a proud, resolute man—someone who knew what he wanted and went after it.

Only, he was making no attempt to go after her.

She had no sooner given it thought when he surprised her by placing a hand on her shoulder and giving it a light caress.

Heavens, this man's touch.

But the moment of tenderness ended in the blink of an eye, passing so quickly she questioned whether he had meant anything more by it than a comforting pat. He drew the sleeve back in place. "It looks terrible. But it will heal. Just be sure to keep it clean. Has Dr. Stratton stopped in to see you today?"

"Yes, and he put an unguent on it that smelled like chicken fat."

He laughed. "It's worn off you then. You smell like orange blossoms."

She cast him an impertinent smile. "I think you just gave me a compliment."

"It is merely a statement of fact." He arched an eyebrow and then added, "Tell me more about that book you spoke of earlier."

"*The Book of Love?* So we are through discussing Mr. Pierson?"

He nodded.

"What do you want to know about the book?"

"How does one tell the difference between love and merely a passing interest?"

"I'm not sure. You know more about men and women in romantic relations than I do. But the strength of this book is that it teaches us how to look upon something and see the truth of what is before our eyes."

She tucked her feet under her as she made herself more comfortable on the bed.

If he was not worried about the appearance of impropriety, then she would not worry either.

She liked this man and enjoyed having him beside her. "This is perhaps the most profound thing I've learned, the importance of looking at a thing with clarity and not twisting it into something we hope to see. People lie to themselves all the time. Pretend things are fine when they are not. Make excuses for why the object of their affection is not behaving as they would like."

She waited for him to comment.

He said nothing, merely grunted.

She took it as encouragement to continue. "Love matches are not common among the Upper Crust, but we Farthingales always marry for love. It has been this way for generations. And most recently, there have been several love matches between Farthingales and Braydens. What do you think of that?"

He arched an eyebrow. "I'm not surprised. If the Farthingale women are as pretty as you and your sisters...not just pretty, but as clever and strong in heart as you, then I can see my cousins falling in love with them."

"Aha, now that is compliment."

He smiled. "No, still a statement of fact."

"Fine, be stubborn. Who needs your compliments anyway?" she teased, quite flattered by his description of her. How could he regard her as pretty, clever, and strong in heart and not hold some feeling for her? Nor would he come around to see her as often as he did if he cared nothing for her.

However, she refused to give her heart free rein because she might be misconstruing his attentions. What if he was curious about the book because he wanted to rekindle his romance with the elegant lady he had been seeing in London?

"For a match to be successful," she continued, since he appeared to have no inclination to speak, "one ought to start with the five senses. Sight, touch, taste, sound, and scent. The object of our affection must be pleasing to all our senses, or else we are not likely to move forward in the courtship. For me, that would mean liking the sound of his voice, the way he looks, his scent. His touch. I'm not sure how taste comes in, but I think it has to do with kissing on the lips."

He grinned. "So that was what you were going on about last night?"

"I have no idea what you mean." She cleared her throat. "But love is not merely about pleasing the five senses. This is where we often make the biggest mistakes. We cannot be starry-eyed and ignore the faults of another even though our senses may decide he or she is perfect. This is very important because everyone has faults, and we cannot overlook them. Yet too often we do."

She cast him an impertinent grin. "Even you have faults, Shayne."

He chuckled. "I know. Arrogant, overbearing. Like to be in command. Which goes along with hates to take orders from others."

"Because you think you are always right and know everything better than others."

"Ouch," he said with a wince. "Yes. But I am listening now, aren't I? At least I am aware of what I don't know, and I am always willing to learn. Go on, Willow. Tell me more."

"Certain faults are hard to overlook. Drunkenness. Lying. Cheating, whether at cards or in business. Being unfaithful." Oh, that struck a chord with him.

Was he the unfaithful one in his London courtship, or was his sweetheart?

"So, even if someone is pleasing at first glance, it may be that his or her character is not. But it is also a matter of perspective. In many *ton* marriages, love is not an issue. The parties expect to spend very little time around each other and do not particularly care if they are unfaithful to each other."

She paused, hoping he might say a word.

He seemed lost in his thoughts but was looking at her with interest, so she pressed on. "Both parties having the same expectations is what makes a marriage work, or so the book seems to indicate. I can see the logic in it. I'm sure there have been instances of one party wanting a true and solid marriage, while the other one expects to live separate lives and have discreet liaisons. That difference in expectations can only lead to unhappiness."

He rose and crossed the room.

She thought he was going to leave, but he merely picked up a chair and drew it over to the side of her bed. "I should not have been sitting on the bed with you."

"I wasn't afraid. You know I feel comfortable around you. I have no fear you might do something untoward."

He cast her a wry grin. "Willow, I've warned you. Men cannot be trusted, and that includes me."

She frowned. "Should I kick you out? I was enjoying our conversation."

"So was I. No, I want to stay. Still, it doesn't mean you can trust me."

She scooted off the bed and grabbed the hearth shovel, then scooted back on and placed the shovel across her lap. "There. I will hit you if you are out of line. Does that make you feel better? Shall I continue? I rather enjoy lecturing you."

His eyes crinkled as he smiled. "I knew you were a bossy bit of goods. Continue."

"Love is very much about mutual expectations…compatible expectations. Working together to build a happy family life, a solid future. This is why I could never be happy in a typical *ton* marriage. Going to London to be tossed into the marriage mart simply felt wrong to me. But I did not know how to explain it to my parents."

She sighed and shook her head. "Those in *ton* marriages

spend their lives avoiding each other. Why would anyone ever wish to do that? It is sad, don't you think?"

He nodded. "Yes, especially if one party wants more and the other does not wish to give it."

"What do you hope for in a wife, Shayne?"

He had turned the chair around and now sank onto it with his legs astride, as though seated on a horse. He leaned his arms on the chair's back as he faced her. "I have no idea. This is why I'm curious about the book. What should I be looking for?"

She wanted to hit him over the head with the shovel. "Are you serious? Have you never given it thought? But why should you? It is only the most important decision you will ever have to make in your life."

He reached over and tweaked her chin. "I shall overlook that sarcastic remark. Stop frowning at me. Of course I've given it thought. I haven't come up with any answers. We grew up in a household of men except for my mother."

"I see. Boys do not have heart-to-hearts with their mother?"

"We don't even ask for directions when we're lost. I'd put my eyes out with hot pokers before confiding in her about such matters. She passed away a few years ago."

"Oh, I'm so sorry."

"Thank you, Willow. She's at peace now, resting beside my father. Beside him is where she always wanted to be. I loved her, and she was a great mother. But she was my *mother*. Why are you grinning?"

She held her side to stifle her laughter. "Until this very moment, I never thought of you as having parents. In my mind, you were Neptune arising from the sea. All powerful and just...*here*, ruling over Taunton."

He cast her a smile that melted her heart. "So, you think I am a Greek god?"

She could not contain her laughter as she said, "Neptune happens to be a Roman god. Poseidon is his Greek counterpart. And stop giving me that smug smile. My remark was merely a statement of fact, not a compliment. So do not get too full of yourself."

"Very well, I am put in my place. Then you do not think I am magnificent?"

She blushed. "Heavens, no."

But she doubted he believed her, for she was terrible at hiding her feelings, and he was all too aware of his appeal. The women of Taunton were in a swoon over him. The women of London would have responded no differently. After all, a handsome man was a handsome man. Add smart, wealthy, and honorable, and who would not fall wildly in love with him?

"We've gotten off the topic, Willow. Tell me more about this book. What are the danger signs of love?"

"Danger? Is this what you think of us? Is this why you have never made a commitment?" Now was her chance to get at the truth. "Have you ever asked a woman to marry you?"

"Answer my question first. What should I be looking for?"

"I want to grab you by the scruff of your neck and shake you soundly. First of all, do you wish to marry for love?"

"Yes, of course. Braydens are like Farthingales when it comes to marriage. Love is a must in the marriage. Commitment. Faithfulness. We take our vows seriously."

Did that mean the woman he was courting had been unfaithful to him?

How was it possible?

There was no better man than Shayne Brayden.

She shook her head and continued their conversation. "Then the next question is, what attributes in a woman please you? We are talking high brain now. We have moved beyond the low-brain male urges. Think about the five senses, but also beyond them. What traits appeal to you? Do you want a woman who is chirpy or quiet? Thoughtful or merry? Helpless or capable? Educated? Elegant? Able to play a pianoforte?"

He chuckled, then stopped. "You're serious? Why would I care if my wife can play the pianoforte or not?"

"I only tossed it out there as a possibility. Obviously, this is not important to you at all. But I want to point out that I was quite pleasantly surprised by your artistic ability. It isn't something I would consider important, but I liked it in you. It softens your hard edges because, otherwise, you can be quite overwhelming."

"Do you play the pianoforte?"

"Yes, it so happens I do. But I cannot sing to save my life. My cousin Violet is the singer in the family. She has the voice of an angel. My cousin Dillie also has a nice voice and can play the pianoforte, too." She grinned impudently. "Doubly talented. I'm sure this is why she landed herself a duke. She is Duchess Dillie now."

He laughed. "As a man, I can tell you for certain that her musical talents had nothing to do with why the duke married her."

"Then why do you think he married her?"

She expected a brash retort, but he suddenly turned serious. "I happen to know the Duke of Edgeware and the torments he faced in his life. He married your cousin because she touched his heart. He married her because he trusted her, knew she truly cared for him, and was never after him for his title. She is probably beautiful, made more so because of her warmth and caring. He gained a trusted friend, a valued confidante, someone he could rely on to tell him the truth. Someone he knew would love and protect their children. Someone who would keep to her wedding vows and love him always."

She inhaled lightly and bowed her head in dismay. "Then you must think I am an utter failure."

He tucked a finger under her chin and raised her gaze to his. "Why would I think that of you?"

"Dillie is everything you've said, and brave, too. She saved her husband's life. What have I done other than plague you?"

"You cannot compare yourself to your cousin, Willow. People don't go about facing death every day. And you don't plague me." His thumb grazed along the line of her jaw. "At worst, you mildly irritate me."

He dropped his hand but continued to gaze at her, his eyes so sharp and assessing, she did not think he missed anything. "You lack confidence in yourself," he said quietly. "I think this is because you are young and have had little experience outside of Barnstaple. But honesty, loyalty, and kindness count no matter where one resides."

"Those traits seem to be most important to you."

He nodded. "They are everything to me. Love and trust must go together. There cannot be one without the other."

"Yes, this is exactly what *The Book of Love* says."

"I'm sorry your book was lost in the fire. It sounds as though it offered good advice. However, I still think you place too much reliance on it."

"How can I not? I have no experience of my own, as you've pointed out. The marriage mart can be treacherous, and the consequences of my making a mistake would be dire. Women are not given the same chances as men. Men can be caught in compromising situations and be forgiven for their improprieties. Women are never forgiven. Men can survive a broken betrothal. Women cannot. Oh, perhaps an heiress might be forgiven everything. But I am no heiress." She shook her head and sighed. "Women are held to a much higher standard of behavior. And you know I am not all that well behaved."

He chuckled. "You do have a way of forcefully expressing your opinions. Just don't punch anyone in the face, and you'll do all right."

She rolled her eyes. "I am not a violent person. You are the only one I've ever…well, I've apologized to you for it. But I still believe that book survived the fire. I feel it, Shayne. It is still out there."

"Don't stay up all night fretting about it. I had better get back to my office." He rose and returned the chair to its rightful spot. "These next few days will be busy for both of us. But I haven't forgotten my promise. We will search through the remains of the fire before you leave for London."

She set aside the hearth shovel and came to his side. "You do realize you've still managed to avoid answering my questions."

"About love and marriage? Yes, I know."

"A conversation involves a mutual give and take. I've answered yours. Don't you think I deserve some answers, too? I wouldn't be asking if I did not feel the need for guidance…even from the likes of you. Assuring me that I'll be fine in London is not very helpful. I need specifics."

He glanced at the door, obviously eager to get away from her now that he'd gotten what he'd come for, confirmation about Mr. Pierson and advice about the meaning of true love. She folded her arms across her chest and cast him a stubborn look.

Of course, she was half his size, so he was not likely to be intimidated.

He was big and muscled while she was slender, and the top of her head barely reached his chin. But she knew how to stand her ground, and this was important to her.

"How specific do you want me to be?" He nudged her back inside, stepped back in with her, and closed the door.

She smiled at him. "Now we are getting somewhere. Very specific. I want to know what a man feels when he looks at a woman."

"Such as yourself?"

"Yes. And what he would be thinking when he touches my hand, or if he catches the scent of my skin. Hears the sound of my voice."

He emitted a soft growl resembling the dangerous purr of a leopard on the prowl. She had seen this animal once, its cage unloaded from a ship and handled with utmost care as this exotic gift meant for the king passed through Barnstaple on its way to London. "These are not simple questions, Willow. Every man will respond differently."

"Then let's start with you since you are a typical man." She swallowed hard. "Um, how would you respond?"

"To you?"

She nodded, suddenly worried she might have asked too much. She trusted him, but she wasn't sure what he meant to do next. He had a wonderfully steamy look in his eyes, but jungle cats were dangerous, and she may have poked him unwisely.

However, she wanted answers, and he had them.

She glanced at the hearth shovel, knowing she would never use it on him because she instinctively understood he would never do anything to hurt her. "Shayne, were you ever in love?"

"You want an honest answer?"

"Ugh, you are doing it again, avoiding the question. Of course, I do."

"Then honestly, I don't know. I am still thinking about it."

"Still thinking about it?" How long did it take a man to decide whether or not he liked a woman? He had possibly known the London woman for years. How could he still not know his feelings for her?

She wanted to hit him with the hearth shovel, but he already considered her violent when she really wasn't at all. He had a way of infuriating her. She merely frowned at him instead. "That is not honest. That is avoiding the answer. Denying it. Postponing it. Refusing to face it."

She curled her hands into fists to stem her frustration.

He took them in his, swallowing them up in his large hands.

"Willow," he said with a soft, aching rasp that shot tingles through her body. He released her a moment later, but only to put an arm around her waist and draw her up against his body. The position was scandalous, just the thing she'd been talking about moments earlier.

But she hadn't the slightest desire to pull away from that firm chest and those big, muscled arms.

He cupped her face in his hand. "I am not denying, postponing, or avoiding anything."

She stared up at him. "How can you not know whether you

have ever been in love? Didn't you court the daughter of a marquess?"

"What makes you think I was referring to her?"

"But you were courting her."

"I was escorting her around town."

"Is that not the same thing?"

"No. Courtship implies there is a chance at love. I was not in love with her."

"But you said you were not sure if you ever were in love. Was there someone before her then?"

"No." His gaze was smoldering, the gray of his eyes turbulent and fiery.

"If it wasn't her. And it wasn't someone before her, then was it someone after her?"

He dipped his head the littlest bit toward hers. His breath felt warm against her cheek. "Perhaps."

"Oh, I did not realize there was someone else." She tried to squirm out of his grasp, but he did not seem inclined to let her go. She decided to keep talking. "I suppose you've kept it a close secret since none of the ladies in town seem to be aware of it."

He lowered his lips to hers but held them poised just above her own. "It is still fairly new. She only arrived in town recently."

"How recent?"

"About a week ago."

"But that's when we…*Lord in heaven*…you mean me?" Little explosions erupted throughout her body. She was in his arms, and he liked her. More than liked her if the heat of his silvery gaze was any indication. How was this possible?

"Who else did you think I meant?"

"I was sure it was the daughter of that marquess. Everyone thought you were in love with her? Are you certain I am not your second choice?"

"You are second to no one," he insisted, seeming to be taken aback. "Do you not see yourself for the beauty you are?"

She shook her head because she surely didn't.

"It seems you need convincing."

"No one's ever called me beautiful before…well, my parents have told me, but I do not think it is the same thing. Parents have to love their children."

"Not all do. But you would. You would love them. Fight for them. Protect them. This is what makes you beautiful on the inside as well as outwardly."

Tears formed in her eyes. "Is that a compliment or a statement of fact?"

He caressed her cheek. "A statement of fact…and a compliment."

"Thank you, Shayne." Her heart was racing so fast, it threatened to burst. But in a very good way. Would love be like this? Intoxicating and exciting. She could grow used to being held in his arms because he was pleasing to every one of her senses. "Since we seem to be pasted to each other…rather conveniently…I have a favor to ask of you."

"What is it, Willow?"

Oh, now he was nuzzling her neck, and she was in grave danger of expiring from the pleasure of these new and certainly wicked sensations.

She licked her lips.

She cleared her throat.

Heavens. Heavens. Heavens.

"How soon do we get to the kissing part?"

He laughed. "Be patient."

"But what if Cammy and Aunt Charlotte return before you get around to it?"

"Lord, you are irritating. Very well, close your eyes."

She *eeped* because kissing Shayne Brayden was the most exciting thing she had ever done in her life so far, and she did not think anything to come afterward could possibly be more thrilling. Of course, marriage and children would be joyful blessings, but not quite the same as a first kiss.

Well, Shayne had kissed her before.

But he was the only man ever to kiss her, so this next one still counted as a first as far as she was concerned.

He wrapped his arms more firmly around her. "Ready?"

This man left her breathless.

Unable to speak, she merely nodded.

He was about to crush his lips to hers when they suddenly heard Cammy's cries. "Willow! Willow! You'll never believe—" The door thudded against Shayne's back. Cammy grunted and shoved at it again. "What did you put against the door? Feels like you moved the wardrobe against it. How did you manage to move that big thing? Let me in."

Willow skittered away from Shayne, who was now laughing softly as he stepped aside to allow Cammy in.

"This is no laughing matter," she whispered, frowning at him.

He merely grinned back.

Cammy was now glancing from one to the other. "Oh, Magistrate Brayden. I did not realize you were here. I thought you were done questioning my sister. Or did you have another purpose in mind in coming here?"

"Just seeking independent confirmation about the stub Lorcan found on the hill just beyond the carriage house. I'm fairly certain Mr. Pierson is the culprit. I was discussing a suitable punishment with your sister. After all, she was the victim and ought to have a say."

Cammy arched an eyebrow. "Oh, were the two of you speaking? Wouldn't that require both your mouths to be unoccupied?"

Willow's cheeks turned flaming hot. "Cammy! Mr. Brayden did not kiss me." She once again wished her nuisance of a younger sister had never been born.

He did not appear at all embarrassed. "I'll see you tomorrow, Willow. The remains of the carriage house should be safe to walk through by then. We'll do a thorough search for that book before you head off to London."

"Will you not come by tonight?"

He arched an eyebrow. "Lord Belfy and his friends are all

behind bars. Mr. Pierson has run off to Barnstaple by now. Is there a reason I should?"

Willow felt heartbroken. "No, I suppose…I just…"

Had she made an enormous fool of herself?

Why did he not wish to see her tonight?

He sighed. "I may, all right?"

"No, do not trouble yourself on my account." She was too prideful to show her humiliation and hurt.

She said nothing as he walked out.

But her head was spinning.

First, he was going to kiss her, and then suddenly, he did not wish to see her again.

Had she said or done something wrong?

CHAPTER EIGHT

SHAYNE WALKED OUT of Willow's room and hurried downstairs to find Lorcan. "I think we can close this investigation. Willow confirmed Mr. Pierson smokes and described the paper he uses to wrap his tobacco. I assume her aunt and sister confirmed the same to you."

Lorcan nodded. "They did."

"All these little details, his drinking, conveniently leaving the bar at just that hour, riding off with one of their carriage horses. Everything points to him."

"You're the one with the most investigative experience. If you think so, that's good enough for me. My instincts also tell me he's the one."

They walked in silence to his office.

After checking on their prisoners, they went into the back room. Lorcan stretched out on the cot, casually placing his hands to the back of his head as a makeshift pillow. He stared at Shayne. "You look unsettled. What really happened with Willow?"

Shayne sank into the chair behind his desk and raked a hand through his hair. "I don't know."

"What does that mean?"

"It means she's leaving tomorrow."

"She won't if you ask her to stay. Her Aunt Charlotte won't put up too much of a fuss once she realizes you are serious. Why don't you plead your case to her aunt? I'm sure she will accept to remain here a little while longer."

"No, they have to go. Donal and I have prisoners to deliver to Exeter, and then I'm going to Barnstaple to find their driver and haul his mangy arse back here. He almost killed Willow. Even if she refuses to press charges, he also damaged the inn's property. Mr. Ashcott is not likely to be as forgiving."

Lorcan shot him a scowl. "I can go after Pierson."

"You need to take the ladies to London. I won't trust their safety to anyone else. And don't let them pay for anything along the way. Not the coaching inn. Not their meals. It's all on me."

"Fine," he said with a grunt. "But if you are not in London within a month, I'm going to haul *your* arse there. I know you, Shayne. You may fool others, but I've seen the way you look at the girl."

"How do I look at her?"

"Like you want to devour her. Mum would be boxing your ears for letting her go if she were alive today."

Shane rose and pushed aside his chair. "I had better make my rounds of the town. I'll see you later."

He strode out before Lorcan could stop him.

Not that he expected his brother to do or say anything more. In any event, the walk through town would do him good. He needed to get his mind off Willow. He needed to take a step back and think straight.

Love did not strike like a thunderbolt.

Or did it?

Should it not grow over time?

He could not deny that thunderbolt impact when first meeting Willow, that feeling of coming face to face with the most beautiful girl he had ever beheld, of loving the look of her body and the scent of her skin—loving the lilt of her voice and touch of her hand.

He had dismissed it as mere lust.

And every man knew that lust clouded one's thinking.

Yet, he also thought Willow clever, brave, and compassionate. He enjoyed talking to her. He liked that she was not afraid to challenge him.

He loved looking at her expressive face.

He could look at her for hours and enjoy every moment.

But was this conclusively love?

He had averted disaster with Lady Felice.

He would not risk the same thing happening with Willow. While his body had yet to recover from the frustration of not kissing the luscious girl, he was just as glad the kiss had not occurred.

Kissing her would have led to more, and Willow would not have stopped him. If anything, the girl was too adventurous. But she was nothing like Lady Felice. The wonder of it was that Willow only wanted to be adventurous with him.

He liked the feeling of being someone special to her.

The difference between the elegant marquess's daughter and the straightforward beauty from Barnstaple was glaring. When Willow gave her heart to a man, it would be for always. She believed he was that man for her. He saw it in the starlight shimmer of her eyes whenever she looked at him.

He loved that look, her little hitch of breathless excitement, the slight heave of her chest, and the widening of her beautiful eyes whenever she saw him.

She affected him, as well.

But was this feeling so potent because it was new? Was it mere infatuation or something that would last forever? It seemed impossible, at least for him. Experience had left him cynical and jaded. Would they tire of each other in a week or two?

Well, she would not be around more than another day for them to find out.

He shook his head and resolved to put her out of his mind, for he had just spent the last two hours walking around town lost in thoughts of her. But as he strode back to the magistrate's office, someone shouted out to him. "Mr. Brayden!"

Shayne recognized the voice as that of the Ashcott Inn's ostler, Mr. Geoffries. He watched the man approach, frowning when he noticed how exceedingly troubled he appeared. "Is something wrong?"

Mr. Geoffries began to wring his hands, and his leathery face appeared quite haggard. "You see…she only meant to borrow it…"

"Who meant to borrow what?" Shayne stared at him, trying to make out what he was worried about.

"That book, the one belonging to Miss Farthingale. She had tucked it in one of her travel bags and stowed it in their carriage the night before they were to leave for London."

"Book? You mean the one with a red leather binding?" He gaped at the man. "Are you telling me it did not burn?"

"No, I have it in my office at the stable. Mr. Brayden, I don't know what to do. I want to return it to Miss Farthingale, but please…I cannot tell her who took it. You see, she meant no harm and had every intention of slipping it back in the bag before anyone realized it was ever gone. She was very careful with it, not a single page damaged. Surely, you cannot imprison someone for borrowing a book."

He put a hand on the ostler's shoulder to calm him. "No, I would not. And I can guarantee you Miss Farthingale is more likely to hug this girl than press charges. I assume you are talking about your daughter."

"Oh, Mr. Brayden. Molly's a good girl. She meant no harm."

"I know." He patted the man's shoulder. "Let's get the book, and I will return it to Miss Farthingale. Who took it is not relevant, only that you found it sitting on your desk and sought to deliver it to me as soon as you noticed it was there and realized to whom it belonged."

"Yes, yes. That's right." He nodded fervently.

"Answer me this, Mr. Geoffries," he said as they walked to the stable. "Did it help your daughter?"

The man appeared surprised by the question but hastened to answer. "Yes, indeed it did. Immensely. You see, she had two suitors and did not know which one would be right for her."

The stable was bustling as they strode in, the newly arrived carriage horses being fed and watered, and some brushed down. The scent of hay, horseflesh, and stable muck assaulted Shayne's senses. "Which suitor did she choose after reading the book?"

The ostler laughed. "Neither of them. Can you believe it? Instead, she has now set her cap for our neighbor's boy."

"Tom Grimple?" Shayne knew him. He was a very good lad. "I'm sure Tom won't mind. Your daughter's a very pretty girl."

"Not mind?" He laughed again as they entered his small office that was mostly taken up by a long table cluttered with leather straps, buckles, stirrups, and tools. Bits of hay and dust were strewn on it, but it was organized and clean for the most part. "Why that boy took not an hour to propose to her, and she has accepted."

"Wait, he proposed to her? Already?"

The man nodded. "Seems he has always been in love with Molly but was too shy ever to let her know his feelings. Are parents always the last to find out about these things? Although my wife claims she knew all along. Maybe it's just men who are the ignorant fools."

Shayne grinned. "We are utter dolts when it comes to matters of love. Women are far better at understanding feelings. Men cringe and try to run away from them."

Indeed, he was a prime example.

His brain hurt from his contortions of thought these past few hours. Had he not spent them exploring, dissecting, denying, suppressing what he obviously felt about Willow? He had done everything but admit to himself he cared for her.

He took the musty book from the ostler and brushed a little sawdust off it. "I'm delighted your daughter and Tom have found each other. Give them my hearty congratulations. Be at ease, Mr. Geoffries. Miss Farthingale is not going to press charges against your daughter, especially once she learns she is to be a bride."

He walked out with the book tucked under his arm. Once out

of the stable, he glanced up at the sky, somehow expecting a thunderbolt to strike him down. That this book was spared could not be explained by logic. Molly was a good girl who had never stolen anything in her entire life, and yet, she'd slipped the book out of the Farthingale carriage mere hours before Lord Manton had set fire to the structure.

Divine intervention.

It had to be.

Nor could he overlook Willow's insistence that the book had not burned. She had sensed it. "No," he grumbled, refusing to make too much of the coincidence. What she'd sensed was only wishful thinking. She desperately wanted the book to have escaped the fire.

How could she actually *feel* it had been spared?

And yet, now that he was holding it…something was happening. His arm was tingling as he held it, as though there was a life, a vibrancy to this book that could not be denied.

He started for the inn and then changed his mind.

He wanted to read it before returning it to Willow, not that he believed it held magic. But Willow and her sisters, and now Molly, were relying on its wisdom before making the most important decision they would ever have to face.

He had to know what was written in that tome.

Should he not check it out? Make certain it was not some evil book of spells?

He strode down a winding lane that led to the outskirts of town and the hills surrounding it. There was a pleasant spot on one of the closer hills that offered a splendid view of the town.

A warm breeze rustled the leaves and blew through his hair as he neared the summit of that hill. The sun was shining down upon his shoulders, and the air was pleasantly dry. He intended to settle on the grass beneath a shade tree and skim through this book to make sense of the information it contained.

But he heard the trill of female laughter up ahead and silently cursed.

He would not be alone.

He was about to turn back to the inn when he heard another gentle trill of laughter. He recognized the voice. What in blazes was Willow doing up here? Should she not be resting from her injury?

This morning she could hardly move.

So what was she doing here now?

What if she had tired herself to the point of exhaustion and could not walk back to the inn on her own?

He marched up the small rise and soon came upon Willow, Cammy, and his brother Lorcan seated on the grass, chatting and laughing as though attending some jolly party. "Lorcan," he growled.

His brother ignored his scowl and grinned back. "Join us, Shayne. I thought the young ladies would enjoy a walk in the sunshine. What have you got under your arm?"

Willow gasped and scrambled to her feet. "No! It cannot be. And yet I felt it all along." She rushed to his side to inspect his parcel. "Where did you find the book? How did it survive?"

She stared at him for the longest moment, and then her eyes clouded with tears.

He groaned.

Lorcan took Cammy's hand to help her to her feet. "Come on, youngster. My brother and your sister need a moment alone." He winked at Cammy. She grinned back and allowed him to lead her down the hill.

Shayne watched with annoyance as the pair practically skipped away, thinking themselves quite clever in leaving him alone with Willow.

As for Willow, she had her face buried in her hands and appeared to be silently crying.

He put an arm around her. "Willow…"

"You found it," she said with a sniffle and hugged him tightly. But he noticed she had not raised her injured arm, just thrown her good arm around him and still held the other one tightly tucked against her body.

Was it too painful for her to move that injured arm?

Since she had walked up here without apparent distress and had appeared quite comfortable seated beside her sister and his brother, he decided to leave the matter alone for now.

"How can I ever thank you?" she said, the words flowing between sobs of relief.

"None required." He simply held her, knowing how awful she felt about losing this book and how much she had dreaded telling her family. To now have it back was as though a mountain had been lifted off her slight shoulders.

After a moment, she dabbed her eyes with the handkerchief she had tucked in her sleeve. "I did not mean to turn into a watering pot."

He kept his arm around her, liking the way she fit against him. "I know how important this book is to you. Shall I walk you back to the inn now? I'm sure you want to stow it somewhere safe."

She laughed while blotting her tears. "Yes. I won't let it out of my sight again."

They walked side by side, and he noticed her injured arm still remained stiff. "Willow, has the doctor seen you today?"

"He'll come by later. I've been using the unguent he gave me. He warned the stitches would hurt for the next few days. I'll be all right."

He tucked her good arm in his, now worried that perhaps he had not dug out all the glass, and this was the reason for her continued discomfort. Would the doctor have to open up the stitches and dig around for the lost shard?

He felt a raw ache wend its way through his heart at the pain he knew she would have to endure.

He hoped he was mistaken.

He could not bear to see her suffering.

"Shayne, I'm fine. Uncle George will see to my arm once I arrive in London."

She was right, of course.

London.

The Farthingale ladies would leave tomorrow, and he might never see Willow again.

No, that was not true.

He would ride to London once he had taken care of Lord Belfy and his rabble and dealt with her sot of a coach driver, Pierson.

Perhaps it would ultimately not work out between him and Willow. How could one ever know for certain? But he was willing to give it a chance. "Join me for lemonade when we get back to the inn. We can sit in the garden's gazebo."

She regarded him curiously. "I thought you had no more time for me today."

"I always have time for you. What I needed was time for myself. I needed to think." He took hold of her hand to help her over a bumpy patch that dipped steeply downhill and then simply never bothered to let go of her.

He liked the feel of her soft hand against the rough skin of his palm.

Her fingers entwined so naturally with his.

"What did you need to think about?" she asked, holding onto his arm to maintain her balance when they reached another bumpy patch.

"You, of course."

She looked up at him with those gorgeous eyes. "Because you don't know what to make of me? Is this why you walked to the hill? For time alone to ponder your future? And we interrupted your plans."

"It doesn't matter." He glanced at the book. "I knew I had to return it to you."

She was still looking up at him with those ensorcelling, blue eyes. The sun shone down on her hair, enhancing the lush golds and reds. "I'll lend you the book, Shayne. You really ought to read it. It will explain most of what you need to know."

He smiled at her. "Care to read it with me?"

"Do you want me to?" She regarded him with obvious surprise.

"I wouldn't have asked if I didn't."

She cast him a radiant look of wonder. "I would love to. But are you certain?"

"Yes." He turned serious. "You sensed this book had not been destroyed. You seemed to feel it in your bones. This is the way I feel about wanting to read it with you. Don't ask me how I know, but I am meant to do this with you."

She arched an eyebrow. "And not anyone else?"

"Fishing for compliments, are you?" He could not hold back a chuckle. "I've never felt about anyone else the way I feel about you. Surely, it must be obvious. But I have to be honest, too. I'm not sure what this feeling is yet."

"I understand. You need time to figure it out."

"Yes."

"I think having more time will do us both good, time together now and then time apart while I am in London." She cast him a gentle but impudent smile. "You are a mix of breathtakingly appealing and incredibly annoying. I expect this is the way you feel about me, too. But it is exciting, isn't it? The possibility that we have found something special with each other. We certainly are not indifferent to each other."

He considered it frightening more than exciting, but he supposed most men feared a lifetime commitment to one woman. There were men who would think nothing of breaking their wedding vows, but this was not the Brayden way.

That vow, once uttered, was unbreakable.

All the more reason for caution.

When they walked into the inn, Shayne asked Mrs. Ashcott to bring out a pitcher of lemonade for them. "Miss Farthingale and I shall be seated in the gazebo."

"At once, Mr. Brayden." She cast him a twinkling smile, which was precisely the reason he had walked out earlier, wanting to be on his own to think. The entire town had already paired him with Willow, and he did not like it.

What if he decided she was not right for him?

Wasn't this book a guide about how to avoid falling in love with the wrong person?

The girl would be heartbroken.

The last thing he wished to do was hurt her.

Besides, it would do her good to experience a London season. She may decide that he wasn't all that special and fall in love with a duke instead. Then he would be the one left with a broken heart.

But he was more cynical and would soon get over the loss…wouldn't he?

Foremost on his mind was not to repeat the mistake he'd almost made with Felice.

They settled beside each other in those delicate, wrought iron chairs around the matching table in the gazebo, but he did not set the book down on it until they had been served their lemonade and were left alone once more.

There was nothing improper about sitting out here with Willow.

They were easily seen from the dining room and the rooms overlooking the garden. There could be no scandal when all they were doing was reading a book together.

She inhaled lightly and smiled at him when he set it on the table and opened it to the first chapter. "Read it to yourself, Shayne. Then you can tell me what you think. I've poured over these pages at least a dozen times and am able to recite them by heart. We can discuss each chapter as you finish it. Would that work for you?"

"Sounds good to me." He was a fast reader and not particularly fond of people hanging over his shoulder anyway. Nor did he want to read the book aloud so that anyone might overhear them and make more of his attraction to Willow than was warranted.

Also, he had no idea what was written in the book.

It could be utterly scandalous.

He made quick work of the first chapter, which discussed the two facets of a man's brain with startling accuracy and with some inappropriate detail. The anonymous author had described men as having two brains, the low and the high.

With some shame, he realized he had been using only his low brain when first meeting Lady Felice, never thinking beyond the sexual appeal of her body.

It was only when his high brain had taken over that he realized how bad a choice he'd made. They were incompatible in so many important ways.

Willow had explained some of this to him.

This first chapter also explained the woman's brain and how a woman's urge was to seek the mate who would best protect her and their children. Willow had berated him for his inconsiderate remarks about the marriage mart, and rightly so. One had to use the tools available to them in order to survive. A female at her most vulnerable needed a strong male to protect her. Strong did not mean only physically strong, but also powerful, rich, or intelligent enough to keep them fed, sheltered, and safe.

Losing that male could be catastrophic for a female if she were not able to leave home to provide for her young. What choices did a woman have if she were not independently wealthy?

Willow had been sipping her lemonade and lost in her own thoughts as he had been reading. "What do you think?" she asked when he finished the chapter and turned to her.

"Interesting."

"That's it?"

"You are frowning at me again. No, it isn't *it*. But I'd like to read a few more chapters before we start to talk. Is that all right?"

"Yes. The next ones are about the five senses. Of course, it is important to find a partner who is pleasing to all your senses. But the real importance of these next chapters is in teaching us how to be honest with ourselves. I think it will help to test these senses out on each other. They are like recipes for love."

He leaned back in his chair. "Is this why you keep asking me what I think of you?"

She nodded. "What pleases one person might be loathsome to another. Who can ever know? But I find it fascinating that June and Augustus immediately knew how they felt about each other. It was love at first sight for June. Probably the same for Augustus, although he tried to deny it."

"It is easier for women because they want to be in love," he said, "so they are open to it. They want to find their protector, set up a household, raise their children. Men mostly want to be left alone. Marriage is an infringement on their solitude, an added constraint on their existence. Wife, children, house, and all the responsibility that goes with supporting family life."

She took a sip of her lemonade. "But men marry all the time. Wasn't your father happier because he married your mother?"

He nodded. "It is all about finding that special someone who makes it all worthwhile. You end up wanting to please her more than you want to please yourself. The burdens you take on no longer feel like burdens but enrichments to one's life."

"Shayne, I think that's what love is. Caring for someone that deeply. Everything falls into place when there is love. This is how it was for June and Augustus. My parents also made a love match. My father was happiest whenever he was with my mother. Same for her. All was right with the world when he walked through the door."

"This is what you hope for yourself."

She nodded. "Don't you?"

"I suppose. Let me read these next chapters."

She sighed. "All right. But will you indulge me in one thing when you finish?"

He glanced up from the pages he was about to read. "What do you want me to do?"

"Will you please tell me what you see when you look at me?"

CHAPTER NINE

S HAYNE WAS STARTING to understand the supposed magic of this book. It wasn't so much that it held the secrets to love, but it certainly held helpful insights. The first few chapters were about that primal response, the instinctive sexual urge that attracted a male to a female.

It explained why men felt compelled to look at a woman's breasts and the breadth of her hips. This compulsion was innate, a man's need to determine whether his woman of choice was capable of breeding healthy offspring.

This impulse was not something any man could control.

It was raw and savage, meant purely for survival of one's family, one's clan, one's name, and existence. Only afterward would a man start to think beyond the sexual and begin to whittle down the potential mates.

Perhaps more thought went into his next decisions but using the five senses was, for the most part, still an unthinking response. Does the woman look pleasing? Is her scent pleasing? Her voice? Her touch?

The taste of her on his tongue?

Willow certainly met those qualifications.

But there was so much more to falling in love. It required two people to find each other amid the thousands they might come across in their lifetime and recognize how special they are to each other.

But how would they know for certain?

More was required than mere physical compatibility to bind them.

He quickly skimmed ahead to the opening paragraphs of the next chapters. Expectations. Connections. This was the higher brain at work.

This is where the wonder of love happened.

This is why Willow was eager to learn what he wanted in a wife.

He wasn't sure yet, but this book would help him find the answers.

To understand whether Willow was right for him, he first had to understand his own needs. He hadn't given serious thought to them before. What did he want that only she could fulfill?

The opposite also applied. What needs did she have that only he could fulfill?

For that matter, what faults did either of them have that would destroy their chance for happiness?

No wonder he'd almost made a grave mistake with Lady Felice. Yes, she had pleased his senses at first. Yet, over time, she began to look less and less attractive to him. Her looks hadn't changed. Her scent, her voice, her touch…all the same. But their outlooks and desires were so different, the more he got to know her, the less he liked her.

Was it any surprise her manner began to grate on his nerves?

Her smile was no longer dazzling but appeared feigned.

Her elegance was no longer alluring, just cold and condescending.

She was not sophisticated, just shallow and indulged.

He cast Willow a furtive glance.

She was nursing her glass of lemonade, her lithe fingers absently stroking along the glass. His mind, of course, went immediately to thoughts of her hand on *him*.

He silently chided himself for his low-brain response.

One thing for certain, Willow was much more than that to him.

He cared for her.

Worried about her.

Felt an apish need to protect her.

He noticed the way she discreetly continued to hold her injured arm against her body. It frustrated him that he could not prevent her pain. Not only frustrated but distressed him. The need to comfort and protect her was overwhelming. "Willow, let me summon the doctor now."

"No." She cast him a stubborn look because that was who she was, stubborn, determined, strong-willed. Irritating. And he loved this about her. He loved that she looked delicate and yet had the heart of a lion. "The discomfort is no more than to be expected, Shayne. I will let you know if it becomes unbearable."

"All right." He understood getting through the book with him was the most important thing to her.

Perhaps it was best for them to simply continue.

She was not going to admit to being in pain and would be angry with him for interrupting their precious time together. Well, he would watch her pallor, her ease of movement, and summon Dr. Stratton if she seemed to worsen.

Another thing he understood about Willow was that she rarely complained.

She could have made a fuss over so many things, the loss of her clothes, her injury, their delay in reaching London.

She could have cast blame and criticized, but she never did. Not to him or the Ashcotts or any of their serving staff.

He eased back in his chair and stretched his taut muscles. "I've read these chapters on the senses. Go ahead. Ask your questions."

She laughed softly. "I will try not to sound like a Spanish inquisitor. You know the one I am most keen to ask. What do you see when you look at me?"

He took a moment to collect his thoughts, then leaned toward her as he spoke. "I could state the obvious. I see a beautiful young woman with fiery gold hair and stunning blue eyes. A young woman with lips as fair as a rose and a body so breathtaking, it can stop a man's heart."

Her eyes widened in surprise.

"But you are far more than that to me." He shook his head and chuckled. "You stand up to me when I am too full of myself to listen to what you have to say. You think for yourself and are not afraid to share your opinions."

She grinned back at him. "Also known as mouthing off irreverently."

"I like your mouth."

"Oh, you are being nice to me because you think I am in pain, and you cannot bear to inflict more."

"I am being nice to you because my body is in spasms over you. I should not desire you the way I do. But this feeling grows stronger in me by the day. You are beautiful and do not seem to know it. You are smart, and yet you doubt yourself. I know it is from lack of experience being out in the world. Who you are pleases *me*. Everything about you pleases me. Strengths. Weaknesses. Faults. Perfection."

She leaned her elbow on the table and strained toward him. "Do go on. This is quite fascinating."

"There's a wonder to love, I think. An incredible beauty in these feelings, to know there is someone special out there just for you. Someone who is not merely pleasing to the senses, for there are many pretty people in the world. But someone who will make you a better person, whose strengths are compatible with your weaknesses. Someone who will enhance your life and make it happier. I think this is who you might be to me, Willow."

Her eyes rounded in surprise, and her beautifully shaped lips formed a silent 'O' as they dipped slightly apart.

"However, I am not going to make you any declarations yet. Our situation is not that of your sister June and her General MacLauren. There was a good chance they might never have seen each other again. For this reason, they had to take that leap of faith and marry. But I know I will see you again."

"Truly?"

He nodded. "I intend go to London to properly court you if you will allow it."

She laughed. "I could put on airs and pretend it means nothing to me whether you do or not. But you know I cannot hide my feelings. I would love it. I will count the minutes until your arrival."

He ran a hand across the nape of his neck. "Just as my thoughts will be on you until I see you again. But do not close your eyes to other suitors. I avoided disaster with Lady Felice because I pursued her thoughtlessly and for all the wrong reasons. We were never meant for each other, and I almost took too long to realize it."

"And you think the same might happen with us?" He could see the disappointment reflected in her eyes because what Willow had said was true. She did not hide her feelings.

He loved this honesty about her.

He reached out and gave her hand a light caress before drawing it away. "You are nothing like her."

"But neither does it mean I am right for you." She was now staring at her glass of lemonade instead of looking at him. "I understand. You know so little about me. How can you be sure of my character? Or if our goals and dreams are similar? I hope you come to see me in London. Please do. I will not dismiss other suitors in the meanwhile, assuming I have any," she said with a snort. "But I sincerely doubt any will be as fine as you."

"Dukes, earls, and barons will be lining up along Chipping Way, blocking all access to your street. You will be the season's diamond."

She laughed. "Stop. You are ridiculous. Read the next chapters, Shayne. Those are all about the high brain issues. What connects us? What are our expectations? Which aspects of our character make us right for each other and which will tear us apart?"

"All right."

"While you do, I am going up to my room to grab a..." She stopped and groaned. "I forgot. I do not even have a shawl to put around my shoulders."

"Here, take my jacket." He took it off and wrapped it around her slender body, studying her closely as he did so. She appeared suddenly paler, and although she tried to hide it, he could see that she was shivering despite the warmth of the breeze.

He sighed and sat back down to face her. "Willow, you overdid it today. Do not bother to deny it."

She frowned at him, pursing her lips in displeasure, but it only drew attention to her kissable lips, and this is what he wanted to do...kiss her...and keep kissing her.

And kiss her some more.

He tweaked her chin. "Why don't you go back to your room and rest? I'll escort you. But I won't stay. I'll return down here and finish reading the book, if that is all right with you."

"I'll be fine in a moment. It was just a passing discomfort. Let me stay, Shayne. I'll sit quietly and not disturb you while you read. It is important to me."

He gave in.

Gad, is this how their married life would be...assuming they married? He giving in to her because her happiness meant more to him than anything else. This was his father. He understood now why his mother won every argument. Nothing mattered more to his father than seeing her happy.

"Would you care for something to eat, Willow?"

She nodded. "Mrs. Ashcott's marvelous crumble pie. It has apples, raisins, and cinnamon. Utter heaven."

He handed the book to her. "Wait here. I'll order it and some hot tea for you."

She arched an eyebrow. "I can do it, you know. I am not helpless."

"I know. But let me be overbearing and worry about you this

once. You were shivering a moment ago, and it is not cold out here. You haven't moved your arm the entire time we've been sitting in the gazebo. Your face is pale, and your eyes look strained."

"I thought you said I was beautiful."

"You are, even when you are obviously ill." He stood, then leaned over to plant a kiss on her forehead. "Don't chide me. I know everyone's probably looking and will now gossip. It was just a kiss on the brow. But you are beautiful, and I would be lying if I said I felt nothing for you. That is a statement of fact…not a compliment. Don't make too much of it."

"Rest assured, I won't," she said in a dry manner that revealed he had hurt her feelings.

He sighed. "It isn't my way to flatter and fawn or spout mawkish poetry. I need to take my time and think about what I am doing, Willow."

She nodded. "I know. This is unexpected for the both of us. I didn't think I liked you until a few days ago. You kissed me, and suddenly everything changed."

"Kisses have a way of doing that. This is why they are so dangerous. The taste of love, even more dangerous than a touch." He strode away, leaving her wide-eyed and not certain whether to smile or scowl at him.

He found Mrs. Ashcott and ordered tea and pie, then noticed Lorcan seated by the inn's entry with Charlotte and Cammy. He walked over for a word with him. "I'll be right back. I think I had better check on Lord Belfy and his rabble. I trust Ezekiel, but he isn't used to handling hardened criminals."

Lorcan shot to his feet. "No, stay. I'll go. How is Willow?"

"Yes, please do tell us," her aunt said.

He frowned and turned to Charlotte. "I think your niece is in pain, but she won't admit it. Mrs. Ashcott is bringing out some tea for us. Once we're done, I'm going to insist she return her chamber, and I'll fetch the doctor."

Charlotte put a hand to her throat. "Oh, dear. Shall I take her upstairs now?"

He shook his head. "I doubt she will agree to go. Your niece is stubborn."

Cammy looked up at him. "Yes, she is. Especially about that book. I wish she did not think of it as some magic talisman, but she's convinced you will never fall in love with her unless—"

"Cammy!" Charlotte said, casting her a disapproving glower.

"It is no use, Aunt Charlotte. Willow is in love with Mr. Brayden. We all see it, don't we? It is a Farthingale curse, I think. We fall in love, and it is forever. Having a season in London won't change anything."

"Yet, she must have it," her aunt insisted. "She is too young to know her own mind. Is this not so, Mr. Brayden?"

He nodded. "It is."

Lorcan, who had not yet left, grunted in agreement. "For many reasons, including getting you away from Lord Belfy and his jackals, London is a good idea. I'll stop by after supper to finalize arrangements for tomorrow's journey." He bid them farewell and strode to Shayne's office.

Shayne turned to the ladies. "Won't you join us for tea?"

"No," Cammy insisted before her aunt had the chance to respond. "I may not believe that book is magical, but Willow does. You have to finish reading it with her. Please, Mr. Brayden. Do it for her sake."

He nodded and returned to the gazebo.

Yes, he would do it for her sake. She would be gone tomorrow, and he wanted her to have no regrets over their parting. He was also doing it for his sake, for he had a lot to learn about commitment and marriage, and the book was teaching him plenty.

The teapot and pie had been set out by the time he returned, but Willow hadn't touched any of it. "I'll pour you a cup," he said, resuming his seat and studying her. "How about some of that crumble? Smells delicious."

He was pleased when she nodded. "Yes, thank you."

She looked almost lost in his jacket, but he was big, and his shoulders were broad. He took hold of her hand and was relieved to find it warm. "Are you feeling better now?"

"Yes, but do read on. I'm curious to know your opinion about these next chapters."

So he did, sparing a glance at her from time to time.

Her arm was still stiffly at her side, but she had regained the color to her cheeks. More important, she was no longer shivering. Her appetite was good, for she finished the slice of crumble and was enjoying her tea.

It was late afternoon by the time he finished the last chapters, and he knew he would have to return to his office soon. Lorcan and Ezekiel had carried the burden of guarding the prisoners for most of the day. It wasn't fair to place all the responsibility on them.

But he felt better knowing Lorcan was watching them.

Those lords were no match for his brother, for he had the instincts of a predator. Sharp, fast, lethal...merciless when necessary.

"What do you think?" Willow asked him after taking a sip of her tea.

So many thoughts were whirling in his head. "Would you mind terribly if we put off discussion of these chapters until tomorrow morning? We'll talk as I walk you through the carriage house remains before you leave for London. There is a lot of information to absorb within these pages."

She nodded. "I understand. In truth, I found the chapter on connections particularly difficult."

"How was it difficult for you?"

"Confusing. Take you and me, for example. What connects us?"

In truth, he found this part fairly straightforward. Feelings were difficult for him, and yet they were easy for Willow. "Well, family ties connect us, for one. Several of your cousins are married to mine. Similar upbringing for another. Parents who were happily married and raised their children with certain values. Honesty. Loyalty. Kindness toward others. Strength in ourselves."

She smiled at him, casting him that look of wonder he was growing to like quite well. Yes, if this worked out, he could see himself bowing to her every whim.

He drank the last of his tea and set his cup down. "We each care for our siblings and consider them an important part of our lives. We are bound in many ways. It is the expectations that confuse me. This is what I have to think about."

"I've given it thought." She looked up at him hopefully. "Do you wish to know what I think?"

"Yes, of course."

"I think the trick is not to think of them down to the minutest details but merely in broad strokes. What are the most important things to you? A true marriage or a *ton* marriage? Raising children together or handing them off to nannies, tutors, and governesses? I know what I'd like."

"You do? Tell me, Willow. What is important to you?"

"I would like what my parents have, a true partnership. No separate residences. No separate bedrooms. No separate lives. Being with our children to watch them grow. Being together as a family as much as possible. Making family decisions together. Being friends and companions to each other."

He reached for her hand again and touched it lightly. "I think we are of the same mind on this."

She nodded. "Yet, you still look troubled."

"This is a lot to share with one woman. I still don't know what else I should be looking for in a wife. Honesty, faithfulness are a must, but what about the rest of it? You said it yourself. Will I get along best with a chatty wife or a quiet one? A wife who is biddable or independent? Merry or reserved? Do I care if she is musical? Do I care if she embroiders perfect initials on my handkerchiefs? Do I care if she likes to dance or prefers to read?"

"Shayne, you won't find anyone who fits perfectly in the

image of your ideal. Nor will you be perfect for her. But as long as you are willing to compromise on your differences, that is what matters. I do not mean compromising faithfulness and honesty. Those cannot be bent. And wouldn't it be dull as dishwater if we were perfect matches in every way? I think it would be the most boring household imaginable."

He laughed as he rose and offered his arm to her. "You've given me plenty to think about. We'll continue the discussion tomorrow. Your aunt and sister are seated by the entry hall. Let them take you upstairs. I'm going to summon the doctor for you. I don't like the way you are holding your arm so stiffly by your side."

She surprised him by offering no protest.

He had not known Willow very long but already knew her well enough to realize she had to be in pain if she was not arguing with him.

He placed his hand over hers as he led her inside, once again feeling that sense of apish protectiveness coming over him. "If the doctor needs to undo those stitches, ask Mr. Ashcott to send one of his boys over to summon me before he starts."

"Why? Cammy and Aunt Charlotte will be with me."

"I want to be with you, too. I want to be the one holding you."

She shook her head and smiled up at him. "Yes, I'd like that. But once he gives me laudanum for the pain, then I want you to go away. If I'm to start gibbering idiotically about kissing you, I don't want you to hear it."

She handed him his jacket once they were back inside. "Thank you, Shayne. It warmed me."

The scent of her would cling to the fabric, soft and sweet, and making him ache. Was he thinking too hard about the perfect woman? Wasn't she standing right before him?

He'd spent hours with Willow and still felt as though it wasn't enough.

He handed her the book. "Have me summoned for any reason. Promise me."

"I promise."

When she reached her aunt and sister, the three of them bid him good day and went upstairs to their quarters. He watched them go, his gaze fixed on Willow.

Lord, she was beautiful.

And smart.

Smart enough to handle him.

His heart was telling him not to let her go to London.

Ask her to stay in Taunton.

But to what end?

He strode to his office, immediately tense and on alert as he entered. Gone were thoughts of Willow. His attention was on his prisoners.

His brother and Ezekiel were watching them, and all appeared calm. But he remained wary, for all hell could break loose at any moment.

Those prisoners were plotting an escape.

He saw it in their eyes.

He saw it in Lord Belfy's unsettling gaze, the look of a madman. Cold, wily, desperate, and with a hint of wicked amusement. He was a spider spinning webs in his head and plotting to lure his captors into his demented trap.

These were all desperate men who would do anything to avoid their punishment.

Lord Belfy stared at him through the bars. "Did you enjoy your time with the luscious girl, Brayden? Willow's her name, I believe. Did you strip her naked? I bet she's a tasty morsel. She must have looked exquisite with her fiery hair fanned out upon the white bedding and her legs spread to take you in. Perhaps I'll have her next."

"You slime!" Ezekiel cried. "She's a lady."

Shayne stopped him when he started toward Lord Belfy. "Don't, Ezekiel. This is what he wants you to do, draw you close so he can grab your weapon. Pay no attention to him. Do not let him rile you into doing something reckless."

But Shayne understood his companion's anger. He wanted to kill this man himself.

He would without hesitation if given the slightest reason.

This exchange, however brief, proved one thing, however. He could not ask Willow to stay in Taunton. Not another day, not another week. Not until Belfy was securely delivered to the Exeter prison.

He wanted to see this man hang and his fellow lords permanently imprisoned or sent into exile.

This answered the question of whether or not to ask Willow to stay.

Absolutely not.

He wanted her away from Taunton as soon as possible.

His heart was not going to win this battle.

He had to let her go.

Lorcan had taken a position against the wall with a clear view to the cells, the door, and out the windows.

He motioned for Shayne to come to him.

"What now?" he muttered, wondering what Lorcan was staring at.

"Your carriage just arrived," he said quietly. "If the horses weren't likely spent and in need of rest, I'd pack up Charlotte and her nieces this very hour and start for London. Every time I look at Belfy, I feel spiders crawling up my spine. I'll rip him in half if he hurts those girls."

"He won't. He can't. Just don't lose your head and play into his game."

"I'm too well trained for that," Lorcan assured him. "But he's got Ezekiel riled."

Shayne glanced over at his trusted guard, who was still glowering at the locked-up lords and now pacing back and forth with weapon in hand. "I've noticed a change in him over the last day or two. Whatever Belfy has been saying to him is working to overset him. I think I had better send him over to the inn right now. You and I will watch the prisoners tonight."

"I wish Donal was here."

"He'll be back tomorrow to help us out. In the meanwhile, he's with the Earl of Monkton and his family. They're as much on edge over these jackals as we are."

"I'm sorry, Shayne."

"For what?"

"Willow, of course."

"Let's not talk about it here, Lor. There's nothing to say. I have to send her away until the danger has passed."

"I know. Duty first."

Shayne nodded and called Ezekiel over. "Let's check on the inn before nightfall."

They walked out of his office together. "You're my best man, Ezekiel. You know how I feel about Miss Farthingale. I need you to guard her and her family this evening."

"You're getting rid of me because you're worried what I will do to that devil's spawn, Belfy."

Shayne kept his manner calm. "If I meant to be rid of you, I would be sending you home. I meant what I said. I need you guarding the ladies. I need my mind to be clear. It won't be if I'm worried about them."

Ezekiel snorted, but cast him a grin. "You know I'll protect them with my life."

"I know. That's why I need you there." Having dealt with him, he strode to his coach driver and greeted him. "You made good time, Mr. Baldridge. How are you?"

"In the pink, Mr. Brayden."

"Good. Mr. Geoffries will take care of the horses and get you settled. Then go around to the kitchen and have yourself a proper meal."

"Thank ye, sir. I will admit my throat is parched. I could do with an ale. But just one, never ye worry. I never imbibe when I'm on duty. The horses can tell when their driver is not sober."

Shayne nodded. "I'm hoping you can get an early start tomorrow."

But he had not forgotten his promise to Willow. She wanted to walk through the ashes to see if there was anything to be rescued from her burnt-out carriage. It would not take long now that she had the book back in her possession. Then she would be off. He watched his coachman head to the rear of the inn, his thoughts still on Willow.

Would her feelings change for him once she arrived in London and was caught up in the glittering whirl?

CHAPTER TEN

WILLOW AWOKE THE following morning to a burning pain along her swollen arm. She inhaled sharply, unable to put the slightest pressure on it without feeling a piercing jolt throughout her body.

Her soft cry must have alarmed Cammy, who hurriedly tossed off her covers and scampered out of bed to her side. "Willow, how bad is it?"

"Very bad, I think. We had better summon the doctor. My arm feels like it is on fire."

"Oh, dear. Lie still. I'll wake Aunt Charlotte and then run downstairs to ask Mr. Ashcott to summon the doctor. I know it is still early, but I'm sure most of their staff will be up by now." She tossed on her robe and slipped her feet into her slippers before rushing into their aunt's room. The connecting door between their rooms had been left ajar all night.

Willow leaned back and closed her eyes as another wave of pain overcame her. She heard her sister urgently whispering to her aunt and then heard her aunt's response. "Stay with your sister, Cammy. I'll alert Mr. Ashcott."

"The magistrate wanted to be told as well," Cammy said in a hushed tone. "Have Mr. Ashcott alert him as well. He will be angry if we fail to tell him."

Her aunt sighed. "Yes, I think you are right."

Willow heard the door swing open and then quietly click

closed as her aunt left them.

Cammy returned to her side and put a cold compress on her head. "I hope this will help. You feel a little warm. I'm sure you have a fever."

Willow licked her tongue across her parched lips. "I think I do."

"You certainly do. So much for our trip to London. We cannot possibly leave for another day or two, perhaps longer." She crossed to the window to draw aside the drapes and open the window. "Does the sun bother you? I think a little light will do you good. The room was dark and sweltering."

"I don't mind. You sound jubilant," Willow said with a strained laugh, fully understanding the reason for her sister's glee.

"I am not at all. Relieved is a better word for it. How can I be jubilant when you are in pain? But I've made no secret of my desire to return home. I don't want to go to London to be ogled by strangers and drawn into their manipulative courtship games."

"I don't think any of us were eager for it, but Uncle John and Aunt Sophie will be disappointed if we don't visit them. So will our cousins. They've all managed to enter into love matches for themselves, so you should not reject the marriage mart out of hand. They found good men to love them. With their guidance, I'm sure you will do very well."

"Me? What about you? Or has the handsome magistrate already claimed your heart?"

"Cammy, please do not say anything to him. I think I am in love with him, but he hasn't made up his mind yet about me. And now I think the doctor will have to cut open my arm again. I will be a scarred mess by the time he is through."

"Dr. Stratton is an experienced doctor and highly regarded in Taunton. As for Shayne Brayden, he is not so shallow as to dismiss you because of a little scar." Cammy dabbed the cloth in water again and gently ran it across her brow.

Tears formed in Willow's eyes. "What if I lose my arm?"

Her sister gasped. "Do not even think of such a thing! You

cannot. You will not. *The Book of Love* would never be so cruel as to—"

"Oh, ho! Now, who is suddenly a believer in its magic?"

"I don't, Willow. I mean, I know there is something special about that book. But you are the one who places too much emphasis on it. Since you do, why would you think it would abandon you now?"

She shrugged. "Perhaps to warn me that Shayne is not the right man for me."

Her sister scowled at her. "Or perhaps to show you that he is as noble and perfect as you hope him to be. You are in pain and obviously not thinking clearly. I am beginning to understand why so many of our cousins fell in love with Brayden men. They are quite like baboons, aren't they? Territorial and protective? It is infuriating at times. But also a bit wonderful, don't you think?"

Willow laughed. "Yes, I suppose. But all the more reason I will not allow my heart to dwell on him. You know what the book says about a man's low brain urges. They are primal. Beastly. What if his low brain now views me as imperfect and dismisses me as a suitable mate? He may not even realize this is happening because it occurs on such an innate, instinctive level. I wouldn't blame him. How can it be his fault?"

A soft growl at the door caught their attention.

Willow turned to the sound and groaned.

Of course, Shayne had run over here the moment he was alerted. He looked magnificent, of course. His hair was still damp from a recent washing, and he was clean-shaven. She caught the scent of lather and sandalwood soap as he approached and drew up a chair beside her bed. His shoulders looked broad, but she attributed it to the fact that he had not donned a jacket, vest, or cravat. The white lawn of his shirt seemed to stretch for miles across his chest. Dark breeches hugged the muscled contours of his legs and disappeared into his boots. "Do you think I would ever abandon you?"

Heat rose in her cheeks, and her body began to tingle in response to the deep resonance of his voice. "How much did you hear?"

"Enough." He emitted another soft growl to mark his irritation, but it only set her body tingling again. "I'm glad your aunt summoned me. I was going to walk over here in another hour anyway since I had promised to escort you through the ashes of the carriage house before you left for London. I doubt you will be going anywhere today." Despite his obvious turmoil over her injury, he managed a soft smile. "Seems I will not be rid of you that easily."

She managed a small smile in return. "Seems not. I shall be here to plague you for at least another day."

He caressed her cheek. "I am not complaining."

But he rose a moment later and strode to peer out the window. "Doctor's on his way. I see him hurrying down the street. He'll be here in a few minutes."

"I'll go down to greet him," Cammy said and scurried out of the room.

Willow groaned. "My matchmaker. She's convinced that…well, it does not bear discussion."

He turned to look at her, and she was once again struck by how handsome he was. "Willow, I know you are in pain and overset. All the more reason to put aside that low brain, high brain nonsense for now."

"It isn't nonsense. Haven't you done everything to prove what the book says is true?"

He was now frowning at her. "And you think that I must now dismiss you as a suitable mate because you think a scar on your arm will leave you imperfect?"

"Won't you?"

She thought he was angry with her, but his expression softened, and she saw only his compassion. "No."

"No? That's it? That's all you have to say to me?" In truth, the one word was more than enough to hearten her. Not flowery or flattering. Just to the point.

"That's it. What more do I need to say to convey my meaning?"

Nothing else, she supposed, loving the silvery heat in his eyes and his quiet strength. "Shayne, will you hold me as the doctor cuts open my arm?"

He returned to her side and gently gathered her in his arms. "Of course, I will. I'll remain by your side for as long as you need me."

"What if it is for always?"

"Then always it shall be."

The import of his words took a moment to wend through her dazed brain. By the time she realized what he had said, Dr. Stratton entered the room. Cammy and Charlotte walked in behind him. Both stood quietly at the foot of her bed while the doctor set down his medical bag and approached to examine her arm.

Shayne had moved aside to allow him near, but he kept hold of her hand and gently ran his thumb across the top of it to calm her when the doctor turned to her aunt and sister and said, "You ladies had better wait downstairs."

"Shayne," she whispered, understanding this would require more than undoing a few stitches.

"I'm here, Willow. I won't leave your side."

She tried not to sound like a coward, but she was afraid. Her mind could not help leaping to the worst possible outcome. What if the arm was infected and had to be cut off? Clearly, it was infected. Her skin was red and bruised around the area of the stitches and terribly swollen.

"We'll get dressed in Aunt Charlotte's room and then be waiting just downstairs. Mr. Brayden, will you please send for us as soon as the doctor finishes." Cammy had set out their gowns at the foot of their beds last night since they had intended to dress, grab a quick breakfast, and be on their way to London this morning. She now took her gown and gathered a few other articles of clothing in order to dress in Charlotte's room.

But she paused at the door and cast the doctor a worried glance. "How long do you think it will take, Dr. Stratton?"

He rubbed the nape of his neck. "I could be a while with your sister. Have your breakfast and linger over a cup of tea. I hope to be finished by then. But kindly do not return up here until you are summoned. It is not a good idea. There is nothing you can do for your sister and…it is not a good idea. You will only overset yourself."

Aunt Charlotte nodded. "Come along, Cammy."

Cammy burst into tears.

Willow wanted to do the same, but her sister would never leave otherwise. They had always been close, she, the adventurous one, and Cammy, the sensitive, affectionate one. The two of them would be bawling like babies if she did not remain strong for both their sakes.

She held tightly to Shayne's hand and only allowed her fear to show once her sister was out of the room and the door had closed behind her. "Doctor, what will you do to me?"

"Explain it to her, Dr. Stratton. She will feel better knowing exactly what is to happen," Shayne said, surprising her because he was not used to sharing information himself. "Tell me how I can help as well. Just so we are clear, I have every intention of remaining by her side."

"I believe a small fragment of glass or a bit of cloth must still be lodged in your arm, Miss Farthingale. This is what is causing the swelling and discomfort. I shall have to remove the stitches and dig around for these stray bits. Because they are likely so small, this may hurt. I am going to give you a concoction devised to minimize the pain. I discovered it during my years as an army doctor in Spain. These are Moorish medications and more refined than our own."

"Is that vinegar I smell?"

"Yes, this is another thing I learned from my time in Spain, their practices on cleanliness. I wash my hands and instruments with it before every procedure."

He cast her a fatherly smile as he began his preparations.

Oddly, the array of odors assaulting her nose calmed her, even though most were unpleasant. Once finished with the vinegar scrub, he began applying a pungent liquid that smelled like a potent brandy to a sponge and added a powder to it. "This is laudanum at its essence, but with a little variation to provide a deeper numbness to ease your pain. The morphine extract is a slightly higher dosage than ordinary laudanum. Used only for my surgeries. Never anything more. It is far too dangerous for general use."

"I see." She did not really understand the science of it but hoped the man knew what he was talking about. He probably did because one did not develop a fine reputation if patients died, and Dr. Stratton was very well regarded.

"Afterward, I will apply a salve of alcohol and yarrow to help cleanse the area of the wound once I stitch your arm again. That should do it."

She nodded. "You do not use isinglass?"

He turned to her in surprise. "You know of fish bladders? We used it when amputating on the battlefield because we had to work fast, and there was no time for neat stitches. So we cauterized the arterial vessels then wrapped them in the fish paste we made out of those bladders. It worked remarkably well. But my stitches are neat and will leave you with very little scarring. Trust me, Miss Farthingale."

"I do. Um…I'll need help slipping my arm out of my sleeve." She glanced down at herself and realized it would be no simple task to accomplish. Someone would have to draw the sleeve of her nightgown off her shoulder. She could not do it herself because her arm was too sore to move.

She turned in dismay to Shayne.

He immediately understood what she was asking. "I'll help you, Willow."

Somehow, this made her feel better. She was not going to be able to hide much of her body while he slipped it off her, but he was not going to leer at her. Having him be the one to partly undress her did not feel humiliating.

Surprisingly, it felt right.

She had her bedsheet drawn up around her at the moment but allowed him to pull it down to her waist.

"Will there be a lot of blood, Dr. Stratton?" she asked, desperate to keep her mind off Shayne's intimate touch.

The doctor had turned away a moment out of discretion while Shayne bared her shoulder. "There will be some, but most will be absorbed by the balls of cotton and yarrow tincture. You shouldn't bleed too badly."

"But the bedding…"

Shayne seemed to understand her concern. "No reason to fret if it's ruined, Willow. I will compensate the Ashcotts for any damage done. Also, if my presence here threatens to damage your reputation…I will make it right."

The doctor turned to face him, an eyebrow arched in surprise. "Never thought I'd hear those words out of you," he said with a grin.

Shayne cleared his throat. "Let's get started."

She was properly covered up once more, all but her arm and shoulder, which had to remain exposed.

Willow was scared, but she wanted this to be over with already.

"Close your eyes, Willow," Shayne murmured, brushing aside a few of her curls with gentle care before taking her hand in his.

She did so and held onto him with all her strength. Then she felt nothing, remembered nothing once the doctor administered the laudanum. He had mentioned using a particularly potent extract of morphine, aptly named after Morpheus, the god of dreams.

Her head began to spin, and within moments, all went black.

When she awoke, Shayne was still by her side, holding her hand. "Willow, can you hear me?"

She groaned.

"It's over, sweetheart. Dr. Stratton found the shard. But you need to rest."

She was trying to blink open her eyes, but her lids felt so heavy, she couldn't quite manage it. "Was there a lot of blood?"

"A bit. Cammy and Charlotte helped me change you into a clean nightgown. One of the maids put fresh sheets on the bed."

"What time is it?"

"Noon. You've been out for several hours. We opened the windows to allow the warm breeze to circulate." He stroked his thumb lightly across her brow. "That ought to make the room more comfortable for you. Your aunt and sister will look after you shortly, just tell them what you want, and they'll attend to it. But you are not to do anything for yourself yet. Dr. Stratton does not want you getting out of bed for several days."

"I don't think it will be a problem. I can hardly lift my head." She inhaled lightly. "Are we in a field of lavender?"

"Something like it. The doctor recommended burning an essence of lavender. He claims the pleasant aroma will calm you and ease your recovery."

She pursed her lips. "Did he think I would awaken and become hysterical?"

"Some people do, and it has nothing to do with your being a delicate woman, which I assured him you were not."

She laughed. "I think you just insulted me."

"Not in the least. You look delicate, but you have the courage of a lion. That is a statement of fact. You may also take it as a compliment if you wish. Did you know lavender was also used in the army when I was a soldier? They would burn it in censors to clear the infirmary of foul scents such as blood and bile. It has to do with morale and healing. It is nice, don't you think?"

"Yes, I like it. Are Cammy and Charlotte here now?"

"Not at the moment. Since you were sleeping peacefully, and I was not going to leave your bedside before I saw you open your eyes, they took a moment to go to Mrs. Albright's shop and pick up their gowns. They'll purchase more nightrails, another robe, and a few more day gowns for you, as well."

"Are you still paying for all this?"

She felt his hand stiffen as it lay atop her brow. "Yes."

She opened her eyes and stared at him. He still appeared hazy to her, and she expected the drug the doctor had given her would take days to work its way out of her body. She could make out the gray steel of his eyes since he was staring intently back at her. "Thank you."

She understood the nature of this man and how helpless he had to be feeling as she suffered. If purchasing gowns for her eased his frustration, she was not going to fight him on the propriety of it. "You mentioned earlier that you helped Cammy and Charlotte change me into a clean nightrail."

"Is this your way of asking whether I saw your body?"

She blushed.

"Yes, I did. Before and after. I had to slip the sleeve off you before the doctor started his ministrations. Do you remember? Afterward, you were unconscious and bloody. You had to be changed, but they could not lift you on their own for fear of hurting you."

"So they asked for your help?" She was surprised. "Did you see me naked?"

He nodded.

"That doesn't make sense. Charlotte is supposed to be protecting me from—"

"We are speaking of love, Willow. Not your ruination. Your aunt understood."

She tried to sit up but could not manage it on her own. "Help me up, Shayne."

He propped several pillows behind her and carefully settled her into a sitting position. His touch felt exquisite, his hands gentle as they pressed around her waist and drew her body up. He made certain she was comfortable, then pulled the sheet over her chest for modesty. "Kindly explain that last statement," she said, still trying to shake the haze from her head.

"About love?"

He'd gone straight to the point, not avoided the *L* word at all. How could it be? She had to look awful. Probably smelled awful as well, for even she caught the scent of blood and alcohol on herself. In that mix was also a scent she did not know how to describe. It was sweet and yet unpleasantly acrid. She also suspected she had thrown up on herself, for although she had been wiped clean, there remained the lingering odor of vomit.

Perhaps it was just her nose inhaling the remains of the morphine-laden laudanum and wreaking havoc on her sense of scent.

Her mouth felt as though a dragon had taken up residence inside it.

She patted her hair. It was still in a braid, but there were stray wisps everywhere. She needed to brush it. "Why make mention of love?"

He cast her a steamy look. "Should I not be?"

"No, not now. You are not thinking straight. I do not want you to say something to me you will regret in an hour. You know how apishly protective you are by nature. Will you deny that you like me best when I am vulnerable?"

He laughed.

"It is true."

"It is not." He leaned forward and kissed her brow. "I like you best when you are mouthy, as you are now. You've hardly regained consciousness and are already going on about what I should and should not feel."

"Oh, so we are talking about feelings now?"

"Yes." He kissed her again, this time on the tip of her nose. "Don't tell me how I ought to feel about you, Willow. What this morning has proven to me is that I value you above anything else in my life. I was supposed to take Lord Belfy to Exeter prison this morning. We were to depart right after you left for London. But you did not leave, and there was no way in hell I was going to ride off while you faced being cut open again."

"I had my sister and aunt beside me."

"And now you also have me."

"You are assuming I want you." But she laughed and shook her head. "I suppose I do, but I will not have this conversation with you before I am fully recovered. Then you can look at me as I mouth off to you and decide whether or not you want me."

He planted a soft kiss on her cheek. "As you wish."

Tingles shot through her as she inhaled the lather and sandalwood scent of his jaw. Was she being an idiot? Would any other woman in England put this man off if he declared his love for her? "It is what I wish."

He did not appear very concerned about it.

Which only proved her point. He was being led by his protective nature, not his heart. "Because if you really loved me, you would not be planting chaste kisses everywhere on my face except my lips."

He ran a hand through his hair, and his expression suddenly turned pained. "Willow..."

"What?" He simply continued to stare at her with that wretched look in his eyes. "I am going to punch you in the nose, Shayne Brayden. Tell me what is going on."

"All right, love..."

This had to be bad, he had just called her his love. "Am I dying?"

"No. *Bloody hell.* No."

She breathed a sigh of relief, for he sounded rather emphatic about her survival. But her relief did not last long when he spoke his next words. "When the doctor began to cut open your arm, the laudanum may not have fully worked its way through your system. We thought you were unconscious. That morphine extract is quite potent. It turns out you weren't quite out."

"What happened?"

"You felt him cut into you and bit down on your lip to stem your pain." He pressed a finger to his lip, pointing to a spot on the lower right corner. "You bit down so hard, it bled open. He had to put two stitches in there."

She brought a hand to her lip, but he stopped her before she could touch it. "Don't, Willow. Your mouth is still numb, and you shouldn't be touching it anyway."

Her eyes widened in horror.

She had fresh stitches on her arm. The limb was still a swollen and bruised mess. Now she had stitches on her lip. No wonder he had been spouting that nonsense about her being the most important thing to him. No wonder he had been calling her *love* and been so gentle with her.

What he was feeling for her had nothing to do with love.

What he was feeling was pity.

She let out a cry and turned on her side to roll away from him. "Go away, Shayne. I don't want you looking at me like that."

"How do you think I am looking at you?" He reached for her hand, but she smacked it away. "Willow…"

"Don't. Just go. Leave me alone." She wanted to wrap her arms around herself and curl into a little ball. She could not even do that because everything hurt too much. His gentle touch hurt worst of all. "I am releasing you from whatever promises you've made to yourself about me. You owe me nothing. You are free."

"What in blazes are you talking about?" The next thing she knew, he was lifting her into his arms. He sank onto the bed and settled her on his lap.

She wanted to struggle, but lightning bolts of pain coursed through her body with every small movement and quickly sapped her strength. Anyway, she was an idiot for struggling. His arms felt wonderful as they wrapped around her to draw her up against his solid chest. "Stop moving. You are only hurting yourself."

When he tugged down on her nightrail, she realized it had ridden up her legs while she had been squirming and struggling against his grip. She had accomplished nothing but scandalously exposing her thighs. Her futile maneuvering had also drawn her bodice down so that her breasts were about to spill out.

She was alarmed and ashamed and yet hopelessly in love with him. More so by the moment because he was sincerely worried about her and doing his best to be gentle while she behaved like a spoiled child.

All she had accomplished was to put her nightrail in a twist.

Attempting to right it only made the situation worse.

"I've seen you already," he said with a growl and held her even closer so that her body was shockingly pressed to his. "Stop trying to hide from me. It's done. There's no going back from it. And by the way, you are the most beautiful woman I have ever beheld."

"Why are you being so thickheaded? I am letting you go. The monster has released you."

He inhaled sharply. "Is this what you think you are to me...a monster?"

CHAPTER ELEVEN

SHAYNE DID NOT know what to say to console Willow or how to convince her he still thought her beautiful. The cut on her lip was minor and would heal completely within the month, if not sooner since yarrow was a potent curative. Once healed, the scar was not likely to be discernable unless someone looked closely. "You are beautiful, Willow."

"How can you say that?"

The cuts and stitches to her arm were more severe but would also heal in time. Those scars might not disappear altogether, but even they would be relatively minor. "I have scars, too. Shall I show you mine? They are quite ugly and puckered. No delicate stitching done. Just quick cauterization."

Her eyes widened. "With a hot iron?"

He nodded. "That's how it is done."

"Were you…alert?"

He nodded again. "I did not have the luxury of a physician as fine as Dr. Stratton."

He did not dare describe his treatment, for it would revolt her. No laudanum to ease his pain. No time to drink himself into a stupor. All he recalled was blinding pain before and after, but he'd survived it. He had told her enough, hoping to convince her she meant more to him than the sum of a few scars.

Did she believe him shallow enough to regard her wounds as imperfections and scorn her? If anything, her courage under pain made him love her all the more.

Yes, he loved her.

"Shayne, I'm so sorry. I would have comforted you had I been there."

"I know, Willow. Can we forget about scars now?"

She sniffled. "No. I'm sure yours only make you look manly. I don't want to look like a man."

He held back a chuckle, for she was miserable and worried that no one could ever love her. "There is not a chance in hell I would ever mistake you for a man."

Any doubts he held about the sort of woman he should marry had melted away while holding Willow in his arms before the doctor began reopening her wound.

She was the one for him, and he had been a fool to resist the obvious.

He felt it even more strongly as he held her now.

He placed his hand to the small of her back and stroked her lightly to calm her. It did not appear to be working, but he had only himself to blame. His own body was a rampant mess and had been ever since the doctor had asked him to remove her injured arm from the sleeve of her nightgown. He'd done so, having to pull it down over one breast in order to get it off without hurting her arm.

His heart had yet to recover from that jolt of desire.

But he had pushed the gown back over the creamy mound immediately and held the fabric modestly in place for the sake of propriety.

He had not been trying to look at her.

But how could he not be mightily affected by the sight of her body?

Seeing it, feeling its exquisite softness, and holding his hand to the side of her breast while the doctor cut into her, had created an intimate connection between them. An unbreakable connection, as far as he was concerned. "Willow, love. Look at me."

This is not the way he had ever intended to see her, but he

had, and it could not be taken back. His palm still tingled from the feel of her against his hand.

He would act on his desire once she was healed…but as a husband bedding his wife, because he wanted Willow in his life forever.

"Don't call me your love. It only makes me feel worse. I am nauseated, probably drooling out of the side of my mouth because it is numb and drooping, my hair's a mess, and I have stitches all over my face and limbs. How can you not find me revolting?"

"You'll heal and will feel better in a few days." He stroked her hair once more since she refused to turn back to look at him. "You won't see much of me this week anyway. I intend to take our prisoners to Exeter first thing tomorrow. Lorcan, Donal, and I are going to deliver them a few at a time, so we'll be occupied much of this week."

"Be careful, Shayne."

"I will, love." He sighed since nothing he said seemed to make her stop crying. "Willow, wait for me to finish with the prisoners. Don't leave Taunton. There's much I need to say to you."

She moaned between sniffles. "I won't listen if you continue to behave in this foolishly protective way."

"Then you can refuse me, but it won't stop me from asking."

"Asking what?" she asked amid more sniffles.

"Surely, you must understand. I want to marry you." He scooped his arm around her waist and carefully turned her to face him. Her face was blotchy pink and tear-stained. Her hair was an unfashionably beautiful mess. Her body was exquisite even as she tried to remain curled in a ball. "I want to marry you," he repeated more forcefully, "if you will have me. Will you have me?"

"Do not say another word! I will not accept your pity proposal."

"Then how about the proposal of a man who fell deeply in

love with you the moment he set eyes on you? Because that's what I did. Only I was too busy trying to deny it because I had made a hell of a mistake my first time around and almost ruined my life for it. But reading that book with you taught me so much."

"It obviously did not teach you to keep your mouth shut."

Lord, would she always be this irreverent? "You accused me of being taciturn and never talking. Well, I am talking now. I love you. Would you care to say it back to me?"

Pain filled her eyes, and she sniffled again. "You are not playing fair."

"Fine. You don't have to say it back to me. I know you love me."

She gazed at him through her tears, her face small and achingly sweet. "How do you know that?"

"Because you were talking as you began to wake. Laudanum does that to you, as you discovered the first time around. Do you know what you said to me?"

"Oh, dear heaven. Did I ask you to kiss me again?"

He smiled. "Yes, among other things."

"Other things? What else did I say?"

"You asked me to remove my clothes and lie beside you. You thought it only fair since I had removed yours."

She gasped. "I did not."

"Ask Charlotte and your sister."

"They heard me?" She wriggled in his arms, now turning fully to face him. "You are jesting. You must be jesting."

Since she was still on his lap, as she turned, her shapely bottom brushed against parts of him that he dared not mention. It was his fault for putting her on his lap in the first place. But he could not hold himself back, for he was overwhelmed by this need to comfort and protect her. Not to mention fireworks were still exploding behind his eyeballs after catching sight of her full breast and the rosy area surrounding its perfect tip.

He'd caught little more than a glimpse before slipping the

sleeve off her shoulder and down her arm.

Then, he had quickly turned away.

But Lord help him, that glimpse was enough to put his body in spasms.

The girl was spectacular.

How was he to convince her when she was determined to believe the worst?

He dared not show her a mirror yet because her arm did look awful, and her face was not at its best. He saw only the beauty in her, but she would only notice her puffy, tear-stained eyes, the droop of her mouth that was still numb, and the dark stitches poking out at the corner.

She groaned. "What else did I say?"

"Other than deciding you wanted me in your bed?"

She began to cry again. "Everyone heard that?"

"Well, your aunt and sister did. But they'll understand."

"And Dr. Stratton?"

"No, he'd already left before you started rambling." But the maids had been there, changing her sheets. And she had been talking up a storm, most of it about him and how he needed to kiss her on the lips…and anywhere else he thought would be helpful. But he had warned them not to repeat a word of it to anyone, or he'd toss them in his gaol.

They would likely ignore him, for the gossip was too juicy.

But nothing bad would come of it since most of the women in Taunton felt the same way. He was no coxcomb, but he understood the look of desire in a woman's eyes. He understood the ogles and nervous giggles he routinely encountered. He was no stranger to brazen overtures, either.

He liked that Willow was remarkably curious about many things, especially his body. The gossip was not likely to be malicious and would die down once they were married. And he was going to marry her. All her questions would be answered after their wedding night.

Perhaps before their wedding night if they could not keep

their hands off each other.

He sat quietly holding her on his lap, his arms around her until he heard her aunt and sister returning. Willow had stopped crying and was merely resting her head on his shoulder, her eyes closed and cheek pressed to his chest.

She seemed comfortable, so he did not bother to move her.

"What happened?" Cammy asked, setting aside her bundles and coming to his side.

"I had to tell her about the stitches to her lip."

Charlotte had gone to her quarters to deposit her packages and now joined them. "Poor dear. Was she terribly overset?"

He nodded. "I'm sure she'll feel better about it tomorrow. She's still nauseated and feeling hazy. I've asked her to marry me, but she won't hear of it. She believes I proposed to her out of a sense of pity."

"She refused you?" Cammy put a hand to her stomach. "Oh, dear. Will you ask her again?"

He smiled wryly. "I am wildly in love with your sister. Yes, I will ask her again…and again, if this is what it takes." He rose and carefully set Willow back down on the bed, tucking the covers about her. "I think she's cried herself to sleep."

"Poor dear." Charlotte nodded. "I know she adores you, Mr. Brayden. Give her time. But I must think on it as well. She is young and has seen little of the world. Perhaps she needs a few months in London to be sure you are her right choice."

Cammy emitted a small *eep*. "Aunt Charlotte, is there any doubt? Do you not see the wonder in her eyes whenever Mr. Brayden approaches her? And Barnstaple is not isolated. We have assemblies and musicales. At times, Father has had to beat the young men away from us with a stick. However, we showed no interest in these suitors by our own choice. None of them ever caught our fancy. But June knew her feelings for Augustus the moment she met him. Willow knew Mr. Brayden was someone special, too. She does love you. I could see it right away."

"Thank you, Cammy." He cleared his throat. "I had better get back to my office now. I'll come by again in a few hours."

"Please do."

He turned to Charlotte. "I understand your point. I had wanted her to go to London as well. I thought it would be good for her. But now…well, talk it out with Willow. Not now. Her head's too clouded. Wait a few days until she calms down. She has a good, sensible mind. I'll respect her wishes."

Cammy cast him a look of dismay. "You won't fight for her?"

He arched an eyebrow. "Of course, I will. But I want her to have no doubts. Marriage is forever. I don't want her life to be a living hell if she decides she has made a mistake."

He strode out, knowing Willow would be well looked after by her family, and tried to turn his attention to his prisoners. These next few days would have him quite busy riding to Exeter and back.

His thoughts needed to be on that business now.

Willow would also need time to settle down and think. He knew she loved him. But at the moment, she did not love herself. For this reason, she could not trust his motives in wanting to marry her. He understood what she was feeling, that whirl of doubt and fear.

He strode into his office.

Lorcan was seated in his usual spot against the wall with a view of all windows and entrances. He looked quite comfortable with another chair drawn close and his feet casually propped on it.

Ezekiel, to Shayne's consternation, was also present, pacing like a caged lion. He could feel the man's agitation and did not like it one bit. "Ezekiel, why are you here? I assigned you to the inn."

"You were busy with Miss Farthingale. I thought I would come over and see if Lorcan needed relieving."

"I'm back now. You can resume your post. Miss Farthingale is sleeping comfortably. Her family is watching over her now." He turned to Lorcan. "We'll start taking the prisoners over tomorrow morning. A few at a time, as we discussed."

"What about me?" Ezekiel asked, obviously put out he was not included in Shayne's plans.

"You'll join me on the second trip when we deliver Manton, Simmel, and Kearns."

"Why not take me with you for Belfy? Am I not your best man?" He was holding a rifle in his hand and carelessly pointing it at their prisoners.

"You are my best. But Lorcan is a trained agent for the Crown," he replied calmly, motioning for Ezekiel to follow him into the back office for no reason other than to get him away from the prisoners. The man was a tinderbox about to blow. No doubt Belfy had been playing games with his mind and now had Ezekiel right where he wanted him. One more remark would set him off and have him lunging for Belfy.

That's when Belfy would grab him and slit his throat.

Lord help them all if he managed to grab Ezekiel's rifle. He'd fire it with deadly aim, taking him down or Lorcan, for he was a crack shot.

For this reason, he had given the keys to the cells to Lorcan to hold. They were no longer left on a peg for any of his guards to grab—no doubt this further agitated Ezekiel.

How was he to talk sense into the man?

He shut the door and motioned for Ezekiel to take a seat in one of the chairs beside his desk.

The man grudgingly did so.

Shayne then settled behind his desk. "I'm worried about you," he said, deciding it was better to simply speak honestly. "Lord Belfy is a madman, the worst sort if such a thing exists."

"What do you mean, Shayne?"

"He is diabolically clever, a master at manipulation. What has he said to you? You are not yourself, Ezekiel. Do not bother to deny it. We both know he's gotten under your skin."

"He means to hurt the Farthingale sisters. He says the lewdest things about them. His friends laugh and urge him on."

"But we know this is how they operate. They have been doing this for days. Why do you care? They can do nothing to the ladies while we have them behind bars. It is just desperate talk." He leaned forward and rested his elbows on his desk. "Why are you taking it so much to heart now? Has he said something else to you? This is…"

Blessed saints.

He understood now. "What did he do to your sister?"

Ezekiel blanched.

At first, he tried to deny anything had happened, but his pain and grief could not be suppressed. After a few more lame attempts at denial, he broke down and told Shayne all. "She works at the Earl of Monkton's manor house. Lord Belfy found her hanging out the wash one morning. She was alone…he took advantage."

He burst into tears. "She was too afraid to tell anyone. He threatened to kill her if she reported it to the earl. The earl is his brother, he told her. The earl would protect him and discharge her, he assured her."

Shayne grunted in disgust. "He is an odious person, but justice will prevail."

Ezekiel slammed his fist on the desk. "What justice? Do you really believe the earl will not step in at the last moment and ask for clemency for his brother? Then he will be right back here, working his malice, no one able to touch him because he is the earl's brother." Darkness shimmered in his eyes. "It will destroy my sister if he is set free. Her mind is so frail now. She is terrified of everything, even a meek fieldmouse scampering across the floorboards sends her screaming in fear. Let me kill him, Shayne. Let me do it and rid Taunton of this pestilence."

Shayne met his gaze with an icy one of his own. "No. Go home. Take these next few days off. Come back to work next week."

Ezekiel stood up so abruptly, he knocked over his chair. "What? Am I not even permitted to guard the Farthingale ladies?"

Shayne stood as well. "No. Your sister is not the only one whose mind is in danger of snapping. You are one of my best men. I will not deny it. But I must have you back with your mind clear. Right now, it is filled with bile and thoughts of vengeance when it comes to Lord Belfy and his companions. Leave them to me. Go home, Ezekiel."

"The hell I will." He stormed off, slamming the door behind him as he left the building.

"Do I detect trouble in paradise?" Lord Belfy taunted.

Shayne ignored him. "I'll relieve you, Lor. You haven't gotten much sleep these past few days."

His brother cast him a questioning look. "I'm all right."

"I'm sure you are, but I need us both alert and on guard to-night." He lowered his voice. "I think Ezekiel is going to try to kill Lord Belfy."

Lorcan said nothing, merely rose, and went into the back office to lie down on the cot.

This was typical of his brother, to say nothing and show nothing of his feelings. But Shayne was so relieved to have him by his side.

Donal would soon be here, too.

Those two were his best friends as well as his brothers. He trusted them with his life, just as they trusted him with theirs. He was not much of a praying man, but he gave a silent prayer of gratitude that the three of them happened to be together this week.

He could not have captured Lord Belfy and his companions without them. Now, all he had to do was prevent all hell from breaking loose tonight, or someone was going to die.

Would it be Belfy? Ezekiel?

Or, in trying to stop those two, would it be him or one of his brothers?

CHAPTER TWELVE

To Shayne's relief, Donal rode in just before nightfall and offered to guard the prisoners with Lorcan. "You are a sight for sore eyes," Shayne readily admitted. "I could do with an extra hand now that I've taken Ezekiel off this assignment."

Donal frowned. "You're worried he will do something foolish."

He'd said it as a statement, not needing to ask the question.

Shayne nodded. "I want to find him and talk to him, perhaps keep my eye on him tonight. He's a good man. I won't have his hatred for Lord Belfy turn him into a murderer."

They had been speaking in the back office, outside of the prisoners' hearing, but now walked back out. Lorcan was in his usual spot guarding all the potential entrances. Donal took up a position behind the door so that anyone bursting in would not notice him until they were brought down from behind.

Of course, they all had Ezekiel in mind.

"I'm going to look for him," Shayne said.

Donal patted him on the back. "Be careful. A man in that state is a danger to everyone, even a trusted friend like you."

He nodded and strode out, ignoring Lord Belfy's jeering taunt. "Tell Ezekiel I send my regards to his sister."

Lord, this man could not be hanged soon enough.

He walked through town, his instincts on alert more than usual as he strode to Ezekiel's house. His mother and sister were home. "He isn't here, Mr. Brayden," his mother responded in answer to his request to speak to her son.

The sister appeared ready to burst into tears.

He regarded her kindly. "It is nothing important, Millie. Just let him know I stopped in if he returns within the hour. He isn't to come looking for me. He was feeling poorly, so I sent him home for a few days' rest, that is all."

She nodded, watching silently as he bid them good evening and left. But he had only made it as far as their front gate before Millie scurried after him. "He is overset about Lord Belfy, isn't he? Please find him, Mr. Brayden. Find him before he does something foolish."

He nodded. "That is my plan."

She sighed. "You know, don't you? About me, that is."

He had no wish to lie to the girl. "Yes, your brother confessed all to me today. It will go no farther, I promise you. Are you all right?" He sighed and shook his head. "Stupid question. I'm sorry. Of course, you cannot be fine. Lord Belfy will be hanged soon, and we shall soon breathe easier. Millie, I wish you had come to me at the time."

She clasped her hands together and began to wring them nervously. "You could not have done a thing for me or any other of the girls on his brother's staff. I was not the first."

Shayne wanted to howl in frustration. "And no one said a word to the earl?"

"How could we? He always protected his brother. Harmless fun, he called it. So sorry it got a little out of hand, he would say whenever Lord Belfy and his companions got into a brawl and damaged property or broke a few noses. So, what were any of us to do?"

Shayne did not know how to respond, but he was in silent outrage.

Millie cast him a wistful smile. "I know not all men are bad. You, for one. I wish there were more like you."

"There are."

She laughed. "Oh, dear me. No. You are one of a kind, Mr. Brayden. Don't you worry about me. I will not forget what Lord Belfy did to me, but I shall move on. Such a thing takes time to overcome. My brother is overwrought because he was not able to protect me. Now, he needs to be protected before he does something irreparably foolish."

"That is why I am looking for him."

She breathed a sigh of relief. "And I will hold him here if he returns. Even if I have to keep a rifle aimed at him all night."

Shayne nodded and walked on toward the nearby taverns. With luck, Ezekiel would drink himself into a stupor and not wake up until midday tomorrow.

He did not find Ezekiel at the first two establishments but spotted him immediately at the White Horse Tavern, for he was off by himself in a corner. His behavior was so loud and belligerent, the other patrons had moved away from him.

Mr. Seaver, the tavern keeper, mopped his brow and rushed over to Shayne when he walked in. "Thank goodness you're here. Your man is out of control. Betty's been trying to distract him, but not even she will go near him now."

"I was afraid of that. Keep your girls and the patrons away while I talk to him."

"Won't be a problem," the tavern keeper muttered.

Shayne strode toward him. He sank onto a chair across from Ezekiel and said nothing as he watched him down the last of his ale and shout for another.

When Betty refused to serve him, he cursed at her.

"Is this how you treat women now, Ezekiel?"

The words took a while to penetrate his fogged brain. But when they did, he bowed his head in shame. "I am nothing like Lord Belfy."

"Then stop behaving like him. Your sister is worried about you." He kept his gaze on him. "Go home and sober up. She needs you to be strong for her. She needs you to be honorable and kind as you have always been, not turning into a depraved beast. This is how you help her. This is how you protect her. She needs to know she can depend on you."

"I have to kill him."

"No, the law will attend to it in Exeter." He nodded toward the empty ale mug. "Being drunk will not help you. Nor will it numb you enough to turn you into a cold-blooded murderer. This is what you are doing, is it not? Trying to drink up the courage to shoot him down."

Ezekiel burst into tears. "He deserves to die."

"He surely does, but not by your hand or mine." Shayne rose. "Come on, I'll walk you home."

"You needn't. I can manage by myself." He staggered to his feet, almost knocking over the table in his clumsiness. "Or don't you trust me?"

"I trust you with my life, but not with Lord Belfy. Promise me you will go straight home and forget your idiotic plan of revenge. Say it, Ezekiel. Give me your word of honor."

"I will go home. Upon my oath."

"Look me in the eyes and say it."

"Damn you, Shayne." He looked around the tavern and growled upon noting all the faces staring back at him. "All right. I will go home."

"And only home. Nowhere else."

He shoved Shayne out of the way and staggered out of the tavern into the night. It was dark now, and Shayne was still concerned about his best guard. The simple solution would have been to lock him up for the night, but there was nowhere to put him now that his cells were packed with Lord Belfy and his cohorts.

The last thing he needed was to play nursemaid to Ezekiel tonight.

He caught up to him, which was not very hard to do since he was staggering down the middle of the road, obviously headed for the magistrate's office instead of home to his mother and sister.

"Bloody fool," Shayne muttered. "Ezekiel!"

"Let me do it, Shayne. You can't stop me."

He punched Ezekiel hard enough to knock him out and caught him just before he toppled.

"You are going home, my friend." Shayne hauled him over his shoulder and strode back to his house with the man slung over his shoulder like a sack of grain. "Millie, I need some sturdy rope," he said calmly when she opened the door to him.

"What is going on?" Ezekiel's mother placed a hand over her heart as she watched him stride into the parlor with her unconscious son. "Oh, dear! Is he hurt?"

"It's all right, Mama," Millie responded. "We must keep Ezekiel tied up until about…um, midday? Is that long enough, Mr. Brayden?"

He cast her a wry smile. "Yes. Thank you, Millie. Do not release him any sooner. My brothers and I will be escorting a prisoner to Exeter first thing in the morning. I want us to be too far away for your brother to catch up."

"I understand. He will be." She turned a moment to her mother, who was now crying and fussing over Ezekiel, confused as to what was going on.

Millie turned to Shayne. "It is time I told her what happened and why Ezekiel is behaving the way he is."

He nodded. "Do you wish me to stay when you do?"

"No, you needn't. I think it will be easier for her if she and I can speak alone, but thank you for everything." She turned back to her mother and placed a comforting arm around her shoulders. "Do not fret, Mama. It will all be fine. I shall be fine."

She turned once more to Shayne. "I will be fine, Mr. Brayden. In a way, this has helped. I cannot stay weak and frightened. My brother needs me to be strong, and so I shall be…even if it terrifies me at first."

"Millie, that strength has always been inside of you. But we all need help at times," he said, glancing at her brother, who was still slung over his shoulder. "Come see me if you ever do."

"I will." She scurried out, fetched a suitably sturdy length of rope, and led the way upstairs to Ezekiel's chamber, where Shayne deposited him on the bed. She cast him a look of fierce determination. "Make sure you bind his hands and feet securely, but also bind him to the bedpost so that he will have to break the bed apart to escape. He'll wake the dead if he tries."

It was good to see that glint of ferocity in Millie.

One problem now solved.

He returned to his office and spent the rest of the evening guarding the prisoners in shifts with his brothers.

At dawn, he and Donal prepared to ride out alone with Lord Belfy, for they needed to get him to Exeter and away from his companions. He was the cruelest and exerted an almost mystical pull on his friends.

This first shift was only him, Donal, and Lord Belfy, while Lorcan and his regular guards remained behind with the other prisoners.

"Avenge me!" Lord Belfy cried out maniacally as they led him out of his cell.

A few of them gave tepid assurances, but it was the crack of dawn, and these spoiled lords were not about to rouse themselves when they had their own troubles to worry about now. But Shayne wanted to be sure they understood their circumstances. "Lord Belfy is sentenced to hang. You are not. I suggest you think about salvaging the remains of your lives, for you will surely hang with him if you attempt to interfere."

Lord Simmel turned to him with a sneer. "You don't understand, do you? You are the first one we shall kill as soon as we are let out."

"No, not him," Lord Kearns said with a curt bark of laughter. "His sweetheart. That luscious Willow. But we won't kill her right away. We'll all have her first."

Lorcan rose and cocked his rifle. "Not if I cut off your balls, Kearns."

"Ah, the stoic one rises," Lord Simmel mocked. "Who is your

sweetheart, *Lor*? Or are you too ugly to have one?"

"Blessed saint, they are all idiots." Lorcan turned to Shayne. "Get going. I don't know how much longer I can stand their whining."

"We will kill you," Lord Mercer growled.

Lorcan stared at him.

Mercer paled and backed away from the bars, falling back on his cot. "Bastard. I'll get you."

Shayne stifled a grin. Lorcan did have a frightening way of looking at a man when staring him down.

Lorcan rolled his eyes at Shayne.

He grinned at his brother. "We'll be back tonight."

He wanted to stop in and see Willow before he left, but it was not possible. He had to concentrate on Lord Belfy and could not risk a moment's distraction. Also, Willow probably looked worse today, since the bruises would start showing and turning purplish-yellow. He did not mind for himself. She was beautiful to him no matter what.

She needed time to understand this.

Fortunately, the day was spectacular as they rode to Exeter. No rain or mud-soaked roads to slow them down. They stopped several times to rest and water their horses, but not in any towns where Belfy might do harm to innocent citizens.

Shayne knew the man's mind was awhirl with plots of escape.

If the situation weren't so serious, he might have taken great pleasure in thwarting him. All he felt when they reached Exeter in the early afternoon and delivered their prisoner into their cousin's custody was a great sense of relief. "Good to see you, Rafe," he said, for their cousin, Raphael Quinton, happened to be Exeter's magistrate.

"Been a while, Shayne. Seems you've had your hands full." He nodded toward Lord Belfy, who was still manacled and now being led away to a much sturdier cell than any they had in Taunton. "How are you, Donal?"

"Enjoying my time off," he said with a grin. "Lorcan and I

intended to spend the week fishing on Shayne's estate and eating up all his food, but he's put us to work. Be careful with Belfy. Keep him isolated from the other prisoners, or you will find yourself with a prison uprising on your hands. He's mad, dangerous, and has a way of luring those of lesser minds to do his evil bidding. Do not underestimate him. And watch your guards as well, for he will surely try to manipulate them. He has an uncanny way of sensing a person's weakness and preying upon it. No one is safe."

Rafe nodded. "And what of the others you'll be bringing over?"

"They follow him blindly," Shayne said with a frown. "Keep them all apart. Make sure the guards cannot be bribed to deliver messages back and forth. They may behave like soft, pampered lords, but they are not harmless. More important, they will do anything to help Lord Belfy escape."

"And themselves?" Rafe asked, offering them seats in his office.

Shayne settled into one of the comfortable chairs with a sigh. His cousin's office was far more elegant than his, but Exeter was also a more important town than Taunton. More commerce, more banking, and situated along the main route to London. "Those fools would die for Lord Belfy, without hesitation. I'll release a breath of relief once he is hanged. But do not think it will make his companions less dangerous. I'm certain they have made a pact to seek vengeance on those who put them away."

"Nasty fellows, aren't they?" Rafe shook his head. "Born in privilege and appreciating none of the advantages they have been given in life. I know their sort, resentful of not being the firstborn son and feeling constrained by their meager allowances, which would keep any ordinary man's family comfortably fed, clothed, and sheltered for life. But they wish to live like kings, and no amount will ever be enough."

Donal nodded. "That's it in a nutshell."

After dining with their cousin, he and Donal rode back to

Taunton with a contingent of Rafe's guards. In truth, Shayne was relieved to have them. His own men were good and decent but not used to handling the more dangerous sort of prisoners.

Also, having Rafe's guards would allow him time to look in on Willow.

He had promised himself he would not do this, but his heart had other ideas.

So it was with great eagerness that he called upon Willow the following morning. Donal had ridden off at daybreak with Rafe's guards and three more of their imprisoned lords. Lorcan was now guarding the four who remained behind.

He strode into the Ashcott Inn and immediately spotted Cammy and Charlotte finishing their breakfast in the dining room.

Cammy waved him over, flashing a glorious smile. "Good morning, Mr. Brayden. Have you come to see Willow?"

Charlotte was not quite as pleased when she noticed him. "Don't tell me you have finished with your prisoners already. I expected you to be busy for days yet."

"Donal has taken the next three to Exeter. Lorcan and I will take the last four tomorrow. My cousin happens to be the magistrate there," he said, reminding Willow's aunt, for he knew he had mentioned it several times. "He was kind enough to spare some of his guards to help us out."

"And you couldn't wait to see my sister," Cammy said, smiling so gleefully, he had to laugh.

"Something like that. How is she?" He turned to Charlotte. "May I see her?"

He merely asked out of politeness, hoping she would not give him a hard time about it. No one was going to keep him away from Willow.

Cammy was his ally in this. "She would love to see you, Mr. Brayden. Give me a moment, and I shall make certain she is presentable."

She ran upstairs before anyone could stop her.

Charlotte eyed him dubiously. "I do like you, Mr. Brayden.

But this does not alter my opinion. Willow ought to have a London season before she leaps into marriage. It was different with June and General MacLauren. She is the eldest and was of an age to marry. We could not have stopped her even if we wished to do so. Also, she is the sort who always knew her mind."

"And you think Willow does not?"

"I could see the strength of their love. You could not be in their presence without feeling the fire between them."

Shayne rubbed a hand across the nape of his neck. "What are you saying, Charlotte? That you do not think I know my own mind? Do you doubt I love Willow?"

She cleared her throat. "No, I think you do. The problem is, you don't trust your feelings yet. I will not have my niece's heart broken because you waver."

"And what of Willow's feeling for me?"

"She is also uncertain."

Shayne felt as though he had been punched in the gut. "Are you suggesting Willow does not love me?"

"I am merely saying she is distraught right now, and I would not like to see her pushed in a direction she might regret. You know she is not at her best with those ugly stitches still in her." She frowned as she looked him in the eyes. "You are a handsome man, Mr. Brayden. Willow believes you are the handsomest she has ever met."

"Is this not how a wife should feel about her husband? You needn't fear it will swell my head. I am well aware of my faults."

"But she does not see them. To her, you are perfect. In my mind, this cannot be real love but merely infatuation. I am especially concerned because she feels so vulnerable. Give her these next few days to recover her spirit. If you press her for a marriage commitment now, she might refuse you again because she believes she is grotesque."

"There's also the chance she will accept my proposal."

Charlotte cast him a pained look. "And spend the rest of her life worried you married her because you felt sorry for her? Oh, Mr. Brayden, will that not be ten times worse?"

CHAPTER THIRTEEN

S HAYNE RESENTED EVERYTHING Willow's aunt had said but had to agree with her. Wasn't this why he had originally resolved to keep away from Willow all week? Not only keep away but encourage her to go to London. "You win, Charlotte. I will visit her only after the last of the prisoners are delivered to Exeter."

He rose and strode out of the dining room, about to leave the inn when someone called his name.

Blessed saints.

He recognized the female voice, one he never expected to hear again. What was Lady Felice doing here? And how long would it take him to be rid of her?

He stifled a groan as he turned to greet her. "What brings you to Taunton, Felice?"

She ignored his frown and sidled up to him, the shimmering green silk of her gown too elegant for this quieter society. The fabric *whooshed* lightly as it rubbed against his leg.

She cast him a coquettish smile, her eyes innocently widening in that practiced way she had mastered to bring out the deep emerald of her eyes. They were striking eyes, quite beautiful, and she knew it. Her gown and accessories matched their color, even her jewelry enhanced their perfection.

But was she demented? Those gems were too lavish to be worn when traveling and would attract thieves to her like bees to honey.

This was the magistrate in him thinking of all the potential dangers.

Did he not have enough worries with the last of Lord Belfy's cohorts still to be transported? Then he had to track down Willow's driver, that sot Pierson, and bring him back to Taunton. Not to mention Ezekiel was still intent on seeking justice for his sister.

For this reason, he was not paying close attention and was caught by surprise when Felice boldly pressed her body to his. "Is this any way to greet your betrothed?"

"My…" He shook his head and laughed. "You are nothing of the sort. What happened with your dupe of an earl? Did he come to his senses and drop you?"

She frowned at him. "No one *drops* me. I break it off with them. But I think I made a mistake with you."

He had allowed the courtship to simply die out by no longer visiting her, but if she needed to think she had been the one to break it off, so be it. He did not care, other than to be rid of her now.

All he had learned from the book he had read with Willow the other day came flooding back now. The scent of Felice was overpoweringly floral, not sweet or subtle as Willow's was. It might have been suitable for an overly crowded ballroom with all those sweating bodies on the dance floor, but here in Taunton, it was simply too much.

Her touch was not gentle, either.

Her voice grated, and he cringed whenever she gave that fake laugh of hers he had once been foolish enough to find attractive.

"Come back to my guest chamber with me," she said in what she considered a seductive purr. Well, she was a beautiful woman. No doubt about it, but he felt nothing for her. It was as though his low brain, having once considered her as a potential mate, had now ruled her out forever.

"I'm busy, Felice. You should not have come here." He tried to ease out of her grasp, but she was not yet ready to let him go.

"How busy can you be? You had time to talk to that old biddy," she grumbled, referring to Willow's aunt. "Who is she, anyway?"

"None of your business." The last thing he wanted was Felice getting her claws into Willow, which would happen if she had the slightest hint of her existence. For this reason, he avoided mentioning even her Aunt Charlotte.

"Something dull and official, I suppose."

"Yes, quite." He tried to end the conversation and turn away, but she burrowed herself against him and held fast in a manner he found annoying and proprietary.

The feel of her body against his was not at all arousing.

She felt bony.

Willow was also slender, but there was a softness to her body that he adored. Of course, Willow also had magnificent breasts. *Blast.* This is not what defined Willow or why he cared for her so deeply. But when comparing these two women, Willow's natural beauty and her forthright honesty were far more appealing to him than Felice and her elegant snobbery. "Go back to London. I do not have time to be dragged into your latest game."

She gave him a practiced pout. "You are beastly, Shayne. Why should we not resume our courtship?"

"Because there was no courtship. We each learned early on that we would not suit."

Her eyes rounded in obvious surprise. "You've found someone else."

"No." He was never going to mention his feelings for Willow and have her subjected to Felice's spiteful games. "My life is here, not in London. More important, when I marry, I shall expect my wife to be faithful to me. Do not even pretend to be capable or willing to do this."

She tipped her head up in indignation. "There is someone else, isn't there?"

"No one else, as I've just told you. This is about you and me."

"You are angry that I encouraged the Earl of Everell."

"I am not angry with you. I do not care who you encouraged and to whom you give your attention next. I do not care, Felice. I am truly sorry if this hurts you, but you will land on your feet as you always do."

Indeed, this woman was like a cat, agile and not easily led or subdued.

She also had sharp claws that left many a man scratched and bleeding. He shuddered to think how narrowly he had escaped being one of her victims.

And if he had married her?

Lord help him, his life would have been a living hell.

But he had every faith she would find herself a suitably titled husband who would allow her to do as she wished.

"You truly do not want me?" she asked with an undertone of menace that could not be overlooked.

"I truly do not. I'm sorry you came all this way to find out. Go back to London. A glittering ballroom is where you belong, not in this backwater town of Taunton."

She cast him a feline smile, one he surely did not trust. "We ought to at least share a farewell kiss."

"No."

She grabbed him anyway and tugged his head down to ravish his lips, crushing her mouth to his with an ardor neither of them had ever felt in the months they had known each other. In truth, not even when making love.

For pity's sake.

She would not let up.

Everyone in the inn's entry hall and dining room had to be watching this ridiculous scene.

He did not know which was worse, dealing with Lord Belfy and his cohorts or trying to handle a spurned Lady Felice. He could punch a man or toss him behind bars. What could he do about Felice other than try to keep out of her line of fire?

"Enough," he said with a quiet growl, finally easing free of her. "You've sufficiently made a joke of me."

He saw nothing but contempt in her eyes and knew she was not yet done with him.

She tipped her head up and cast him a feral, predatory smile. "Your desperate kiss has done nothing to change my mind," she said, her voice shrill and easily carrying through the inn. She removed a ring from her hand and gave it over to him. "I am sorry, but I do not love you. I cannot accept to marry you."

"What's this?"

"I am returning your love token to you."

He hadn't given her any.

He expected what she'd handed over was one of her fake gemstones. The other jewels she wore were real, however. This was Felice, arrogant and contemptuous of those who lacked wealth. She enjoyed flaunting hers, even if it was a stupid and dangerous thing to do.

Her father, although never able to control his daughter, was no fool.

Felice appeared to be traveling alone, but he knew she wasn't. He spotted an older woman quietly seated in a corner and surmised this was her downtrodden chaperone. A glimpse at some of the other guests revealed a few who had the look of Bow Street runners. Added to that would be the able-bodied footmen attending her coach.

He handed the ring back to her. "Keep it as a remembrance of me."

He had meant to be sarcastic, but his words only spurred her to create more of a scene. Gad, he just wanted her to leave Taunton.

Having finished her performance, she tucked the ring inside her bodice, shoving it between her breasts as she cast him a pitying smile. "I am sorry I broke your heart. Please know this was never my intention. Be happy, and do try to forget me."

He could be cruel and assure her that he would.

But he allowed her to save her wounded pride. "Just go, Felice," he said quietly. "You've made an ass of me, and I allowed it this time. Do not try it again."

She slapped his face. "No, you may not follow me to Bath. Everell will be there, and we intend to marry."

So, she had caught herself an earl after all. Well, Lord Everell was a good-natured idiot, just the sort who would accept Felice's antics without too much rancor.

Shayne watched with relief as Felice strode into the dining room. The haggard, older woman bustled in after her.

Mr. Ashcott, who had been at his desk and watching the entire time, cleared his throat and grinned at him. "You've been a busy man, Mr. Brayden."

"Lord Almighty. When is she scheduled to leave?"

The innkeeper studied his guest ledger. "She arrived yesterday evening and will be off for Bath later this morning. Her coachman was going on about her exploits to Mr. Geoffries. Seems he is quite fed up with her. They were supposed to go straight to Bath for her wedding to Lord Everell, but she diverted them here. Still holding a torch for you, I expect. Wanted to give you a last chance to propose."

"That will never happen. Send word to me once she's gone. I'll be hiding in my office."

The man chuckled. "Dealing with the likes of her is like tangling with a hungry jungle cat. One of you is going to get eaten alive, and it won't be her."

Shayne grinned. "Am I not the bloodied proof of it?"

"Oh, aye."

He was about to walk out of the inn when he glanced up and saw Cammy peering down from the railing.

He groaned inwardly.

How much had she seen? Or heard?

Then he realized it was worse…so much worse.

Willow stood behind her.

His heart gave a violent tug.

Her beautiful face was ashen.

How much had Willow seen and heard?

She could not seriously believe what Felice had been spouting, could she?

He considered climbing the stairs to talk to her, but what was he going to say? Felice kissed me; I did not kiss her. I never gave her that ring. I have no intention of following her to Bath. Sounded lame even to his ears. Worse, he was concerned about what Felice might do if she realized Willow was the woman he loved.

He strode out and did not look back.

Why was love suddenly so complicated?

CHAPTER FOURTEEN

WILLOW WISHED SHE had remained hiding in her room and not followed Cammy into the hall in time to see Shayne kissing that exquisite woman. So much for his declarations of love and not caring about her stitches.

Cammy hurried after her as she fled to their chamber like an utter coward. "He called that woman Felice. I'll wager she is the one he left behind in London."

"Precisely, and now she is back in his life. Did you get a good look at her, Cammy? She is beautiful. An Incomparable. A diamond of the first water. And what am I? An ignorant peahen from Barnstaple without a proper gown to my name."

Cammy folded her arms over her chest and frowned at her. "You forgot to mention your stitches."

Willow felt tears well in her eyes. "Now you are just being cruel. I did not mention them because I consider them obvious. How can I compete with Lady Felice?"

Her sister released a huffed breath. "Compete with her? Why are you being so dense? Shayne has made up his mind, and he loves you. He chose you."

"And he showed it by kissing her?" Willow shook her head as she tossed off her robe, her angry motion sending jolts of pain up her arm and into her temples. She sank back on the bed, still wincing and feeling miserable.

She stared down at herself, noting her newly purchased

nightrail. Shayne had acquired it for her. She would have ripped it off and put on one of her gowns, but he had bought those for her as well.

He made her feel like a kept woman.

Dr. Stratton's insistence that she rest in bed these next few days only made her feel even more constrained.

His clothes.

Trapped in bed, one he was paying for at the moment.

Nothing to do but wait for him to visit.

He had her neatly wrapped up.

Not that any of her injuries were his fault.

But while he had her conveniently tucked away in this bedchamber, Shayne had not wasted a moment in renewing an old acquaintance. "He chose her first and then changed his mind. What makes you think he will not break it off with me now that he has seen her again? She is perfect in every way. He is once again realizing it."

Cammy shut their bedchamber door with a light slam and turned to her. "You are making this up in your head. Why won't you just admit that you are perfect for each other? Did you not see his expression after that kiss? He looked horrified and could not wait to be away from that woman."

"First of all, Shayne's expression was stoic, revealing nothing. He is very good at hiding his feelings behind a stone facade."

"And you are becoming very good at wallowing in your misery." She went to the wardrobe and withdrew one of the new gowns Mrs. Albright had delivered to them. "Here, get washed and then put this on. I'll help you. I don't care what orders the doctor gave you. This is no time to be lolling in bed. Since when are Farthingales scared minnows? We are fighters, and this is what you are going to do, fight for him."

"Like this?" She pointed to the stitches at the corner of her lip and winced as she raised her arm to show those ugly stitches, too. Both wounds were a horrid mix of raw red and purplish-blue from the residual bruising.

Cammy curled her hands into fists. "I am going to give you a matching cut on the other side of your mouth if you insist on remaining spineless."

Willow shook her head and laughed.

Until this very moment, her sister had been a sweet and gentle thing, never a fighting word or harsh remark out of her. But right now, she looked like an invading general leading a battle army of savage Huns. "All right. Don't bludgeon me. I will wash and dress, perhaps sit in the garden gazebo with you for tea since I am bored to tears lying in bed anyway. But I will not chase after Shayne Brayden."

"Then I'll have one of Mr. Ashcott's sons send a message over to him."

"Don't you dare. He will find me in the garden if he decides to return."

"Fine, have it your way. But you do realize he will spend the next few days hiding from Lady Felice, don't you? He will not stop by the inn until she is gone. Ugh, I wonder how long before she flies off on her broomstick?"

"She is awful, isn't she?" Willow pursed her lips, hoping her sister was right. "What if he decides he wants her to stay?"

Cammy rolled her eyes. "He will not. Were we not watching the same comedic scene unfold? Only it wasn't funny. She is a woman scorned and not about to take the insult lightly."

"And you now want me to go downstairs and tangle with her?"

"Well, no. But I want you to show everyone you are not afraid of a little competition. More important, you need to show Shayne that you trust him."

"You are asking too much of me, Cammy." But Willow did finally agree to walk downstairs. It was late morning by then, and the day was another glorious one, filled with sunshine and birds merrily chirping in the trees.

"Stupid birds," she muttered, wishing she could shake off the sight of Shayne kissing that woman and simply smile and twitter the day away.

Cammy snorted a giggle. "Still feeling peckish, are we?"

"Yes, we are." She had taken along *The Book of Love* and asked Cammy to join her in the garden, even though her sister was still being annoying in her eagerness to defend Shayne.

Aunt Charlotte had gone to run an errand in town, leaving the two of them to themselves.

One of the serving maids delivered a pot of tea and lemon cake to the gazebo. Willow poured a cup for Cammy and was about to pour one for herself when she noticed Shayne striding toward them. "What's he doing here?"

Cammy *eeped* in delight, immediately made an idiotic excuse about forgetting something important, and scurried back inside.

Shayne settled into the seat Willow's sister had just vacated, grinning as she skipped away. His expression became serious when he turned to Willow. "I'm sorry about that scene this morning."

Willow did not know what to say.

Shayne sat beside her, his dark hair thick and beautiful under the rays of sunlight, his gray eyes sharp and utterly stunning. She was riveted to his handsome face and its masculine features, confused as to how such a man could want her and not the elegant beauty who had kissed him with unbridled ardor earlier today. "You don't owe me any explanations, Shayne."

He frowned lightly. "Yes, I do. I want nothing left unsaid between us. Whether or not you wish to commit to me yet is beside the point. I have committed to you, and that will not change."

"Until Lady Felice convinces you otherwise." She sighed and set aside her teacup. "I'm sorry. That isn't fair of me. I know you are not fickle or a cad. It's just hard for me to understand your feelings when she is so beautiful. Her father is obviously titled since she is *Lady* Felice. By the fine cut and fabric of her gown, it is obvious she comes from wealth."

"I have no need of her wealth when I have my own."

She blushed. "Which you have lavished on us." She could not forget that he had paid for their new gowns and expenses at the inn. "But my father will pay you back."

"He needn't, as you well know."

"He must, as you well know."

"Why? I do this freely for the three of you and expect nothing in return. The last thing I wish to do is *buy* your affection."

"It is for the sake of my own pride. I do not wish to feel like a kept woman."

"How can you even think…" He shifted in his chair, looking quite uncomfortable since he was a big man and the chair, although quite sturdy, was designed for delicate ladies. "Willow, I love you."

Tingles shot through her as he uttered the words with aching tenderness. Such sweet, heart-melting words. But this was Shayne, always direct and to the point. She clasped her shaking hands and stared into her cup, wanting to return the sentiment, for she felt the same way about him.

She had never been a coward in her life, nor was she one now.

But how could he kiss another woman this morning and barely two hours later look her straight in the eyes and tell her that he loved her?

To say those words back to him simply did not feel right, no matter how strongly she felt them. What if he gave the matter more thought and chose to resume his courtship with Lady Felice? It would destroy her.

He cast her a wry smile. "Silence? No opinions, Willow? Very well, have it your way. I know you love me. I feel it every time you look at me, even now, as you are glowering at me. It is the way I feel whenever I look at you, even when I glower at you."

He leaned over and tucked a finger under her chin to raise her gaze to his. "I'll come by later. I just wanted to see you now to clear away any doubts you may have had because of Felice's unexpected arrival."

She arched an eyebrow. "It isn't her arrival that troubles me. It is what you did when you saw her. You *kissed* her."

"I did not. She kissed me."

"And this makes it all right? You did not appear to be struggling very hard to free yourself from her attentions."

"That kiss was awkward and unwanted." He slipped his hand off her chin and frowned. "I did not instigate it. I did not encourage it. I did not like it."

"And now am I supposed to forgive you and pretend everything is all right?"

"I am not asking for your forgiveness. I did nothing wrong."

She gasped.

"Willow, for pity's sake. What was I supposed to do? Shove her away?"

"You could have done it gently."

He laughed and shook his head. "Gentle does not work with Felice. She is a nasty and vindictive creature. No one controls her, nor can she be appeased when she has a specific objective in mind. She does as she pleases until she gets bored and walks away."

"You kissed her."

"I waited for her to stop kissing me. There's a difference." He rubbed a hand across the nape of his neck, obviously finding their conversation not to his liking. "Once you are better, I will show you what a proper kiss feels like."

"Do not insult my intelligence. First a pity proposal, and now a pity promise of a kiss? Am I supposed to be grateful to you?" She rose, too unsettled to care that she might have hurt his feelings, even though she knew he was telling the truth.

Worse, she did want him to kiss her.

But how could he when her mouth was bruised and filled with ugly stitches? "You let her kiss you. You didn't even try to pull away. Don't pretend there wasn't the littlest bit of curiosity, that lingering doubt you may have been wrong in ending your courtship with her. Do not put me in the middle of whatever is still going on between you. Do not think to appease me by telling me you love me while her kiss is still warm on your lips."

She ran back upstairs, ignoring his calls to her.

But she paused at the top of the stairs, her hand curling around the newel post in frustration. "Oh, drat. The book." In her haste to leave, she had left *The Book of Love* in the gazebo.

Were it any other item, she would have left it there and returned for it later. But she had almost risked her life in a fire to reclaim it. Having miraculously gotten it back a few days ago, she was not going to leave it out there for anyone to steal.

She owed it to Cammy, at the very least.

Shayne was still seated in the gazebo leafing through its pages when she returned. She plunked herself in the chair next to his and cleared her throat. "I may have been a little harsh with you."

He looked at her, an almost imperceptible smile twitching at the corners of his lips. "No, love. I handled the situation with Felice very poorly. I did a rather poor job with you, as well. But I don't know how else to tell you that she means nothing to me. How can she when it is you I love? I started looking through this book in the hope it might give me some guidance. After all, it is a book about love. But how do you handle someone wily and vindictive who would go to any measure to destroy what I feel for you?"

"Did you find your answer?"

He set the book aside. "I think so."

"And?" She tried not to appear too eager, but the hurt of seeing him kiss another woman was still fresh, and she really wanted to hear the answer to ease her pain.

He took her hand. "I think the answer is quite simple. It is not about her at all. It is about us and how we feel for each other. Willow, the answer is that true love cannot be destroyed."

She arched an eyebrow in disbelief. "Why do you say that?"

"Because this sort of faithful and eternal love can only happen when we have unshakable trust in each other. And before you blast me again, I realize it is you who must put your faith in me and trust me this time. I hope you do, but I will also understand if you don't. We've known each other for so short a period. It is a lot to ask."

"It is, Shayne." She studied him for a long moment. "So, you are saying that if you found me with another man in my bedchamber, you would still trust me?"

His eyes turned a stormy gray. "Once you committed to me? Yes. I would trust you. But I would not stop to ask for explanations before I pounded him to dust."

She emitted a strangled sound of astonishment. "That is utterly unreasonable."

He tossed her a possessively hungry look. "It is completely reasonable. I would trust you, for I have no doubt you would always honor your commitments. This is who you are, Willow. This is one of the many things I love about you. But that man would not be in your bedchamber for honorable reasons, and I would take pains to let him know he risks his life in trying to take what is mine."

"You make it sound as though I am merely one of your possessions."

"My most precious possession, just as I hope I am yours. And I would give my life to protect you because your heart is my treasure. It will always be the most valued possession I have. Valued above my own life."

She sighed. "I hate when you do that."

"Do what?"

"Say something apishly arrogant and then follow it up with something breathtakingly sweet."

He cast her a wry grin. "Still angry with me?"

"Hurt is a better description of my feelings."

"I know, love. It was not a pretty scene, and I was unprepared for it. But she is gone now. She packed up her entourage and rode off for Bath about twenty minutes ago."

Her eyes widened as she stared at him. "You waited for her to leave before coming to see me?"

He nodded. "I did not want her meeting you. It has nothing to do with cowardice on my part, although there was a little of that. Nor was I trying to keep you apart because of any feelings I may have for her. I assure you, I have none. But she would have come after you with her claws sharpened."

"Are you certain she is gone for good?"

"Lord, I hope so."

Willow pondered what he had told her.

She wanted so much to trust him, and in truth, she did. But she hadn't quite gotten over the shock of seeing him with his lips on another woman.

Nor could she blame him for trying to behave like a gentleman, even to a woman who did not deserve his kindness.

"Shayne," she said, trying not to melt in response to his tender smile. "What will you do if she returns?"

CHAPTER FIFTEEN

"FIRST OF ALL, I doubt Felice will return." He and Willow were still seated together in the gazebo. A light breeze ruffled through her beautiful curls, and the sun had pinkened her cheeks.

She looked so lovely, and she made him ache.

Of course, she was still too caught up over her stitches and bruises to appreciate how captivating she looked.

"But what if she does?"

This discussion sealed the decision for Shayne.

No one was going to keep him away from Willow, not Felice and her malicious intentions, not Charlotte, not common sense or reason, not even Willow herself. It would have been different had she not cared for him. He would not have imposed himself on her if she did not love him.

But this was hardly the situation.

She could not help loving him just as much as he could not help loving her. But how was he to convince her of this when she was experiencing more than mere physical hurt? Her heart was aching, and nothing he said or did seemed able to fix it.

He ran a hand through his hair in consternation. "Then I hope to handle her better than I did this time. But I doubt I will. She is an angry, feral cat. I'm sure I will be left bloodied in our next encounter as well."

Willow tried to hide a smile.

"You think it is funny," he said, laughing softly as he cast her an affectionate glance. "How does anyone handle such a woman? I will admit, I do not have a clue. Nor do I ever wish to find out. There is a big difference between liking a woman who will keep you on your toes and tangling with one who will cut off your toes if she happens to be irritated with you."

Willow remained silent a long moment. "I think I am just as angry with myself because I want to kiss you and these dratted stitches are in the way. This is why seeing Felice kiss you hurt me so much. I wanted to be the one."

He took her hand in his. "You are the only one for me. Forever, only you. I want you to know this. I had to tell you now because I won't have the chance to see you tomorrow. We'll be taking the last of the prisoners to Exeter at daybreak."

She nodded.

"But when I return, you and I are going to talk seriously."

She blushed, and stammered, and ultimately smiled at him with a sweet sparkle in her eyes. "Not too much talking, I hope."

He cast her a tender smile. "As little as possible, I assure you."

He thought back to her comments while under the influence of laudanum, her chattering about her desire to be kissed, to be held in his arms, and thoroughly kissed. "Willow, love. I'll let my actions speak for me."

"Does that mean I shall have my scandalous kiss?"

"Yes. Burn-in-hell scandalous, I promise." He escorted her inside and left her by the innkeeper's desk. Her aunt was just coming down the stairs and did not appear too pleased to see them together.

Had Willow and Cammy told her about Felice and the kissing incident yet? He did not wish to wait around to find out.

He nodded to acknowledge Willow's aunt, then hurried on his way.

It was only a few paces to his office.

He poked his head in to check on Lorcan. "Want to take a break? I'll take over."

Lorcan shook his head. "No, you had better go find Ezekiel."

Shayne frowned. "Damn it. Was he in here? I warned him to stay away."

"He didn't stay long, but he had his eye on the remaining prisoners. Lord Manton in particular. I suppose now that Belfy's gone, he has focused his retribution on the arsonist instead of the treasonous attempted murderer. He tried to appear calm, but I could see he was quite agitated."

"The bloody fool. Seems nothing I said penetrated his thick head. I'll look for him. I'm sorry, Lor. I wanted to give you a break. I'll return as soon as I can."

He found Ezekiel at home with his mother, seated outdoors on a tree stump with an ale in hand while the old woman was hanging out the wash. He looked as though he'd already tucked a few under his belt, for he appeared cheerfully sotted and relaxed. Shayne was not fooled. His visit to the prison had given him away. Ezekiel was still determined to destroy his own life by avenging his sister in his own twisted way. "Shayne, I did not expect to see you. Is something wrong?"

"No, just wanted to be sure you are all right."

He nodded. "I am, and eager to return to duty."

"Looking forward to having you back, but not for another few days yet. I'll need you at your best next week, for I may need to take some time away."

"A trip to London to follow Miss Farthingale?"

"Something like that." He would follow Willow to the ends of the earth if he had to, but he sincerely hoped she would stay in Taunton and marry him.

However, this was no one's business but his and Willow's.

"I just want to be certain you and I are square, Ezekiel." He had knocked him out and bound him, ordered his family not to release him until Lord Belfy had been safely delivered to Exeter. This had to have stuck savagely in his craw.

"We are, Shayne. I understand that you did what you had to do. No hard feelings."

"Good." He nodded to Ezekiel's mother. "Good day to both of you. I'll come around later to see again."

He returned to his office, hoping Ezekiel got the message he was going to keep an eye on him until he left Taunton with his prisoners.

Lorcan cast him a curious look. "You saw him?"

Shayne nodded. "I'll take a turn guarding these men now. Take a break, Lorcan. I'm going to need you on alert tonight."

"Hell, I knew it."

"Oh, he smiled and was all politeness. But as soon as the sun sets this evening, he is coming after Manton."

"Coming after me?" Manton said, his bravado fleeing as he listened in on their conversation. "It is your duty to protect me. I demand you protect me!"

"Shut up, you arse." Shayne had spent hours, day in and day out, listening to Manton and his friends goad him about Willow. They spoke incessantly about what they were going to do to her if ever they got out.

Crude, lewd. Explicit comments designed to rile him.

He had maintained a stoic expression, not wanting them to realize how badly they had gotten under his skin.

He wanted to rip each of them apart. Slowly. Painfully. Mercilessly.

He was even tempted to turn his back and allow Ezekiel to shoot down every last one of them. It would be no more than they deserved. But that would make his friend a murderer, and he could not allow that to happen.

Nor could he allow Ezekiel to return as his second in command, no matter what he'd told the man about needing him back next week.

There was not a chance he would ever trust Ezekiel again.

A trust, once broken, could never be restored.

Bloody hell.

Is this what Willow thought about him after seeing the kiss between him and Felice? He knew she loved him and wanted to trust him. But would that kernel of doubt always remain?

Had he shattered Willow's faith irrevocably?

He relieved Lorcan and took over guard duties for the next several hours, keeping his attention on his prisoners who remained overset and demanding he protect them from Ezekiel's wrath.

He ignored them as best he could.

They were the most annoying prisoners he had ever guarded.

Did it never occur to them that their actions had consequences? Well, he supposed it took a certain narrowness of mind never to consider the repercussions of their bad behavior. Of course, their families had not helped by always rushing to protect them.

Until now.

The king had gotten involved because these idiots had tried to kill Augustus MacLauren, not only one of England's most capable commanders, but also one of his closest friends.

Faced with incurring stiff fines or loss of title and property if they lifted so much as a finger in aid, their families were going to sit by quietly and avoid doing anything to draw the king's attention and stir his wrath.

Lorcan returned shortly after supper. "Is your head splitting yet?"

He laughed. "They haven't shut up once in the past four hours."

"Good, that means they'll be hoarse now and give me some peace. I'll take over guarding them."

Shayne grabbed the opportunity to see Willow again.

He hoped it was not a mistake, but after listening to those miscreants curse, complain, and threaten him for hours, he needed to see her lovely face once more before he departed at dawn.

Cammy and Charlotte were having supper in the dining room when he walked over to the inn. He was relieved to note Willow was not with them.

No doubt she had remained upstairs.

He took the stairs two at a time and knocked softly at her door.

After a moment, he heard her light footsteps. "Who is it?"

"Shayne."

The latch squeaked as she raised it. In the next moment, the door was thrown open to reveal her in her nightrail and robe, her hair long and loose as it tumbled in dark amber waves down her back. "I did not expect to see you tonight."

She looked stunning, her big, blue eyes shining up at him and her body so little and sweet, it made his heart sing. "I couldn't stay away."

She cast him a vulnerable look that put an ache in his heart. "I didn't really want you to stay away," she admitted.

He opened his arms to her and lifted her up against him when she rushed into them. He wanted to kiss her, needed to feel the soft give of her mouth against his and not come up until they were both gasping for air.

But her bottom lip was still stitched and swollen.

He dared not hurt her.

So he kissed her cheek instead, then slowly trailed kisses along her lovely neck, spurred by her soft moans and breathless sighs as he teased and suckled the little pulse at the base of it. He kicked the door closed behind him, wanting her with a fiery need. "I missed you."

She laughed. "It's hardly been more than a few hours."

"It's been an eternity." He felt her hot, perfect body mold to his hard frame. Mold to it, belong to it, as though she was made just for him. He tipped her head back and gently buried his fingers in her long, loose curls.

This is what she was, sweet and delicate silk. Her hair, her body, her soft, lilting voice.

But he set her down gently and drew away with a wrenching groan, needing to stop before he took things too far, for he was aching to touch her. To undress her. To put his lips to her body and taste her. "Willow...I..."

She placed a hand on his arm. "I know, my stitches. You cannot bear to look at them."

"What? No." He caressed her cheek as he stared at her. "I was thinking that I had better stop before you and I wound up naked on your bed." *Him inside her.*

He felt her hand tremble on his arm. "Naked?"

He cast her a wicked smile. "Utterly. But I don't wish to hurt you while I take my plunder."

She blushed. "Shayne! You are not a pirate, and I am not your booty. And stop giving me those hot, I-am-going-to-strip-you looks."

She put a hand delicately to the bruising at the corner of her lip.

This is what worried her, he realized.

This is what always made her feel inferior and doubt herself…doubt his love. He took her hand and gave it a soft kiss. "I may not be a pirate, but you are my treasure."

She slipped her hand out of his. "Ah…um…has there been a change in plans with the prisoner transportation to Exeter?"

"No, love. All will continue as scheduled." He caressed her cheek because it seemed safest, and he could not keep from touching her anyway. "We'll take the last of them tomorrow morning. I'll be glad to be rid of those churls."

"So will we all."

He led her over to the bed since she was clad in her nightgown and robe and had obviously been lying down until he had disturbed her by knocking on her door. She had a sleepy, just aroused look about her that shot fire through his veins.

When she sank onto the bed without protest, he brought one of the chairs over and set it beside her so that he could remain close.

She cleared her throat. "You are still tossing me that smoldering look. Are you going to pity propose to me again?"

He shook his head and laughed. "Yes, in fact, I was. But it is not for pitying you. It is for pitying me. The sad fact is, I cannot be without you. I don't ever want to be without you. All those noble thoughts of giving you time to enjoy your season…well, seems I am not all that noble, after all. I want you for myself. I want you as my wife."

He groaned and shook his head. "I did not mean to propose to you again so soon but it seems my mouth won't listen. No, that's not quite right. It is my heart that won't listen."

He caught her faint smile.

Progress?

"I intended to keep away from you these next few days to give you time to heal, time to think. I cannot even do this. My mind was on you the entire ride to Exeter and back. My mind is on you today and will be filled with thoughts of you tomorrow. But I suppose all of it means nothing unless you trust me. I don't know how to make you believe in me after I handled the encounter with Felice so badly."

"Time, I suppose. The fact remains we hardly know each other, Shayne," she reminded him. Not even a month. Hardly two weeks.

Yet, she was in his soul.

She was the fire in his blood.

She was the one his heart recognized.

How could he explain this to her if she dared not trust him?

"We do know each other, Willow. From the moment we came into being, we have been seeking the mate to our heart. Searching amid the moon and stars and earth for the one person who is perfect for us. I knew you were the one the moment I set eyes on you. It is a wonder, is it not? A sense of recognition that transcends time and realms. We just had to wait for our paths to cross as they have now."

"Transcendent love? That is quite a romantic thought."

"Willow, I am a man in love…with you, damn it," he said when she glanced down at herself and then looked at him askance. "You are the only one who sees those stitches."

"Are you suggesting love hides them?"

"Yes."

She frowned at him. "You cannot be blind to them."

"And you cannot let them define you. I am not blind to them. All right, I see them. But I dismiss them as inconsequential to the entirety of who you are." He noticed the faded red leather binding of *The Book of Love* resting atop her bureau.

She followed his gaze to it. "Falling in love with you felt so right and easy, Shayne. Shouldn't it be harder? How can such a complicated feeling ultimately be so simple?"

"That's just it. When it is right, everything falls into place. There is no struggle. There is no doubt."

"Even when you are kissing another woman."

He groaned. "This is why I should have stayed away and not tried to have this conversation with you. You don't trust me yet."

"I do."

"Then what causes your doubt?"

"My lack of experience with men."

"But you have seen enough of life to form your own character and understand the strengths or lack in the people around you." He grinned. "You certainly are not shy about voicing your opinion of me, as we both well know."

She eased his heart with her soft trill of laughter. "I do have a tendency to speak my mind."

"It is what I love most about you. I will always hear the truth from you. I will always be challenged to be a better person. I will always know that despite our differences, we shall always love each other. These differences strengthen us."

"Shayne…"

"We were made for each other, Willow. Our hearts, our stubborn minds. Soon, I will show you how well our bodies fit as well." He rose and paced to the window overlooking the inn's garden. "I swore to myself I would not tell you this, either."

"I'm glad you have. I like talking to you, being with you. More than that, I love you and…I trust you. I could not give my heart and body to anyone but you. I mean it, truly. I have no doubt about your honor and integrity. It is my own amazement that someone as wonderful as you could ever want me."

He turned to her. "I do want you, more than anything on this earth. As my love, my friend, the beauty in my life. I want to fall asleep with you in my arms. Will you take pity on me and accept my proposal? Be my wife."

"I will, Shayne. There is no one else for me."

He strode back to her side and took her in his arms. "Thank you, love."

She cast him that magical look of wonder.

Her entire face lit up with a smile. "Is this really happening?"

He kissed her brow. "It appears so."

He once thought it would take a team of oxen to drag him to the altar. But with Willow, he needed that team of oxen to hold him back. "I'll get the special license when I am in Exeter tomorrow."

She drew back with a gasp. "Shayne, I am not of age yet. What if my parents will not give their permission? They may be of a mind with Aunt Charlotte and decide I must have a London season."

"The license is valid for thirty days. We'll have a month to convince them otherwise." He ran his fingers through her soft curls, brushing them lightly off her exquisite face. "If not, seems we shall have to wait out the season unless we elope to Scotland."

She chuckled, believing he was in jest. "Wait, you're serious? You would run off with me?"

"Just say the word, and I'll take you up there…but not before I deliver the last of our prisoners to Exeter. Nor have I forgotten about your driver, Mr. Pierson. I'll speak to your father when I ride there to collect him. That will be after tomorrow's trip to Exeter. I'll drop the prisoners off and then head straight there. Lor offered to do it, but it makes more sense for me to go, now that I have to speak to your father anyway."

"It would help if you delivered letters from me and Charlotte. Cammy, too. I think she is your strongest ally."

He laughingly nodded. "She is."

Lord have mercy.

He was making wedding plans. "Do you think your parents would join us here?"

She swallowed hard. "For the wedding?"

"Yes."

She threw her arms around him again. "I will return to Barnstaple myself and drag them here if they give you a hard time about it. But Shayne, will you kiss me on the lips now. A gentle one. I do not think I can wait until the end of the week."

He cast her a worried look. "I don't want to hurt you."

"You won't. You cannot. I trust you to be careful."

"Trust," he murmured, drawing her up against him as he wrapped her in his arms, quite enjoying the feel of her delectable body. Her ample breasts pressed against his chest, instantly setting fire to his blood. He wanted to set her on the bed and lie atop her, inhale the orange blossom scent of her skin as he licked and teased and lost himself in her.

She scorched him.

He lowered his lips to hers. "I love you, Willow Farthingale."

He felt the soft give of her mouth on his.

But his heart lurched as he also felt the spiked thread at the edge of her lower lip. He did not dare mention it to Willow, for she was already too concerned about it. He simply took care not to press down too hard.

In truth, there was something quite wonderful in the softness of this kiss.

In the sweet, gentle combination of their lips.

In the perfection of this girl.

"Ahem," Cammy said loudly, forcing the two of them to end the kiss and move apart.

Willow blushed furiously.

Charlotte stood behind Cammy, looking as though she wished to bludgeon him.

"I have accepted to marry Mr. Brayden," Willow said, seeming to think being caught kissing in her bedchamber required explanation. He supposed it did, for there was no getting around what they were doing and where they were doing it.

And she was in her nightclothes, looking quite spectacular, he might add. Her body had a natural grace and lusciousness.

He did not particularly care about the consequences, for he wanted to marry her.

Cammy rushed over to hug her. "I knew it. See, Aunt Charlotte. I told you. True love cannot be denied."

"Oh, for pity's sake." But Charlotte did not appear angry, merely resigned. She turned to him. "Cammy is a hopeless romantic, but I do believe she is right about you two. Willow is incandescent. As for you, Mr. Brayden, you could set the room aflame with the hot looks you are casting her."

"Aunt Charlotte!" Willow regarded her, appalled.

But Charlotte merely smiled. "I am glad you both stopped holding back. You needed to be honest with yourselves and with each other."

"Two sisters happily matched," Cammy murmured.

Charlotte nodded. "I will write to your parents. Goodness, first June and now Willow in a matter of weeks. Shall I lose a third niece before we ever reach London?"

Cammy's eyes widened in horror. "I assure you, that will not happen. I don't even want to go to London. I think we are best off postponing our plans for another year. Is it not enough that both my sisters are so happily matched?"

"Indeed, not," Charlotte intoned. "I was charged with seeing all three of you properly wed, and that is what I intend to do."

Cammy tipped her chin up in defiance. "I'll run away."

Charlotte dismissed her with a casual wave of her hand. "Don't be silly."

Shayne grinned at Willow as her aunt and sister continued to bicker. "I had better return to my office. Set a date, love. We can marry right here at the inn. Do you mind?"

"This is the perfect place." She laughed and shook her head.

"I know we haven't sifted through the remains of the carriage house yet, but I doubt any of my elegant clothes survived. I'll need a gown for the wedding. Do you mind?"

"Order as many as you desire. As for the carriage house, rebuilding it won't start for at least another week when the lumber arrives. We'll have time to walk through the debris upon my return. That fire was intense, and I doubt anything will be salvaged."

"Does your generosity apply to me as well?" Cammy asked, unable to contain her smile. "I'll need at least one suitably fancy gown since I will be standing up for my sister."

He nodded. "As many as you wish, Cammy. You, too, Charlotte."

"I knew I liked you, Mr. Brayden," Cammy teased.

He winked back.

Willow turned to her sister and took her hands. "My heart broke when I thought I had lost *The Book of Love*. Not for myself, but for depriving you. It gives me great joy to be able to turn it over to you now."

Cammy shook her head. "Oh, no. Not yet. Not until you are officially married."

"Cammy—"

"No. That book needs to stay with you until then. It is a magical talisman." She turned to Shayne. "And I think you need all the protection you can get while those horrible men are still in your custody."

"Me?" He wanted to laugh, but Willow and her sister believed in the magic of this book. He doubted it had the power to render him invincible, but he was not going to mock their belief. Especially since he knew there would be danger tonight.

Ezekiel meant to go after Lord Manton.

He meant to stop him.

Could he do it before someone got hurt?

CHAPTER SIXTEEN

S HAYNE STRODE BACK to his office and motioned for Lorcan to follow him into his private back office, ignoring the curses and threats immediately hurled at him by his ever-desperate prisoners, especially Lord Manton.

"What's the matter, Shayne?" his brother asked, frowning as he closed the door.

"Willow accepted my proposal. We are getting married."

Lorcan shook his head and laughed. "You have my hearty congratulations. I thought you were going to wait before asking her again. What happened? You seemed certain Felice's kiss had firmly messed things up."

"Hell, I was afraid it had. But I couldn't leave for Exeter before letting Willow know how much she meant to me. I guess I said something right. In truth, I couldn't keep my damn mouth shut. So I proposed to her again, and this time she accepted."

Lorcan, grinning from ear to ear, crossed his arms over his chest and leaned his shoulder against the wall. "Those Farthingale sisters are something special, aren't they? Look at you with your chest puffed up like a big, old blowfish. I've never seen you this happy."

"I never knew such happiness was possible." But he ran a hand through his hair as he quickly sobered. "I just wanted you to hear the news from me. But I'd like to keep it quiet until we finish with these prisoners."

"One more night, and you'll be rid of them."

Shayne nodded. "Do you mind if I check on Ezekiel before taking over tonight's watch? I should have placed others to guard him, but these men are all friends. I couldn't bring myself to humiliate him, especially if I'm wrong about his intentions. I've told those on the night watch that he is ill, and they're to send him home if he tries to return here. I'm hoping that will be enough."

"I think retiring as an agent of the Crown has turned you soft."

"No, I'm still hard as nails. But being magistrate here is different. I don't get to move on once I've accomplished an assignment. I have to stay and face the townspeople every day, so I must take care in what I do and say. My life is here. My lands and home are here."

"But Ezekiel is still mad and has to be stopped."

Shayne placed his hand on the door, preparing to open it. "And this is what I intend to do now."

Lorcan followed him out and resumed his spot guarding the prisoners. "Be careful."

"I always am." He strode out, walking through town and stopping a moment to peer in at each tavern he passed along the way, on the chance Ezekiel was in one of those establishments drinking up the courage to shoot down an unarmed Lord Manton.

There was no sign of him.

He hoped it meant he was safely ensconced at home.

But Millie came running out as soon as he walked through the gate. "He's gone, Mr. Brayden! I went into his room to talk to him, but he wasn't there. He is nowhere in the house. Let me come to your office with you. He may be on his way there and—"

"No, Millie. It's too dangerous. I don't want you anywhere near there if shots are fired."

Her eyes rounded in horror. "You would shoot him?"

"He is a grown man. He knows better than to point a loaded

weapon at another person. He's been warned repeatedly to keep away. You have begged him yourself, and he refuses to respect even your wishes. I surely do not want to shoot him. I'll do everything I can to avoid it. But I will not let him take the law into his own hands."

Her shoulders sagged, and her expression showed utter dejection, but she knew he was right. After a moment, she nodded her head. "I'll wait here with our mother."

Shayne watched her walk inside and then hurried back to his office. There was still no sign of Ezekiel. "Damn it," he muttered, now standing beside his brother. "He has to be close. It will be dark soon. Where can he be?"

Lorcan shook his head. "Where would you go if you wanted to kill someone and couldn't get near your target? You have guards posted outside this building and inside. We are armed and vigilant. You don't think he is insane enough to set fire to the stables or the Ashcott Inn as a distraction, do you?"

"And risk taking innocent life? No, he couldn't. He's known the Ashcotts and Mr. Geoffries all his life. He would never hurt them."

"He would never do it if he were in his right mind, Shayne. But we both know he is not. Whatever Belfy said to him finally caused his mind to snap. And now that Belfy is out of his reach, he has turned his attention to Manton. Maybe he decided to camp along the road to Exeter and will try to pick off Manton as we ride by."

"That seems more likely."

"Want me to go track him?"

"No, Lor. I need you here. Donal's not back yet, and my men on night watch are already under strain. We'll look for him once we get on the road. There isn't much he can do if we ride fast and place the prisoners in the center of the riders. He isn't enough of a marksman to get off a clean shot under those circumstances. Even he has to realize he's more likely kill one of his friends."

"Assuming there's sense left in him."

He and Lorcan took turns guarding the prisoners once night fell. They worked in two-hour rotations, one standing guard while the other slept. He had organized a similar rotation for his night watch, positioning them to work in pairs, two on and two off throughout the wee hours.

Shayne happened to be on rotation shortly before dawn.

All had remained quiet, but as he went to wake Lorcan, a prickle ran up his spine. "Lor…"

His brother instantly rolled to his feet, rifle in hand. "Do you hear something?"

"I thought I caught a movement by the inn. I don't know. Could be a trick of the shadows."

"Good enough for me." He firmed the grip on his rifle.

Shayne cautiously eased the curtain aside to peer out the window. "Bloody hell."

"What?"

"He has Cammy."

Lorcan paled. "Cammy? What the…he's using her as a hostage?"

Shayne found himself restraining his brother as he was about to rush out the door. "Damn it, you'll get her killed. He has a pistol to her head."

Lorcan joined him by the window and raised his rifle to take aim. "He is a dead man, Shayne. I'll get him right between the eyes. He won't know what hit him until it's too late."

"And what of Willow's sister? Can't you see he's agitated? Any sudden moves, and he'll shoot her. Let me go out and talk to him. But if he refuses to let her go…" He paused and emitted a pained breath. "If he won't let her go, then have your rifle ready. Wait for a clean shot and take it."

"Trouble in paradise, Brayden?" Manton said with a jeering smile as he strode toward the door.

He ignored the man and walked out slowly, holding his arms out to show he held no weapons. "Ezekiel," he said calmly, "what are you doing?"

Cammy was in tears and trembling in his rough grasp. "It's my fault. I shouldn't have left my room."

"It's all right, Cammy. We'll get you out of this." Shayne tried to soothe her, but he was anything but calm himself.

"I was on my way to the kitchen to bring up a pot of tea," she said between sobbing breaths. "It was early yet, and I did not want to disturb the staff."

"Don't blame yourself. You didn't do anything wrong." He paused and swallowed hard as another thought struck him. "Is Willow all right?"

She nodded. "She's still asleep. She doesn't even know I've gone."

His heart hitched in relief, but it was little consolation while Willow's sister remained in danger. "We'll get you back before she or your aunt wakes. Ezekiel, please. Let her go."

"Sure, as soon as you do as I ask. A hostage for a hostage," he said, his eyes alight in triumph. "Tell Lorcan to send out Manton, and I'll give her over to you."

"All right, but I have the keys in my pocket." He patted the pocket of his jacket. "I'll have to step back inside to let him out."

Ezekiel eyed him warily. "No, stay out here where I can see you. Tell your brother to come to the door, and you'll toss him the keys."

"Or you can let the innocent girl go, and we'll forget this incident ever happened. It isn't too late. If this is about avenging your sister, then how is what you are doing to Miss Farthingale making it right?"

Cammy gasped as he once again became agitated by Shayne's words and rammed the barrel of his pistol against her temple. "Shut up, Shayne. Don't take another step, or I'll shoot her."

"All right. I won't move." His heart shot into his throat. The man had lost all reason. He needed to get him to point his weapon away from Cammy. Two or three seconds was all they needed to take him down. Lorcan had slipped out of the building and was now making his way behind Ezekiel, moving with the stealth of a ghost.

Suddenly, Ezekiel's attention darted to the right of him as Willow called his name.

Hell.

Hell.

Hell.

She must have seen what was happening and came running out to protect her little sister. Only, she wasn't thinking. She was angry as a mother bear trying to save her cubs. But anger would solve nothing. "Willow! For pity's sake. Stay back."

She was barefoot and too overset to bother about the twigs and pebbles cutting into her feet. "Stay back," he repeated more sternly when she took another step toward her sister.

But he knew she wouldn't obey.

Her sister was in danger, and she meant to save her, even if it put her own life in jeopardy. "Trade Cammy for me, Ezekiel," she said. "Let her go, and I'll be your hostage."

Cammy paled. "No! Don't you dare. I'm your hostage. Leave her alone."

Willow took another step closer. "Shayne is in love with me. I'll be the more effective hostage. Let me come to you and exchange places with my sister."

"Willow, no." Tears flowed down Cammy's cheeks. "Go back inside."

She shook her head. "Ezekiel, you know I am the better hostage."

Shayne prayed fiercely Ezekiel would not shoot both girls, for they were both talking at him, and he was getting addled.

"All right," he said finally, motioning to Willow. "Come closer. Slowly."

By this time, Lorcan was directly behind him, only waiting for the chance to take him down.

Ezekiel moved the barrel of the pistol off Cammy's head and was about to point it at Willow when Lorcan grabbed the weapon out of his hands and smashed it over his head. "Bastard."

Ezekiel crumpled to the ground.

Shayne rushed to put him in manacles while Lorcan grabbed Cammy and lifted her in his arms when she appeared about to faint. "Willow, go with him," Shayne ordered, motioning for Lorcan to take them both to the safety of the inn.

He wanted to follow them but knew he could not leave until Ezekiel was secured. "Tom. William," he said to the night watch guards who had come running over as soon as Lorcan had knocked their friend unconscious. "Carry him into my office. Chain him to the cot. Keep your rifles trained on him."

The men had just taken Ezekiel inside, leaving Shayne free to check on Willow when Donal rode in with several Exeter guards and their cousin, Rafe.

Shayne gave a silent prayer of thanks as they pulled up in front of him. "You're a sight for sore eyes, Donal. I expected you back last night. Rafe, good to see you. But won't you be missed in Exeter? And what about Belfy? He shouldn't be left without—"

"He's dead." Rafe dismounted and strode toward him.

"What happened?" He shook his head in disbelief.

"He tried to escape. You were right about him being dangerous. He killed one of my guards and tried to overpower another, but that guard managed to sound the alarm before Belfy knocked him out. We gave chase and followed him up to the rooftop. He fell and broke his neck. I know what you're thinking, but he really did fall. No one laid a hand on him. He slipped on a loose patch and just tumbled three stories, landing on his head onto hard stone."

"Needless to say," Donal added, "because of Belfy, we got a late start back to Taunton. The horses were blown since we couldn't stop to rest them as we would have liked. We were all pretty tired as night fell anyway, so we camped by the stream and rode the last few miles this morning. What did we miss? Is that Ezekiel we saw being led inside? What happened?"

"Let me put more guards on to watch the prisoners, then we'll go to the inn, and I'll tell you everything."

"Use my men to guard your prisoners," Rafe said, motioning to the other six riders who rode in with him. "They are better trained."

Shayne nodded. "Gladly. Mine could use the rest. We haven't had a moment's peace since Belfy and his cohorts rode into Taunton about a month ago."

Within minutes, Rafe's men had dismounted and given their horses over to him and Donal, and then taken up their guard duties.

He and Donal roused Mr. Geoffries and his grooms, handing them the horses.

Ezekiel had been unconscious when Shayne's men carried him into his private office and chained him to the cot. "We'll watch him, Shayne," the one called Tom assured him when Shayne entered his office for a moment to parse out the assignments.

Tom was a good lad, the very one the ostler's pretty daughter had chosen to marry after purloining Willow's book.

With the business taken care of for the moment, he led Donal and their cousin to the inn, now eager to see how Willow and her sister were doing. Afterward, he would ride over to the Earl of Monkton's estate to report the news of his brother's death to him, but at the moment, his thoughts were on Willow and her sister.

Lord help him, he wanted to throttle her for running into the path of danger.

What she had done was foolhardy and could have gotten her killed.

But he also wanted to kiss her senseless.

His heart was still racing, and he was still angry over her interference, but it all melted away when he saw her sitting quietly with her sister and Lorcan. They had taken a table in a far corner of the dining room, which was still empty, although it would start to fill soon. The two ladies looked pale and strained, nursing their cups of tea. Lorcan stood behind Cammy with his arms crossed over his chest and a fierce, lethal glint in his eyes.

Cammy was still undone, the sweet innocent sniffling, and her hands were trembling.

Shayne settled in the chair beside Willow and took her hand when he realized she was just as shaken as her sister, only hiding it better. He did not have the heart to berate her. How could he, when he would have done no less to protect his brothers? But he also would have had the strength to wrestle Ezekiel to the ground.

Willow was a little thing.

Strong of will, but still little.

She emitted a trembling breath.

Donal settled in the chair next to him. Willow and Cammy had met him earlier, although they did not know this brother nearly as well as they knew Lorcan. He now introduced his cousin, who had also joined them at the table. "Rafe Quinton, Exeter's magistrate and cousin on our mother's side."

"A pleasure to meet you, Mr. Quinton," Willow said, casting him a warm smile. "Your cousins speak very highly of you."

"The pleasure is all mine, Miss Farthingale." He arched an eyebrow and glanced at her hand, which Shayne had yet to release.

"We are betrothed," Shayne said.

Donal laughed. "Congratulations. I knew I liked Miss Farthingale the moment I saw her smash her fist into your nose. Now there's a woman who can tame him, I said to myself."

Rafe's eyes lit up. "You punched him in the nose?"

Donal was still laughing. "And kicked him in the—"

Lorcan growled. "There are ladies present." He unfurled his arms and placed a protective hand on Cammy's shoulder.

Shayne and Donal exchanged glances.

Lorcan may have fooled the others, but he and Donal were his older brothers and knew him too well.

Cammy did not seem to realize the enormity of what they were witnessing. Lorcan was in love with her.

And Cammy was next to receive *The Book of Love.*

"This should be fun," Shayne muttered.

Willow's eyes widened as she caught on to what he meant.

But he had his own heart to think about now and Willow's parents to convince as soon as he delivered those prisoners. After telling the ladies about Lord Belfy's demise, the conversation soon turned to that chore.

They had just finished reshuffling plans, deciding to leave Lorcan in Taunton with the ladies while he, Donal, and Rafe went to Exeter, when Charlotte hurried in. "What is going on? Why are you all down here?"

Cammy burst into tears again.

Charlotte hastened to her side. "My dear, what happened? How did you get that bruise on your forehead?"

CHAPTER SEVENTEEN

S HAYNE AND DONAL delivered the news of Lord Belfy's death to the Earl of Monkton later that afternoon. Donal headed off to speak to Lady Monkton and her sister, while Shayne spoke privately to the earl.

"Thank you, Mr. Brayden," the earl said, escorting him into his well-appointed study. "I wish I could say I was distraught, but his behavior had gone from bad to worse, deteriorating so badly this past year, we were all afraid of him. He threatened me, my wife, and the child she carries. I am relieved more than saddened."

Shayne nodded. "I will be taking the last of his cohorts to Exeter prison in the morning. However, I wanted to deliver the news before you heard it from other sources."

"It is much appreciated. Ever since his confinement, my staff has been coming forward to tell me of the other sins he has committed." The earl was in his thirties, a few years older than Shayne. However, he had a young-looking face so that he hardly looked old enough to have a wife and a child on the way. At the moment, he looked quite haggard. "It weighs upon my conscience the evil I allowed to go on under my very nose. I think I have much to atone for to the citizens of Taunton. Rest assured, my wife and I will personally help those who have suffered by his hand."

"Thank you, my lord." He and Donal returned to the Ashcott

Inn, arriving late in the evening. Shayne expected Willow would be asleep by now. He had seen her earlier in the day, and in any event, he was exhausted. He returned to his guest chamber, disrobed and washed, then climbed into bed.

He was asleep before his head hit the pillow.

But he was up and alert shortly before dawn, ready to attend to the task ahead. He rode off with Donal, Rafe, and the last of the prisoners shortly after sunrise. They made good time and reached Exeter by late afternoon. However, he and Donal did not tarry there, for they knew the last of Belfy's rabble would now be in Rafe's capable care.

Indeed, the lords who had caused so much damage under Lord Belfy's wicked influence were now bereft upon learning of his death. It amazed Shayne how quickly their evil cabal fell apart without that devil-in-chief to lead them.

It eased his mind considerably.

These men would now live out their lives in exile, kept apart from each other and from the families who had covered up their bad behavior to enable them to indulge in their reckless ways. He was pleased that they would never be permitted to return to England while the king was alive, not even if, by some twist of fate, they inherited the family title.

Having accomplished what they intended, he and Donal made certain their horses were fed, watered, and rested, then grabbed a quick meal and immediately rode off to Barnstaple.

They reached that quaint village the next day.

An odd feeling gripped Shayne as he strode toward the Farthingale residence, a big, rambling house that was in need of a fresh coat of paint but otherwise appeared to be well maintained. The white picket fence surrounding the house also appeared in need of painting, what little of it could be seen amid the colorful tumble of flowers along its expanse.

The gate squeaked as he raised the latch to ease it open and start down the walk.

Someone had to be baking pies, for the aroma of cinnamon,

apples, and raisins filled the air.

"Lord, that smells good," he muttered to his brother who had accompanied him, insisting on lending his support.

Donal heartily agreed. "If their cook is not married, I'm going to propose to her."

Shayne laughed as he knocked on the door.

A distinguished looking gentleman opened it and peered at them curiously. "May I help you?"

He had Willow's eyes, and Shayne knew at once he had to be her father. "Mr. Farthingale, my name is Shayne Brayden, and this is my brother, Donal. I am the Taunton magistrate."

"Brayden, you say? Well, that name is quite familiar to me. Are you related to any of the Braydens who have married into the family?"

"Yes, we are cousins."

The man smiled jovially and called into the kitchen for his wife. "Come in, gentlemen. May we offer you tea? My wife is baking pies, and they ought to be done soon. But you say you are the Taunton magistrate? Dare I ask? What has Willow done?"

Donal could not contain his laughter. "Why do you single out that daughter, Mr. Farthingale?"

He shook his head. "So it is, Willow. I can see it in both your expressions. She has a good heart, but she does have a tendency to speak her mind."

Willow's mother joined them at the door and immediately winced. "We are to blame, Mr. Brayden. We've raised our daughters to think for themselves and do what is right. I hope you take this into account when…" She studied Shayne closer.

Suddenly, she took her husband's hand. "My love, I think we must invite these gentlemen into our parlor. I don't think Mr. Brayden is here because he's tossed our daughter behind bars."

Willow's father remained perplexed. "Oh? Well, what is it then that brings you here?"

Shayne's smile broadened as he entered their home. "Actually…"

He and Donal returned to Taunton one week later with a sullen Mr. Pierson in custody and the consenting signature of Willow's father on the special license. "I'll take care of locking up Pierson," Donal said, knowing Shayne was leaping out of his skin to see Willow again.

"Much appreciated." He dismounted and tossed him the reins, then strode into the inn. "Mr. Ashcott, where are the ladies?"

The day was overcast and cool, but the blood pumping through his veins was already in a hot simmer at the mere thought of seeing Willow.

"They were going to Mrs. Albright's shop for a fitting for their new gowns and then planned to stop at Mrs. Guinn's tea shop for refreshments. Has Miss Farthingale's father given his consent? Are we to have the pleasure of hosting your wedding?"

"Indeed, you are." Shayne nodded. "Ask Miss Farthingale to wait for me here on the chance I miss her in town."

He took off in search of Willow, eager to see her again. Dr. Stratton would have removed her stitches by now, and he hoped there was little of the remaining scar on her lip. Not that he cared, but she did. All he wanted to do was take her in his arms and kiss her until the sun went down.

Willow spotted him before he saw her.

The next thing he knew, she was in his arms, her head of red-gold curls bobbing as she covered his unshaven face with kisses. He picked her up and twirled her in his arms, laughing as she began chattering at him, tossing him a hundred questions in rapid succession.

It felt so good to see her, to hear her voice, and inhale the sweet warmth of her skin. She looked even more beautiful than he remembered. Perhaps this is how love was meant to be, growing stronger over time, whether together or apart. Growing stronger as they forged bonds, built connections, started a life together. "Willow, take a breath and let me kiss you."

She cast him a glowing smile. "I got my stitches out."

"I noticed. But does that cut still hurt you?"

"Only the littlest bit. It's healing nicely. My arm, too." She closed her eyes and tilted her chin up to give him a better angle for the momentous event. "You may kiss me, Mr. Brayden."

"With pleasure, Miss Farthingale."

"Will your beard tickle?"

"Let's find out." He brought his mouth down on hers, his senses exploding as he poured all his heart and longing into the kiss. He tasted the sweetness of her mouth and the lemon and spice of the pie she must have just eaten. But nothing was sweeter than the taste of her or the softness of her lips and her soft moans as he crushed his mouth to hers to deepen the kiss and explore the wonder that was Willow.

"I missed you, love," he whispered against her mouth when he finally eased his lips off hers to end the kiss before they attracted too much of an audience.

He ought to have waited until they were in more private surroundings, but he had been thinking of nothing but this lovely lass the entire ride back from Barnstaple and needed this moment as much as he needed air to breathe or food to eat.

Then again, Brayden men were big and had large appetites.

They ate like beasts in the wild.

He always needed food to eat.

But food for his soul was something different. Only Willow could ever satisfy that ravenous hunger. He wanted to devour her, swallow her up in his arms, and never let her go. But that was merely his low brain desire.

Willow had always been a high-brain girl for him.

She nourished all of him.

"Shayne, I'm so happy you're back. I missed you, too. And your beard does tickle, but I am not complaining. Did all go well with my father?" Her big eyes sparkled as she looked at him.

He set her down and led her over to a nearby bench in the tea shop's small garden that held an abundance of vibrant flowers in bloom. He was not in the habit of paying attention to such delicate things, but he supposed love had turned him soft. "Yes, quite successfully. I have the special license and your betrothal contract. I thought it wise to take care of that matter as soon as possible."

She laughed. "I hope my father did not give you too hard a time over it."

"Not at all. I don't think I've ever negotiated a contract where I had to insist on better terms for the other party than they demanded for themselves."

"Well, he is quite softhearted. My mother has the business sense in our family. If she did not insert herself in the negotiation, it means she trusted you to be fair. I'm sure you were far too generous. I'm glad they liked you. I'm rather fond of you myself."

He tipped her chin up and kissed her again, unable to resist. But this kiss was softer and sweeter and much shorter since the occupants of the tea shop had their faces to the windows and were gawking at them.

He drew away reluctantly and reached into his breast pocket. "Your parents gave me a letter for you."

He handed it to her. "They plan to arrive in about ten days. You'll find it all explained in the letter. We can hold the wedding then. Do you mind that it will be a small affair?"

She cast him an affectionate glance. "Not at all. We would have been delayed for months if we started inviting all the Braydens and Farthingales across England. Perhaps we shall host a country party at your estate once we've settled into married life. That ought to satisfy our families. Does that sound like a workable plan to you?"

"Yes, love. It does."

She smiled, obviously quite proud of the suggestion. "By the way, I have yet to see your home."

"I'll remedy that tomorrow, if you like. You, Cammy, and Charlotte. I'm not sure I'll behave myself if I'm there alone with you."

That brought a blush to her cheeks. "Charlotte will insist on chaperoning anyway, and Cammy will not want to be left behind at the inn. Is it a big house? Do you have a staff?"

"About a dozen to run the house. A few maids, a cook, and scullery. A trusted head butler and two footmen who were soldiers injured during the war, but they are more than capable of attending to their duties and defending my home. They served under my command years ago and are extremely loyal to me. They will be the same to you once we are married and they get to know you."

"I expect it will take time for me to earn their trust. They'll have to be convinced I will never do anything to hurt you. I'm sure they are very protective of you."

This was true.

They also knew the sort of man he was and trusted his honor. They would show Willow due deference as his wife, but she would only gain their loyalty once they knew how much she loved him.

Trust.

It seemed all relations required this to remain strong and thriving.

He left Willow and her family to finish their shopping in town and returned to his magistrate office to catch up on what had happened while he was gone. Tom Grimple was seated at the desk beside the holding cells, which were empty save for a morose Mr. Pierson, stretched out on a cot.

Tom's feet were upon the desk, and he was leaning back in his chair, reading a newspaper.

He scrambled to attention when Shayne strode in.

Shayne waved him back down. "Enjoy the quiet, Tom. Let's hope we'll have plenty of it now that Lord Belfy and his friends are no longer around to plague us. Anything new that I should know about?"

"Just Ezekiel, Mr. Brayden."

He felt a deep sadness over this man who had so recently been a trusted second in command and friend.

"He's been taken to a sanatorium up north." Tom shook his head sadly. "I don't know that he'll ever be well enough to come home. He started laughing when he learned of Lord Belfy's death and would not stop until he lost his breath and nearly passed out. How does something like this happen to a man? He was one of the best among us."

Shayne shook his head. "I don't know. Perhaps there is something fragile in all of us, something that causes so much pain we can no longer bear the reality of it."

"I hope I never face such a thing." Tom contemplated the matter in all seriousness for a moment, then glanced up at Shayne and smiled. "But I think being happily settled helps us, don't it? Having a good woman by our side to comfort us through difficult times. I owe my happiness to Miss Willow and her book."

"You earned your happiness all by yourself, Tom. That book did not change who you are inside. It just helped Molly open her eyes and recognize you for the good man you have always been."

A blush ran up the shy young man's neck. "The Farthingale ladies paid a call on Ezekiel's mother and sister while you were gone."

Shayne arched an eyebrow in surprise. "They did?"

The lad nodded. "Miss Willow wanted to know if they were all right and told them to come to her if ever they needed anything. She then purchased some supplies to bring over to them, seeing as they had lost Ezekiel's wages, and she worried they would be struggling."

He wanted to ask how she had managed to purchase anything without a shilling to her name, then realized she must have put it on the account he'd set up for her, Cammy, and Charlotte.

He smiled inwardly.

He would have done the same for Ezekiel's family, and she had to have known it. But he was glad she made the personal gesture. Being new to town and about to assume the mantle of Mrs. Brayden, he wanted the townspeople to like her.

How could they not when no one would have blamed her for

ignoring that family after what Ezekiel had done to her and Cammy?

Since all was quiet, he left Tom to his reading and Pierson now snoring in his cell and walked over to the Ashcott Inn. Lorcan had taken a room for himself, since it was easier to keep watch over the Farthingale sisters by staying there as well.

He and Donal had also taken rooms. Although his estate was not far from Taunton, it was at least a half day's ride, and he was not about to make the trip back and forth each day. He intended to take Willow and her family there tomorrow and have them remain for a day or two before returning them to the inn.

But they would all keep rooms here until the wedding.

Mr. Ashcott began gushing over him the moment he walked up to his desk. "I'd like a bath and a meal brought up to my chamber."

"Right away, Mr. Brayden. You'll have the very best."

Shayne chuckled as he climbed the stairs. The very best meant he was going to get a walloping bill from the innkeeper after the wedding. In truth, he did not mind. It was an expense he could easily afford, and he could not be happier.

It meant a lot to him to have his brothers with him, to have Cammy and Charlotte, and most of all, to have found Willow.

The tub and food arrived in short order.

He quickly stripped out of his clothes and gave them to Mr. Ashcott for his staff to refresh. He also gave over his boots to polish, then settled in the steaming water with a sigh. He had brandy and a basket of scones within arm's reach and intended to remain soaking in the tub and sipping his brandy until the water turned cold.

After quickly soaping up and rinsing the dirt off himself, he washed his hair and shaved his growth of beard. In truth, he was surprised Willow had not minded kissing his scruffy face earlier. Once done, he poured himself a little of the brandy, eased back in the water, and closed his eyes.

He had just gotten out of the tub when someone knocked

lightly on his door. He wrapped one of the drying cloths around his waist, not particularly concerned since he expected one of the men on the inn's staff to return his clothes and boots. "Come in," he called, taking a bite of the raisin scone that must have been freshly baked because it was hot and soft and rich in delightful flavors that poured into his mouth.

Lord, that tasted good.

But he choked on the next bite of scone as Willow poked her head in, saw he wore nothing but his towel, and gasped. Instead of hurrying out and shutting the door behind her, she scurried in and shut the door, closing them in the room together.

Her eyes were as big as full moons as she took him in.

"Willow, I—"

"Oh, my goodness. You are even finer looking than I imagined." Her cheeks were stained bright pink, and her chest was heaving. Her heart had to be racing like that of a rabbit being chased out of a farmer's cabbage patch.

He wanted to say something clever like "Care to take off your clothes and join me?" But she had no experience with men, and it seemed the sight of him had her brain in spasms.

Her luscious little body wasn't functioning too well, either. Her eyes were about to burst from their sockets, her skin was moist and flushed, and her heart was still in an obvious flutter if the rise and fall of her glorious breasts were any indication.

Even though they were betrothed, he knew it would not do for her to be found in his chamber. However, he meant to have a few minutes of fun with her before he nudged her out the door.

"May I touch you?" she asked breathlessly.

"Lord, yes." This was another thing he liked about her. She was innocent but not priggish. She had a sense of adventure as well, especially when she thought she was doing something naughty.

She had no idea just how naughty they could get.

He would enjoy showing her.

She came to his side and reached out tentatively to touch his chest, splaying one hand over his heart to feel its steady beat. She slowly trailed a finger down the front of him, running it lightly down his chest, along his ribs, and down his stomach, pausing at the towel at his waist.

Mother in heaven.

He sucked in a breath, wondering what she would do next.

Just how adventurous was she?

She cleared her throat and moved her hands up to run them along his arms. She closed her eyes and felt along their muscled contours.

"You can touch me with something other than your hands, Willow."

Her eyes widened again.

He gave her a prompt. "With your mouth. Your tongue. Shall I show you how it's done?"

Apparently unable to speak, she merely nodded.

"Let's make you comfortable." He loosened the ties of her gown, then hooked the fabric under his fingers and slid the gown off her shoulders to bare them. "Are you all right, love?"

She nodded.

He bent his head to hers and kissed her as he slid the muslin further down, unlaced her linen corset, and then slipped it and her sheer chemise off her shoulders as well. Now bared to her waist, he cupped a bare breast in his palm, loving the way it filled his hand.

Soft. Lush. Warm. "Willow, you're so beautiful."

She had her eyes closed and gave a soft gasp as he ran his thumb over its rosy tip. He bent lower and put his lips to it, flicking his tongue over the exquisite bud and then suckling it gently.

She gasped again and held onto his shoulders as she arched into him. "Shayne, I—"

A knock at his door sent her into silent panic.

He put a finger to her lips to warn her to be quiet, then led her to the large wardrobe, which was empty because he hadn't brought any clothes over yet, and lifted her into it. He put his finger to her lips again to warn her to stop squirming, for she was frantically attempting to raise the fabric over her breasts, which were on the verge of spilling out again.

Lord in heaven, she had his blood on fire.

He shut the door to the wardrobe and then opened the door to his room to take his clothes and polished boots from the innkeeper's son. "Thank you, Matthew."

He gently shoved the boy out and shut the door before he could comment on the noise emanating from the wardrobe. Willow must have knocked her elbow against the wood because he heard a soft thump and then an *eep*.

Matthew had to have heard it as well.

He hoped the boy would keep it to himself.

He opened the door, caught Willow as she tumbled out, and kissed her long and deep. She returned the kiss eagerly as he carried her to his bed. But he merely sat her down on it and bent to help her put her gown back in order. "Shayne, do you think he heard me?"

She looked worried.

Of course, the boy had heard her.

His wardrobe had been shaking as though a cat was chasing a rat inside it.

And whoever heard of a wardrobe *eeping*?

"No, love," he said, smothering his grin. "You were as silent as the fallen snow."

"Oh, thank goodness! My heart is still racing. Perhaps I am not as adventurous as I thought I was. Will you peer down the hall and make certain no one is about while I sneak back to my room?"

She stood behind him as he opened the door and looked around.

"You smell so good," she whispered and kissed him lightly on the back.

Lord, her lips were soft.

"I'm going to keep you shut in here with me if you don't stop that." It did not help that the front of her was pressing against his back.

"Sorry," she said, still whispering. "But you really do smell divine, sandalwood and shaving lather. I like your muscles, too."

He shut the door and turned to face her.

"Oh, dear. Are there people in the hallway?"

"Lots." Perhaps an exaggeration since there wasn't a soul to be seen.

She nibbled her lip in consternation. "Shayne, what shall we do?"

He put an arm around her waist and cupped the back of her head to draw her closer. "Just be patient. I'll think of something."

CHAPTER EIGHTEEN

WILLOW'S HEART WAS soaring by the time her wedding day arrived.

She poked her head out the window and peered up at the sun, unable to believe this was really happening. This past week had felt endless despite having been kept quite busy. First, Shayne had taken them to his estate and shown them around his magnificent manor house, an excursion that had taken a total of three days.

Those days had included mornings of fishing in the fully stocked stream that ran behind his house, an afternoon's ride through the hills and farmlands comprising his estate, and succulent meals throughout the day prepared by his very able cook.

In the evenings, she and Cammy had taken turns singing and playing the pianoforte, a beautiful instrument upon which their meager talents could not do justice. But the Brayden brothers did not seem to mind, clapping eagerly as she and her sister finished their recitals.

Honestly, these Braydens were too easily pleased.

Shayne's home turned out to be far larger than she had expected yet still felt warm and inviting. The staff had been welcoming and clearly fond of Shayne and his brothers. She hoped they would grow to accept her and was surprised by how quickly they did seem to adjust to her presence. They were genuinely thoughtful and kind to her and her family.

Her parents had arrived at the Ashcott Inn two days ago, and much of her time since then had been taken with them, showing them the town and introducing them to the various townspeople she, Cammy, and Charlotte had gotten to know during their stay.

But today was her day, so her thoughts returned to the present.

She would be Mrs. Brayden within a matter of hours.

Her stomach was in a mad flutter as Cammy fashioned her hair in an elegantly loose sweep of curls that fell over one shoulder. Mrs. Ashcott had pressed her gown, a lovely peach silk with delicate lace trim and pearl beading at the bodice, and now returned it to her chamber.

Willow's mother and aunt were in the adjoining room, already dressed and excitedly chattering about prospects for Cammy's upcoming London season. "I am going to run away if they don't stop talking about me," her sister whispered, setting aside her hairbrush and adding two jeweled clips to Willow's hair.

"Let's just get through my wedding, and then we'll discuss it," Willow assured her, rising to don her gown. "You are getting *The Book of Love* now and cannot avoid it. Use it whenever you are ready, but I want you to have it, Cammy. June feels the same. We both want you to be happily matched. In your own good time, of course."

"I can assure you, it will not be this year. I never thought I would be going to London without you and June."

"I know." Willow gave her sister's hand a light squeeze. "But all our cousins are there, in addition to Uncle John and Aunt Sophie. They are looking forward to your staying with them. It's all been arranged. Shayne and I will join you next month, I promise. June and Augustus will also be passing through London sometime next month. In the meantime, you'll have plenty of family to turn to if ever you are lonely. Violet lives next door to Uncle John and Aunt Sophie on Chipping Way. Dillie, Daisy, Honey, Belle, Dahlia, and Holly all live close by, too. Half of them are married to Braydens, and the other half are married to dukes and earls."

"Is this supposed to give me comfort? They'll make me attend all the *ton* affairs."

"You needn't if you don't wish to, but it seems an awful waste to avoid all these invitations. Just enjoy yourself, and do not push yourself to make a match. You needn't dance with anyone who does not appeal to you. Spend the evening sitting with our cousins if you prefer. Donal and Lorcan will be in town, too."

"Assuming they are not sent off on other assignments."

"I'm sure they will take the time to look after you while they are in London. You can rely on them to chase away any unwant-ed rogues." Willow laughed and shook her head. "Lorcan has the fiercest gaze I've ever seen. I think he would have sent Attila the Hun scurrying back home in fear."

Cammy managed a smile. "I'm sure he will enjoy scaring those pampered lords. And I suppose Mama and Papa will be very disappointed if I don't go."

"They have scrimped and saved all their lives to provide us this opportunity. You ought to give it a try."

"But how can I attend these balls and other elegant events if our gowns have all been destroyed? All I have are the few Shayne was kind enough to purchase for me."

Willow sighed. "I'm sure our cousins—"

"Am I to spend my season in borrowed gowns?"

"Now you sound like some pampered duke's daughter. What is wrong with a borrowed gown? The three of us were going to share clothes with each other."

"I am trying to be brave, Willow. Truly, I am. I love our cousins. I will adore visiting them, but they are all married now and have their children and husbands to look after. I won't be sharing my season with anyone. I'm the only one to be thrown amidst the wolves."

"You really are opposed to London, aren't you?" Her sister

had always been painfully shy, wanting to hide from the young men who flocked around her, and they all did flock around her because she was so beautiful.

Willow nibbled her lip, feeling bad because she and June had assured Cammy they would look out for her. But they were now abandoning her. For happy reasons, of course. Still, they would not be with their youngest sister to lend her their support.

"I'm simply not ready to do this on my own. I'd like to postpone my debut for at least another year. It is not unreasonable."

In truth, it was not unreasonable. Her sister was only eighteen. "Very well, I will speak to Mama and Papa after the ceremony. All right?"

Cammy gave her a light kiss on the cheek. "Thank you."

They said no more as their father rapped on the door. "Ready, my little love?"

Willow gave him a hug. "Yes. He's wonderful, isn't he Papa?"

Her father chortled and tweaked her chin. "I don't know about that. He's a terrible negotiator. Kept insisting on giving you *more* than I was willing to ask for in our contract negotiations. But I suppose he is a man in love and wants to give you the moon and stars."

The day turned out beautiful, not a cloud in the sky and a gentle breeze to keep the temperature comfortable. The ceremony was held in the gazebo in the inn's garden. Chairs had been set out on the grass for their two families and the few other guests in attendance.

Shayne and his brothers were already standing beside the gazebo when Willow came down with her parents, Charlotte, and her sister.

Shayne's two brothers shoved him forward when she approached, the sort of thing brothers did to irritate their eldest sibling, for Shayne needed no prodding to greet her. "You look beautiful, Willow."

"You are looking quite handsome yourself."

He kissed her lightly on the cheek. "Ready to get married?"

She nodded.

He took her hand and held it throughout the ceremony, his eyes a silver gleam and his smile broad as he spoke his vows. She cast him a beaming smile as she spoke hers. These vows held special meaning, one they both understood and heartily appreciated after reading *The Book of Love*. Marriage was about honesty and trust. Compromise and commitment to building a life together. "I promise to love, honor, and obey—"

Shayne coughed and put a hand to his mouth to cover his grin.

Fine, he knew she was not going to blindly obey him. But did he have to find it so humorous?

She pinched his hand.

He cast her a hot look that made her weak in the knees.

"I now pronounce you man and wife," the minister said as the two were ignoring him to cast looks at each other, hers warning her new husband to behave himself, while his was steamy and held promise he would absolutely not behave.

She was blushing furiously when he bent forward to kiss her lightly on the cheek once more. "I love you, Willow."

She shook her head and laughed. "I love you, too. But you are still a wicked, wicked man."

He cast her a smug smile. "I'll take that as a compliment."

"It is a fact, not a compliment."

He kissed her other cheek. "We'll see about that tonight when I turn you into a wanton and have you howling—"

"Shayne!" Dear heaven, how much had the minister heard?

Shayne grunted. "Gad, you have sharp elbows."

The rest of the day passed merrily, but while their families remained in the inn's dining hall celebrating their union well after the wedding breakfast was over and into the early evening, Shayne stole Willow away to the guest chamber they would now share. Her meager possessions had been moved there immediately after the ceremony.

He still had that smug, steamy look on his face. "The last time we were in here together, I stuffed you into my wardrobe."

Willow tried to look offended, but she was too happy and laughingly groaned instead. "Young Matthew knew all along I was in there and blabbed to the Ashcotts! He still smirks every time he sees me, the horrid boy."

"Well, we are married now. It has all turned out as it should."

Although it was almost eight o'clock in the evening, the sun was still out, and the day was bright. Shayne lit several candles and then strode across the room to draw the drapes. "Damn sunshine. We should have gotten married in the dead of winter. It would have been dark hours ago, and I would have had you in bed and *had* you at least twice already."

He turned to her with a wince. "Not very romantic, is it? But I have been half-crazed all week long, low brain at full hum. Desperate to get you out of those clothes and into my arms."

"I'm sure you'll think of something nice to say once your low brain is sated and your high brain can resume functioning again." She smiled, not at all angry with him because she knew he loved her. Indeed, she wanted to rip the clothes off him and touch and lick his beautifully muscled body. She was just better at hiding her desire.

He removed his jacket, vest, and cravat and set them over the back of a chair.

She sighed, watching him move about and loving the play of those muscles beneath his shirt. The fine lawn fabric accentuated his broad shoulders and powerful arms. Yes, she would quite enjoy being held in those arms.

She started to undress, but he stopped her. "I'll do it, love."

She liked when he called her that.

And very much liked when he came to stand behind her, put his lips to her neck, and began to kiss the most sensitive spot. Kiss it. Lick it. Suckle it lightly.

Every one of those thousand butterflies in her belly began to flutter wildly.

She leaned against Shayne, her back to the solid heat and

hardness of his front, suddenly unsure her legs could hold her up.

He undid the silk laces along her back and nudged the gown off her shoulders. It fell to the carpet in a soft, slippery *whoosh*.

He loosened the laces of her corset and slid his hands beneath it to cup her breasts.

She sighed and closed her eyes, feeling those rough hands of his as he gently stroked the sensitive tips with his thumbs. "Dear heaven…Shayne."

"I know, love. Your skin is like satin, so soft and sleek to the touch."

He soon had the rest of her clothes off, stripping her bare and turning her to face him in the gentle candlelight. "Don't hide your body from me, Willow. I've never seen a lovelier vision. You make my heart soar."

He unpinned her hair and made a comment about her lush mane resembling the reds and golds of the candle flames as he shook it out gently. The curls fell down her back, and a few tumbled over her shoulders and onto her breasts. He brushed those back for an unimpeded view of her body.

Her cheeks were on fire.

She had never been like this with a man before.

Yes, Shayne was her husband, but…

He removed his shirt, seeming to understand her consternation. "I fell in love with you the moment I set eyes on you," he said in a husky rumble. "I would have found a way to take you in my arms in that very first moment, but I had Lord Belfy and his cohorts in need of subduing, and I had my hands full."

She tried to respond while gawking at his sculpted torso, bronze and beautiful on magnificent display. "And there I was demanding to speak to you, giving no thought to what you had to do because I was too impatient and wanted to give you my witness statement right then and there. I'm so sorry. I should have allowed you to finish with him and his horrid friends. But I was afraid you would release them."

He laughed. "You were the fieriest little thing. I knew that if he somehow got away, you were going to chase after him and pound him to dust."

He drew her into his arms and kissed her deeply. "But you scared the wits out of me when you tried to run into the inn's burning carriage house. If you died, a part of me would have died, too. Hell, I would have run in after you and not come out unless it was with you in my arms. I was never, ever going to abandon you. I loved you then, and I love you now."

He wrapped her in his glorious arms, drawing her close so that she felt the heat of his skin against hers. Her lips blew lightly against the spray of dark curls across his chest as she exhaled. "Shayne, I had no idea. I would have thought twice if I realized I was putting more than my own life at risk." She shook her head. "But it's done and over. I promise you, I will never do anything so foolhardy without considering your feelings first."

He glanced at the still healing cuts to her arm where the stitches had recently been removed. "How about, you will never do anything foolhardy again. Period. Nothing to consider. Just don't do it. Seeing you hurt just about killed me, Willow."

"But I'm on the mend now. I'm fine."

"And I would like to keep you that way, love."

She gazed into his worried eyes, those silver orbs that pierced her soul and stole her breath away. "This love business is a wonder, is it not? I loved you, too, in that first moment. I loved you even more deeply as you held me while the doctor was stitching me up." She grinned at him. "I even loved you after you dropped me in the trough when the fire broke out."

She reached up and drew his head down to kiss him on the lips. His mouth felt hot and possessive against hers, for he took over the kiss and crushed his mouth to hers, dominating the kiss and yet managing to keep it achingly tender.

She smiled up at him. "I love you even more now, Shayne. I know I shall love you more with each passing day. This is the true wonder of love. It is like a tree that plants itself in the ground and grows deep roots that spread and grow stronger over time. Our children will be the seeds we sow from our love."

"Speaking of deep roots and sowing seeds," he said, lifting her into his arms. "I think it is time I did some deep planting of my own."

"Shayne!

"What? I cleaned up what I was really going to say."

She curled in his arms and eyed him curiously. "What were you going to say?"

"Not telling you. It was dirty, and I don't want to overset your delicate sensibilities."

She tugged on his ear. "My sensibilities are not delicate. What were you going to say?"

"Something that would get my face slapped. I think you'll enjoy my showing you what I was thinking a lot better."

He set her on the bed, then sat beside her and removed his boots and breeches so they were now both wearing nothing at all. She eyed him hungrily, for he looked splendid, and since they were talking about trees and roots and planting…was that part of him really going to fit inside her?

He arched an eyebrow, understanding exactly what she was thinking. "It will, love. But we're going to take it slowly. There's lots to show you before we get to the actual coupling. Will you trust me to know what I am doing?"

She nodded.

He eased her onto her back and stretched out beside her, propping himself on his side as he looked upon her. He ran his hand in a light swirl along her body, his artist's eye seeming to take in her every curve and line and liking what he saw. Then his big hand began to move over her with greater purpose, cupping her breast—which he seemed to enjoy very much—and taking its rosy tip into his mouth to suckle it.

He then moved to the other breast, working similar magic with his tongue.

She wanted to touch him, too. But he now held her hands in his, raising them over her head and entangling his fingers in hers while he settled his large frame over her and used his mouth to explore her body.

The weight of his big body on her ought to have felt crushing, but instead, it felt divine. Of course, he must have taken care to keep the brunt of his weight shifted off her. His mouth felt exquisite on her body.

She marveled at how well he knew her sensitive spots. Perhaps it was the same for all women, but he was particularly attentive and attuned to what she found pleasing. She wanted to do the same for him, but he seemed determined to initiate her to intimacy before he freed her hands to explore him.

Finally, he released her hands to work his way lower and—

"Shayne!" He was now between her legs and...oh...such a thing could not possibly be legal, even between husband and wife. But it felt...she gasped, clutching the sheets to hold herself together as he touched his mouth to her center, and she practically came undone with the heavenly delight of it.

This is what he'd been talking about when he spoke of spreading seeds and planting roots. Yes, she expected the planting part would happen next. He was preparing her for the moment.

She certainly felt prepared, her body seeming to float on air, her blood a stream of hot liquid. Her bones completely melted.

His tongue slid inside her.

His lips suckled her...*there.*

She clutched his head, began pulling at his hair, and tried to keep quiet as little explosions rocked through her body, but she began to make moaning sounds and could not stop them from escaping her lips. She heard him laugh and felt him shift his big, marvelous body between her legs. "Noisy little thing," he muttered and covered her mouth with his.

His finger replaced where his mouth had been, and then something else replaced his finger, that part of him she was sure would never fit. But he slid inside her with exquisite care and muttered sweet words to her that she could barely make out as more explosions of pleasure tore through her and turned her body to fire and her soul to air.

It wasn't long after he filled her, embedding himself deeper with each purposeful thrust, that he seemed to feel these same explosions and catch this same fire.

He growled low in his throat.

His skin turned hot and damp beneath her palms as he released inside her. Sowing seeds, indeed. If the pleasurable force of his release was any indication, he'd just planted a full field.

She wrapped her arms around his neck and held him close, loving the physical feel of him, his body damp and heavy on hers, his straining muscles and ragged breaths. Most of all, she loved his conquering smile and the treasured way he looked upon her as they both began to calm from their first coupling.

What splendid torment!

He drew out of her after a moment, his powerful body hovering over hers as she lay in breathless wonder. She reached out and traced the bulges of his taut, sinewed arms while he remained just over her, studying her face. "Did I hurt you, love?"

"No, not the littlest bit."

"Good." He eased and rolled onto his back, taking her into his arms and cradling her against him. "I love you, sweetheart."

She turned to face him, her breasts pressing against the side of his chest as they nestled together in an intimate tangle, the bedsheets barely covering them. "It was quite splendid."

He kissed her nose. "You were splendid. Are you sure you are all right?"

She nodded. "Is it done now? Do not laugh if my questions seem foolish, but what happens next? Do we put on our nightclothes and go to sleep? Or is there more?"

He ran his hand through the silky strands of her hair. "Not nearly done yet…unless you've had enough. You have only to say the word."

"And if I am greedy for more?"

He cast her a smug, victorious grin. "I am ever your dutiful husband and will oblige."

He obliged her twice more that evening and then insisted they try to get some sleep, for he feared to bruise her inexperienced body if they continued. "We have a lifetime to explore each other, love. You'll be walking like a duck by morning if we don't stop now. But you needn't put on your nightgown. Come up against my body. I'll keep you warm." He inhaled lightly. "I love your scent. Orange blossoms and silk."

Willow did not think she would sleep a wink, but apparently coupling three times in one night left one quite spent. She slept deeply and awoke the next morning still in Shayne's arms, one of his hands cupping one of her breasts.

Well, *The Book of Love* had spoken of this primal, sexual bond.

Was it not the same for her? She had been clutching his muscled arm, comforted by his strength and power.

Curious as to the time, she tried to slip out of bed.

Shayne immediately stirred. "Willow?"

"I wanted to know the time. How long do you think we have been asleep?" She tiptoed to the window and eased the drape aside. It was still dark outside. She let the fabric fall back into place. "Odd, not even dawn yet. I was sure we had slept till noon."

"No, love. We turned in early and had hours to ourselves. Come back to bed."

She climbed back in and snuggled against him. "This is nice, isn't it?"

"It is heaven, love. Pure heaven." He drew her closer, wrapped his arm around her, and fell back to sleep...or so she thought.

"What are you doing, Shayne?" Apparently, he was not big on talking this early in the morning.

He showed her instead.

"Oh...my...oh..." He covered her mouth with his when her pleasure got too noisy.

CHAPTER NINETEEN

WILLOW'S PARENTS HAD departed for Barnstaple two days ago.

Willow was now seated in the dining room, having breakfast with Shayne and looking quite morose. "What's wrong, love?" he asked, setting aside his cup of coffee and reaching over to take her hand.

"I've let Cammy down. I promised I would speak to our parents about delaying her come-out for another year, but you and I were so caught up in ourselves, decadently locked away in our chamber, that I never got the chance for a moment alone with them. She and Charlotte are scheduled to leave for London today. She was overset last night when I gave her *The Book of Love*."

"Do you want me to talk to her?"

Willow shook her head. "She won't listen to anyone. She and Charlotte have been bickering about London ever since our wedding day."

He gave her hand a light squeeze. "They'll make up once they reach your uncle's home and Cammy settles in. I'm sure your family will put her at ease."

"I hope so. I should have fought harder for my sister. Honestly, I don't see the harm in letting Cammy return to Barnstaple."

Shayne drank the last of his coffee and then gently took Willow's hand. "She's your sister, and you want to protect her, but

I'm sure she will get over her fears once she is there. The Braydens and Farthingales will protect her. Besides, there's lots to see and do. She will have fun once she stops fretting and simply allows herself to enjoy all the town has to offer."

Willow nodded. "I expect you are right."

He checked his pocket watch. "They're running late. I would have expected at least Lorcan to be here by now."

Another half-hour passed before Lorcan and Charlotte entered the dining room. Willow leaped to her feet. "Aunt Charlotte, have you been crying?"

"How can I not?" She dabbed her eyes with her handkerchief. "Cammy's missing."

Willow paled and gripped the sides of the table.

Shayne immediately rose to put an arm around her. "I'm sure there's a logical explanation, love."

She stared at him, her eyes beginning to water. "This is what we were just talking about. She dreaded going to London, and now she has taken the matter into her own hands. But where would she go? Home, do you think? Aunt Charlotte, do you have any idea?"

Her aunt burst into tears. "No. I don't even know when she left. It could have been any time last night or early this morning."

"Hellfire," Shayne muttered and turned a pleading eye to his brother. "Lor?"

"Yes, I will track her. I've already searched through Taunton," he said with a sigh. "I stopped first to check the stables. All the horses are accounted for. Only two of the inn's guests have departed so far this morning, and both were on their way to London, so I'm confident she did not charm her way into those carriages."

Willow followed along, listening intently to Lorcan. "If she hasn't taken a horse and hasn't gone off in any carriage…what does that mean? She cannot intend to walk all the way to Barnstaple. How long a head start do you think she has?"

"Not much of one, for certain," Lorcan said with heartening

confidence. "She is terrified of the dark, so she would have waited until daybreak to run off. She isn't walking. I would have caught up to her at the edge of town if she were."

Willow regarded him with some surprise. "How do you know she is terrified of the dark?"

He folded his arms over his chest, looking far too relaxed about Cammy's disappearance. "Isn't she?"

Willow nodded. "Yes, but…how do you know this?"

In typical Lorcan fashion, he offered no explanation. "I know where she is," he suddenly said, raking his fingers through his hair.

Willow and Charlotte leaped at his words. "You do? Where?"

"She had to have taken the mail coach to Barnstaple. It is the only possibility. I'll go fetch her…unless…" His gaze took them all in. "Do I let her go home?"

"No!" Charlotte said with surprising determination, dabbing her eyes again. "I am not trying to be cruel, but her fear of London and the marriage mart will only get worse over time. There will always be some excuse. This year, it is that she is too young. Next year, her mother will need her at home. The year after, she'll come down with some mysterious ailment that will disappear as soon as her parents give up on the idea of London. Then, she will claim to be too old."

Willow knew Charlotte was probably right. In truth, Cammy was being surprisingly timid about this London visit. If she were the one still single, she would not have minded going on alone, even if only to see her cousins. None of them would have made her attend balls or other social events. None of them would have made her do anything she did not want to do or see any suitors she did not wish to see.

On the other hand, there was an innocent sensuality about Cammy that had boys fighting over her since she was twelve. Now, London's most notorious bachelors would be fighting over her. It had been different for her and June. Yes, they'd had admirers. But men did not throw fists at each other for the mere chance to dance with them or walk them home from a shopping excursion on the High Street.

"Bring her back here, Lorcan," Shayne said. "We'll decide what to do from there. Is that all right with you ladies?"

Charlotte nodded.

"Yes," Willow said, eager to have her sister safe.

Lorcan turned to leave, but Willow called after him. "Lorcan, she'll have *The Book of Love* with her. Make certain she does not leave it behind on the mail coach."

He did not look back, merely tipped his head to acknowledge he'd heard her. "That damn book," he muttered and strode off to collect Cammy.

Shayne stared at the doorway. "Do I tell Mr. Ashcott to prepare for another wedding?"

Willow looked up at him in surprise. "Don't you dare. That's awfully presumptuous of us, don't you think?"

Charlotte was still staring at Lorcan's disappearing back. "She took my pin money, but only one-fourth of it. She's such an honest girl and could not bring herself to steal more than her allotted share. I left all of it out atop my bureau. Oh, dear. I hope she has enough."

Willow blinked her eyes. "You left it out? On purpose?"

"Of course. How else was I to get Lorcan to chase after her? In truth, I wasn't sure she would run. I'm glad to see she has the courage of her convictions. She is quite a determined girl."

"I don't understand." Willow stared at her aunt. "Lorcan was about to escort you both to London. He was going to be with you the entire ride."

"Yes," Charlotte said. "With me in the way all the while. They needed time alone. I think it will all work out as it should." She turned to Shayne and eyed him speculatively. "Do you not think so?"

"I don't know, Charlotte." He cast Willow a worried glance. "Lorcan isn't like me. He may not be ready to settle down. But he won't do anything to harm Cammy or her reputation. He'll track her down and return her safely to the inn as quietly as possible."

Willow tried to stifle her disappointment. "Then you don't think we ought to be planning a wedding? Don't you think Cammy and Lorcan are a match?"

Charlotte spoke up before Shayne had the chance. "My dear Willow, of course, they are perfect for each other. Have you not seen the way Cammy looks at him? As for Lorcan, the man's blood has been flowing hot as molten lava ever since he laid eyes on her. But I do agree with your husband."

"You do?"

"Indeed. There won't be a wedding here, but it has nothing to do with that nonsense about Lorcan not being ready to settle down. There won't be a wedding here because I think they will marry before ever making it back to Taunton."

Shayne shook his head and laughed. "I'd wager you were wrong, Charlotte. But I think I would lose."

"Of course you would, dear boy." She tipped her head up proudly. "When it comes to love, I am always right."

Willow pondered their exchange thoughtfully. How was it possible? Cammy could not be more than a few hours ahead of Lorcan. If all went smoothly, he would have her back before nightfall. Hardly time for them to marry. And how were they to manage it without a special license or their father's consent?

She turned to Shayne. "How long ago would you say the mail coach came by?"

He shrugged. "Three hours at the most, I'd say. But it travels fairly fast. Ten minutes to switch horses at the next coaching inn, then on their way again. They'll repeat the same all the way down the coaching line. Stop at a designated inn. Switch horses. On their way within ten minutes. Lorcan will have to rest his horse at least once or twice before catching up to them. Charlotte, you are quite nefarious."

"Thank you, dear boy."

Willow was going to suggest her husband did not mean it as a compliment, then saw Shayne and Charlotte grinning at each other. Shayne obviously approved of this turn of events. She put her hands on her hips and frowned at him. "He is your brother. How can you encourage such trickery? Even if he does care for Cammy and she for him. What you are both condoning is outrageous and underhanded."

"Thank you." He kissed her lightly on the lips. "My brother knows exactly what is going to happen. He would not have gone unless he wanted to marry your sister. But he might never have said anything to her without this push. Of course, he will never force her. If she does not wish to marry him, he will do all he can to protect her reputation and make sure no one ever finds out about their time alone together."

Willow rubbed her temples. "Oh, dear. I hope neither of them gets hurt."

"They won't. They cannot." Charlotte's expression turned wistful and tender. "True love always wins out. There is no force stronger, is there my dears?"

Shayne nodded. "Stop fretting, sweetheart. Cammy is safe on the mail coach, and she will be safe with Lorcan, as well."

Willow looked up at her husband and clearly saw the love he held for her. She knew Lorcan was a good man, too. "I still think it is outrageous and underhanded."

"Says the beautiful firebrand who risked her life to retrieve that red leather-bound book of spells and ensorcelled me by having me read it with her."

"They are recipes for love, nothing more. And I did not force you to do anything you did not wish to do."

"You cast your magic spell on me," he insisted.

"Do you regret it?"

"No, my love. Nor shall I ever."

She reached up and kissed him on the lips. "I love you, Magistrate Brayden."

He caressed her cheek. "Love you to pieces, Mrs. Brayden. Any chance that book can be passed on to Donal next? Rafe could do with it, too."

She took his hand. "Passing it on to men? Come upstairs with me. You are obviously addled from lack of sleep."

They left Charlotte enjoying her morning cup of hot cocoa and now chatting with Mrs. Ashcott while they returned to their guest chamber.

Shayne cast her a steamy look after she bolted the door and turned to face him. "Addled, am I?"

She felt her body melt under the force of his smoldering gaze. "Yes, indeed. Sadly, there is only one cure for it."

He arched an eyebrow, quite amused and willing to play along. "What is that cure?"

"Lots of bed rest. Lots of bed rest without any clothes on."

His lips twitched upward in a smile. "Is that important? The no clothes part?"

"Vital. And there must be a warm body beside you."

"Also naked?"

She nodded.

"I think I'm catching on to this miracle cure. I assume this warm, naked body beside me must have big blue eyes and red-gold hair and must be married to me." He took her in his arms and began to undress her, his hands skimming over her body with slow sensuality.

Willow tipped her head back and closed her eyes. "Oh…heavens. That feels so good."

He chuckled softly and made quick work of shedding her clothes. "This treatment may take hours."

"Alas, I am sure it will." She cast him an impertinent but endearing smile as he shed the last of his garments.

"And will it have to be repeated often?" His voice was now a silken rumble, deep and smooth as molten chocolate.

This big, beautiful man simply stole her breath. "At least twice more, I am sure."

"Then we had better get started right away." He kissed her with a passionate and devouring longing, then lifted her in his arms and carried her to bed.

He settled over her and wrapped her lovingly in his arms. "Willow, you are the most wonderful thing that's ever happened to me."

She closed her eyes and sighed. "I love you, Shayne."

Yes, love was truly a wonder.

Also by Meara Platt

FARTHINGALE SERIES
My Fair Lily
The Duke I'm Going To Marry
Rules For Reforming A Rake
A Midsummer's Kiss
The Viscount's Rose
Earl Of Hearts
If You Wished For Me
Never Dare A Duke
Capturing The Heart Of A Cameron

BOOK OF LOVE SERIES
The Look of Love
The Touch of Love
The Taste of Love
The Song of Love
The Scent of Love
The Kiss of Love
The Chance of Love
The Gift of Love
The Heart of Love
The Hope of Love (novella)
The Promise of Love (2021)
The Wonder of Love (2021)
The Journey of Love (2021)

DARK GARDENS SERIES
Garden of Shadows
Garden of Light

Garden of Dragons
Garden of Destiny
Garden of Angels

THE BRAYDENS
A Match Made In Duty
Earl of Westcliff
Fortune's Dragon
Earl of Kinross
Earl of Alnwick
Pearls of Fire*
(*also in Pirates of Britannia series)
Aislin
Gennalyn

DeWOLFE PACK ANGELS SERIES
Nobody's Angel
Kiss An Angel
Bhrodi's Angel

About the Author

Meara Platt is an award winning, USA TODAY bestselling author and an Amazon UK All-Star. Her favorite place in all the world is England's Lake District, which may not come as a surprise since many of her stories are set in that idyllic landscape, including her paranormal romance Dark Gardens series. Learn more about the Dark Gardens and Meara's lighthearted and humorous Regency romances in her Farthingale series and Book of Love series, or her warmhearted Regency romances in her Braydens series by visiting her website at www.mearaplatt.com.